MW00467020

DRAGON ON THE FAR SIDE OF THE MOON

Copyright © 2020 by Douglas J. Wood

All rights reserved. No part of this publication may be reproduced, distributed, or transmitted in any form or by any means, including photocopying, recording, or other electronic or mechanical methods, without the prior written permission of the publisher except in the case of brief quotations embodied in critical reviews and certain other noncommercial uses permitted by copyright law.

For permission requests, contact the publisher at the website below.
Plum Bay Publishing, LLC
www.plumbaypublishing.com

Library of Congress Control Number: 2020938448
Hardcover ISBN: 978-1-7335253-8-1
Paperback ISBN: 978-1-7348848-9-0
eBook ISBN: 978-1-7335253-9-8
Printed in the United States of America
Cover Design: Lauren Harvey
Interior Illustrations: Amy Staropoli
Editors: Jeremy Townsend and Kate Petrella
Interior Design: Lance Buckley

DRAGON
ON THE
FAR SIDE
OF THE
MOON

DOUGLAS J. WOOD

PLUM BAY PUBLISHING, LLC

BOOKS BY DOUGLAS J. WOOD

Fiction
Presidential Intentions
Presidential Declarations
Presidential Conclusions
Dark Data

Nonfiction
Please Be Advised
101 Things I Want to Say
Asshole Attorney

"MACHINES ARE MADE BY MEN FOR MAN'S BENEFIT AND PROGRESS. BUT WHEN MAN CEASES TO CONTROL THE PRODUCTS OF HIS INGENUITY AND IMAGINATION, HE NOT ONLY RISKS LOSING THE BENEFITS BUT HE TAKES A LONG AND UNPREDICTABLE STEP INTO THE TWILIGHT ZONE."

—ROD SERLING

"FROM AGNES, WITH LOVE," *THE TWILIGHT ZONE*, SEASON 5, EPISODE 140, AIRED ON VALENTINE'S DAY, 1964. THE EPISODE TELLS THE STORY OF A QUEST FOR LOVE BY JAMES ELWOOD, MASTER PROGRAMMER IN CHARGE OF THE MARK 502-741, COMMONLY KNOWN AS AGNES, THE WORLD'S MOST ADVANCED ELECTRONIC COMPUTER.

CONTENTS

INTRODUCTION

WHEN I BEGAN MY RESEARCH FOR THIS BOOK, I FOUND THAT THE MORE I DISCOVERED, THE more startled I was at how much I needed to learn and how little the press was reporting on the new space race between the United States, China, India, and the private sector. I also learned much about the Moon that added to the mystery surrounding our closest celestial neighbor. I hope this book not only provides enjoyment to my readers but also informs them about developments in space and on the Moon that will affect us for generations to come.

It is ironic that the recent COVID-19 pandemic and China's role in it revealed how little we know regarding China's intentions on the world stage and its dangerous hegemony in the pharmaceutical, manufacturing, and technology sectors. You can add space and the far side of the Moon to the list of issues critical to the national security of the United States.

I hope you enjoy the book.

CHAPTER ONE

LAUNCH DAY

EVAPORATING GASES BENEATH THE THIRTY-STORY-HIGH ROCKET CREATED AN EERIE CLOUD as the rocket sat on its pad. Attached to a gantry, the craft's hoses looked like umbilical cords giving life to an ominous beast. The onboard crew of eight were going through pre-launch checklists under the direction of the mission's spacecraft commander, an accomplished pilot with seven previous trips to space. The launch director and mission management team were a mile away at mission control. It was ten minutes from launch.

This was the sixth launch in thirty days. The third in just the past week alone. Unlike this day's launch, the previous were unmanned rockets filled with payloads of equipment and essentials needed for the mission. Nerves were on edge. Without a successful launch and rendezvous with the other three rockets, all would be lost, and priceless cargos would careen through space for eternity.

Adding to the tension, top political leaders were assembled at a special viewing stand reserved for the historic event. Their viewing stand resembled a Hollywood set. Posh seats sat across from a mile-wide manmade lake, a little less than two miles from the launching pad. That was a safe distance in case the mission went wrong. A fireball could spread devastation as far as a mile out from the pad. Landscaping that included lush greens and subdued annuals and perennials sat neatly trimmed so the view was unobstructed and idyllic. Despite the distance, the launching pad was so large that it seemed to be on top of the visitors, particularly when set against the bright blue sky that greeted this day's launch.

The special guests in their exclusive seats were not people to disappoint. A few hundred yards behind them, reporters and space fans assembled, hoping to see the drama unfold. While their stands were not as luxurious as those reserved for the luminaries, they were quite comfortable and allowed for a spectacular, unobstructed view. The audience was instructed to stay seated for safety, and to wear earplugs to ward off the impending soundwaves. Those admonishments were mostly ignored.

Those watching silently wished the crew a safe flight, but some still remembered the nightmare that befell STS-51-L, the tenth flight of NASA's space shuttle. On January 28, 1986, the ill-fated *Challenger* exploded just seventy-three seconds into its flight, and the crew of seven courageous souls, who were believed to have survived the explosion, suffocated in the minutes that followed. The dark fears of humankind always lurk below the surface.

Over the PA system, the launch director calmly announced, "This is project command. It is T-minus ten minutes and counting. Launch window confirmed. Orbital collision avoidance runs completed. Weather conditions ideal. We are go. Activate flight recorders."

Each minute seemed like an eternity to the crew. They had been training for this flight for two years. Four of the crew had previous space flights. Four were rookies who had expertise essential to the mission.

"T-minus nine minutes and counting. Start automatic ground launch sequence."

The excitement in the crowd began to rise, eager to see the liftoff. Loud chants of "Go, Go, Go" and clapping filled the air. All of the spectators shared the crew's impatience. The last minutes of a launch sequence can seem endless.

"T-minus eight minutes and counting." A four-story tower with the countdown clock, registering time in one-hundredths of a second, loomed on the horizon to the right of the launching pad and about a mile from the stands. Everyone could easily see the time ticking by.

As the crowd looked on in anticipation, the launch abort system was armed. Mission control knew that anything could happen from this point on, so the abort system was ready to jettison the spacecraft away from the rocket in the event of a catastrophic failure once the rocket ignited. The chances of the crew surviving were slim, but at least they would be physically intact for their funerals.

"T-minus seven minutes thirty seconds and counting. Retract spacecraft access arm."

Large clamps attaching the rocket to the gantry dropped, freeing the behemoth from its restraints except for a few hoses and electrical wires.

"T-minus six minutes and counting."

Each pause was excruciating for those who assembled for the show. A new chant of "Launch, Launch, Launch" rose from the crowd.

"T-minus five minutes and counting. Start auxiliary power. Range safety system status is green." Now every safety feature was active to protect the crew in case of launch failure.

Smoke in great billows rose from the rocket. The crowd tensed. As an announcer on the PA explained that it was not smoke from the rocket but steam that results from venting the cryogenic fuel used to power the rocket engines, the tension turned back to excitement. It was perfectly safe. The chants got louder.

"T-minus four minutes and counting. Start aero-surface profile test."

Without human interaction, the rocket dutifully obeyed pre-programmed orders from the computers as various fins, straps, flaps, and rudders moved as if in a ballet to be certain they were ready and working. At this point, the process was machine to machine.

Exhaust billowed briefly out of the various small thrusters on the rocket, testing to be certain they were functioning.

"T-minus three minutes fifty-five seconds and counting. Start main engine gimbal profile test."

The launch computer, now in control, issued another order and the engines at the base of the rocket swiveled to prove the gimbals—much like human hip joints—were working. The engines of a massive rocket ship act like rudders and need to pivot to compensate for thrust that could push the rocket off a straight trajectory and into oblivion.

"T-minus two minutes thirty seconds and counting. Crewmembers close and lock your visors."

The mission commander looked to his left and right, making sure his crew was following commands. He responded, "Confirmed." He didn't need to. The mission control computers knew before he responded that the crew had complied. The ground crew in any launch is nervous, so the computers need to stay well ahead of the commands as traditional conversations between the crew and mission control, despite their irrelevancy, continued. That was the best way to avoid human error while still giving everyone the illusion of human control.

"T-minus fifty seconds and counting. Transfer from ground to internal power."

The command created no visible change. The crowd was now on their feet despite warnings that it was better to sit given the sound wave that would hit fifteen to twenty seconds after the launch. No one seemed to care. They continued to chant.

"T-minus thirty-one seconds and counting. Ground launch sequencer is go for auto sequence start. All second-stage tanks are now pressurized."

The chanting grew louder. "Launch! Launch!"

"T-minus sixteen seconds and counting. Guidance is now internal."

More steam rose from the launch pad and engulfed more than half of the 358-foot rocket.

"T-minus ten seconds and counting. Activate main engine hydrogen burn-off system."

The gantry retracted from the rocket like a baby being placed in a crib. Igniters below the engines came to life with flames lighting the belly below. More steam spewed from the base.

"T-minus six seconds and counting. Main engine ignition sequence start."

The steam continued to billow as computerized orders pumped thousands of gallons of water into a pit below the rocket, in order to suppress potentially damaging sound waves.

The engines suddenly came to life, as flames seemed to engulf the rocket. The audience could literally see the soundwave effect as it crossed the lake that lay between them and the launch pad, now completely ablaze. But they didn't hear it right away, and that delay was disorienting.

"T-minus five. T-minus four. Solid rocket booster ignition. Launch clamps released."

The sound grew. The crowd became frenzied. They could see the huge plume cloud grow as the engines roared, brightly illuminating the sky even in daylight. The moment they waited days to see was seconds away. And in a few more seconds, they would feel its thunder as well.

"Three . . . two . . . one . . . All engines running."

"Zero."

The rocket's kerosene–liquid oxygen main engine, producing more than 700,000 pounds of thrust, burned as bright as the sun. Adding to its power were four hydrolox-powered boosters strapped to the sides of the rocket, each capable of adding 440,000 pounds of additional thrust. The spectacle lit the sky with massive flames and smoke that hid the rocket from view amidst a breathtaking conflagration. If anyone were within a half mile of the blast, they would go deaf even with protective earplugs.

"Liftoff. We have liftoff at thirty-two minutes past the hour. We have cleared the tower."

As everyone watched breathlessly, the rocket seemed to be in suspension, not moving. Then, as if in slow motion, it began to rise above the smoke with the bright blue sky behind it and a fiery column below it.

The full force of the sound arrived to the viewing stands with a deafening boom, knocking over some who foolishly continued to stand. None of that reduced the cheering and celebration. The ringing in their ears that would continue for days for those who refused earplugs was well worth the price of admission.

Gaining momentum with every passing second, China's Long March 9 super-heavy carrier rocket, topped with a spaceship dubbed the Dragon, together with its crew of eight brave *taikonauts*, took to flight without incident from the Jiuquan Satellite Launch Center in Gansu province and began its journey to China's base on the far side of the Moon.

CHAPTER TWO

SPACE FORCE
HOUSTON, TEXAS

Douglas Wright, chief of operations for the United States Space Force, called Phillip Lawson, president of the United States.

Before becoming director of the Space Force, Douglas Wright was a U.S. Navy admiral, the highest rank in the navy. While on active duty, he had a stellar career of more than thirty years. A graduate of the U.S. Naval Academy, Wright earned his Ph.D. in aerospace engineering from Stanford University, where he was a Knight-Hennessy Scholar. An astronaut in his own right, Wright spent two months aboard the International Space Station (ISS) on a mission publicly described as analysis of space debris and its risks to satellites. In truth, the only satellites Wright cared about were the U.S. defensive array critical to national security.

Whenever anyone met Wright, they couldn't help but comment that he looked as if he'd come to his role from central casting. Trim, fit, and handsome, six feet tall with blond hair and piercing blue eyes, he was a commanding figure. He was also uncompromising in what he expected from those under his command: total and unquestioned loyalty. As those experienced in working with him would tell new recruits, both military and civilian, "Don't forget, Wright can never be wrong."

The computers in building 30 of NASA's Mission Control Center, the MCC-H at the Lyndon B. Johnson Space Center in Houston, began messaging to the array of manned terminals in the room. The MCC-H in Houston houses not only the leadership of NASA but also operational officers and troops of the United States Space Force, an official branch of the military formed in 2019 by President Donald Trump. Under Trump's executive order, the supervision of the Space Force fell to the Department of Defense and no longer sat within the U.S. Air Force. Benjamin Bahney and Jonathan Pearl, writing in *Foreign Affairs* in 2019, observed that the Space Force was a U.S. response to fears that China and other superpowers would make the cosmos a new tactical alternative to conventional military deployment. For Bahney and Pearl, space had long been militarized and the United States needed to be as much in the forefront of the race as any other country.

The Space Force operations are located at three facilities: the Vandenberg Air Force Base near Lompoc, California, the Schriever Air Force Base near Colorado Springs, Colorado, and at the Johnson Space Center. Those stationed at Vandenberg support military operations using GPS-based navigation, space-based data, satellite communications, and missile warning. Those based at Schriever monitor and protect military satellites in orbit. The central hub, however, is the Johnson Space Center, purposefully not publicized for security reasons.

The Johnson Space Center is a massive complex of dozens of buildings that house the heartbeat of the U.S. space program. By comparison, Cape Canaveral, where NASA launches most of its rockets, is merely an outpost controlled by the scientists and astrophysicists in Houston. When critical decisions need to be made, they're made in Houston, not Cape Canaveral.

In addition to its oversight of the International Space Station (ISS), the Space Force monitors all launches throughout the globe and reports directly to the president if events warrant it.

"Mr. President," reported Wright, "our Mt. Haleakala, Hawaii, tracking station was the first site in our space fence to confirm China's successful launch of eight crewmembers into space, presumably chasing the three cargo missions they launched earlier this month. In total for the past year alone, the other eleven stations in the space fence like the one on Mt. Haleakala tracked thirty-one launches. We don't believe, however, that any of the missions until this launch were manned."

"Chasing them? Why?" responded President Lawson.

Wright answered, "We can only assume their intent is to catch up to the other flights and accompany them to China's base on the far side of the Moon. That's where the previous missions either landed or crashed. Either way, they all reached the Moon and went out of sight to the far side, never to be seen again. So they're obviously not orbiters."

"Have we confirmed what's in the cargo ships?" asked the president.

"The Chinese continue to claim they're loaded with supplies to complete the research base they've been building for the past two years. They claim it's part of their peaceful exploration of the Moon for mining and topographic analysis. And to be a launch platform for a mission to Mars."

"But you don't believe them?"

"No, Mr. President. Not entirely. While I understand the advantage of using the Moon for a Mars mission and for mining, it continues to be our belief that the base has a military purpose as well. Perhaps its primary purpose. China already controls most of the rare earth elements on Earth. And they ration supplies out in increasingly meager manner. That poses a strategic threat to us that some say we are failing to address. So they may be mining for more rare earth elements on the Moon. Unfortunately, we can't be sure, since it's nearly impossible to monitor what they're doing. Their base is on the far side of the Moon and generally unseen."

"Why can't our orbiting satellites detect what's going on?"

"We have three at the present time: the Lunar Reconnaissance Orbiter and Artemis P1 and P2. They provide some information but there simply isn't enough resolution. They are not spy satellites. They're old and only pass over where we think the base is located once a week, if that. We tried to reposition them but to no avail. Quite often, their transmissions fail for reasons we're unsure of, but we don't discount interference by China. So far, our intelligence is too vague to make any definitive assessment."

"So we spent billions on a bunch of satellites that can't see shit? Is that what you're telling me?"

"I'm afraid so, Mr. President. They're designed as mapping orbiters and are not equipped with the types of cameras necessary to find much. What we've seen is not conclusive. In fact, none of our satellites have yet to even find the old Apollo landers. While we've found some debris of India's Vikram spacecraft that crashed in 2019, it's spotty at best. So I'm afraid they're pretty worthless."

"Unbelievable. So you're telling me you don't know where they are. OK, how about guessing? Where do you *think* China's base is located?"

"That's the odd thing, Mr. President. What we do know is there are various lunar landers, all appearing to be stationary, at various places on the Moon. We believe some are decoys; some are not. So far, we've seen no movement around them that can be explained by our lack of data. So if they're doing anything, they're doing it very stealthily," Wright said.

"That assumes, Admiral Wright, that they're doing anything at all. How can you be certain this isn't all one of China's publicity stunts to give the appearance of success where none has occurred?"

"If it is, Mr. President, it is a very expensive one. I doubt even China is willing to spend billions on a publicity stunt."

Lawson pressed. "Aren't we monitoring transmissions from China to the base? Don't we know their intentions by the chatter?"

"Yes, Mr. President, we monitor all communications. But the Chinese are very good at code and don't use verbal commands. Everything is encrypted. They use something like our AES, the Advanced Encryption Standard. It uses a symmetric algorithm. The same process we use to protect our classified information. But theirs seems even more advanced than ours. So far, it's impenetrable."

"And we've heard nothing from our assets in China?"

Lawson believed human beings were no match for algorithms controlled by machines. Boots on the ground, however, were still the most valuable sources. But no one was better at keeping secrets than China. That made them a most formidable adversary.

"Nothing that is anything more than speculation. Unfortunately, our reliance on technology to protect secrets has made conventional spying pretty much obsolete. Instead, we live in a computer-driven chess match with no one capable of checkmate," Wright said.

"So we're blind," concluded Lawson.

"Yes, Mr. President, we're blind."

"It wasn't a question, Admiral Wright."

"Yes, sir."

"Keep me posted, Admiral," ordered the president.

As if on cue, Christy Rutherford, Lawson's personal secretary, entered and placed a cup of tea on the president's desk. She left, closing the door behind her.

Lawson ended the call and placed his hands around the cup of tea. He gazed at his desk, a fixture in the White House since 1880 when it was presented as a gift by the United Kingdom's Queen Victoria. Built of planks from the HMS *Resolute*, a British arctic exploration ship, it earned the name "Resolute Desk." Lawson often felt humbled when sitting at it knowing that so many past presidents sat at the same desk and made decisions that changed the course of human-kind. It was from the Resolute Desk that FDR decided to enter WWII even before Japan attacked Pearl Harbor. It is where Harry S. Truman decided to drop the first atomic bomb on Hiroshima. And it is where John F. Kennedy made his decision to invade Cuba in the Bay of Pigs, a fiasco that nearly cost him his presidency until he made his decision to stand ground against Russia in its attempt to place nuclear missiles on the island. Lyndon Johnson decided the desk should tour the country after JFK's assassination. Since the JFK tour, only George H. W. Bush removed the Resolute Desk from the Oval Office, replacing it with the one he used while vice president. Upon defeating Bush in 1992, William Jefferson Clinton returned the Resolute Desk to the Oval Office, where it remained. Rumors that the desk has secret compartments are untrue but kept alive by White House historians and tour guides.

Lawson pondered the potential nightmare that lay ahead and how grave the consequences of any decision he made could be. As commander in chief, only his respect for the legislative process tempered his war powers. Despite warnings from the scientific community, the United States was woefully behind in the new space race. Its goal of returning to the Moon remained thwarted by a Congress more obsessed with political infights and legislative gridlock than investing in space exploration, particularly when the suggested price tag was more than $25 billion. Pleas from NASA and the Space Force for more funding and commitment met deaf ears. All the two agencies could do was keep the ISS functioning and launch a few orbiting satellites, but none around the Moon. That was too expensive.

Lawson pressed the button on the intercom. "Ms. Rutherford, please get me Secretary Shapiro. Ask him to come over right away."

Like most personal secretaries, Rutherford knew more about how the president thought and weighed the country's challenges than anyone except, perhaps, the first lady. But unlike the first lady, Rutherford was privy to virtually every conversation President Lawson had with his advisers, particularly those that took place in or from the Oval Office.

At one time, the president's personal secretary was the gatekeeper for anyone who wanted to speak to or see the president. Over the years, however, the president's chief of staff took over that role and the personal secretary became, in the eyes of most observers, nothing more than a clerical assistant who opened doors for visitors and made calls for the president when he wanted to talk to someone. That was fine with Rutherford. She knew how to keep herself in the middle of anything that happened in the Oval Office and didn't care what other people thought of her job. She'd been in Washington politics longer than anyone in the White House and served four presidents, although her youthful appearance gave the impression she must be a new hire.

Within fifteen minutes, Rutherford reported to the president that Secretary of Defense Edward Shapiro had arrived, and she escorted him into the Oval Office.

"Mr. President," Shapiro began. "I got here as fast as I could." Lawson could see Shapiro was visibly winded and wondered if he had literally run the two miles between his office in the Pentagon and the White House.

"Sit down, Ed," responded Lawson. Turning to Rutherford, he added, "And please get Secretary Shapiro a glass of water. He looks like he needs one."

Never one to sit behind his desk, Lawson paced the office as he spoke. It helped him focus his thoughts. It also made it a lot easier for Rutherford to hear the conversation.

"Ed, I assume you have the report from Admiral Wright."

"Yes, Mr. President, I do. It presents a major problem. We're in the dark about China's intentions. And I don't trust them," responded Shapiro.

"Nor do I."

"What do you need me to do, sir?"

"I need you to do your job, Ed."

Lawson's tone revealed his frustration, facing the reality that despite all of his power, he was rendered essentially impotent by an uncooperative Congress, disinterested public, and antiquated satellite system in fighting the growing challenges China presented in trade and space.

Shapiro knew that he should remain silent and not entangle himself in an argument with the president over whether he could do his job as secretary of defense.

Phillip Lawson stood at the window overlooking the White House lawn leading to the Rose Garden. It was one of his favorite views and seemed to calm him as it brought back memories of his mother's gardens and the manicured lawn of his childhood home in Wyoming. His father was a fourth-generation rancher and traced the family's lineage to the first homesteaders who came by wagon train to the wilderness in the late 1800s; settlers who turned the area into some of the most productive cattle ranches in the country.

Ranches are passed down from generation to generation. When the patriarch dies, the eldest son inherits the land and operations. Lawson was the younger of two sons, so he always knew his future was not owning and running the ranch. That spurred him on to both college and law school at the University of Wyoming and eventually into politics.

While Lawson himself was not active in the family business, the ranch was his biggest financial benefactor. His brother, William Lawson Jr., made sure the future president never lacked campaign funds.

The Lawson ranch bred black angus cattle with a herd of as many as four thousand head on nearly two hundred thousand acres, less than half of which the Lawsons actually owned. The rest, as is typical of ranches in the West, was leased from the federal government. Wyoming is lucky to be on the east side of the Continental Divide, where water is not much of an issue and the plains are rich with natural grass to feed the cattle most of the year. Lawson's father was an astute businessman and in 1963 started investing in ranches on the western side of the Continental Divide, where the land values eventually soared as riparian rights became major battlegrounds in the conservation of water. So the family became among one of the richest in the nation, with holdings privately held and free from public or government disclosure.

The ranch also grew hay and other grains. They fed the hay to their cattle in the winter and sold the grain on the open market to processors who would pick up crops from silos that lay alongside the rail lines. Some of the largest purchasers were corporate giants like Cargill, Archer Daniels Midland, and Columbia Grain, but also the Japanese and other foreign companies like Toyota, Itochu, and Zen-Noh. Grain was sold under future contracts as well as spot markets when demand warranted it. When producers called for deliveries, ranchers hauled their crop to the silos, where it was weighed and accounts were balanced. Overseeing the sale of the hay and grain for his father and brother taught the future president real-life economics.

Ranchers in Wyoming do not slaughter cattle. They breed and feed them on plains grass and hay until they reach about eighteen months, at which point they are commonly called yearlings. Once a calf reaches that age, it is transported to a feedlot in Nebraska or another Corn Belt state for fattening and slaughter. Thus Lawson was spared the bloody side of ranching and raising cattle.

A very efficient operation to this day, the Lawson ranch needs only three full-time cowhands, a few horses, and a small collection of dogs. The crew's main job is to make sure the breeding cows survive delivery and to feed the newborn calves and the cattle. While they also tend to the bulls, that part of the job is easy: just feed them and let them at the cows. Breeder cows and bulls in the herd are expensive investments, with breeders running about $2,000 and bulls as high as $10,000. A typical cow can deliver one calf annually and remain fertile for about ten years. While a bull can live more than fifteen years and remain virile for most of its life, the majority are culled from the herd after five or so years due to other maladies they suffer.

The foreman at the Lawson ranch and his crew of two lived in a bunkhouse about a half mile from the main house. The Lawsons also owned a home in Laramie and spent most of their time there, much closer to schools and shopping. On most ranches, help is kept separate from the family. In Wyoming, ranch owners are royalty; the cowhands, their serfs. But that was not the case on the Lawson ranch. They considered their workers as part of their family and treated them very well.

Lawson learned to ride a horse when he was only three and to shoot a rifle at five. Ranchers were always concerned about wildlife feeding on their young calves, particularly coyotes, wolves, and the occasional grizzly bear. Wolves and grizzlies are protected by federal law; coyotes are not. So by the time Lawson was seven years old, he had lost count of the number of coyotes he'd shot. When on rare occasions he mistakenly shot and killed a wolf, the crime was quickly covered up. Luckily, he never encountered a grizzly, although the occasional trespassing hunters regaled him with stories about them. He usually met the trespassers when given the chore to make sure the gates were closed. It was a nuisance to wrangle cattle escaping through a gate carelessly left open by hunters. Even though the hunters are trespassers, ranchers have no real choice but to tolerate them. Policing is simply too time consuming on tracts of lands that cover hundreds of square miles. Besides, if they occasionally shoot some wolves and bears, legally or not, the ranchers are not known to complain.

The Lawson ranch bordered an Indian reservation, so Phillip Lawson came to know Native Americans at an early age. He loved their stories and ceremonies. The ranchers and Native Americans get along just fine and often share grazing land. Lawson had a deep respect for them.

The one chore he disdained was branding the young calves. The cowhands on horseback, along with their barking dogs, corral the calves. Once the animals are corralled, electric prods coax them into a narrow corridor with metal fencing on each side, known as a chute. As they form a single file, each calf enters the "squeeze," where a lever is pulled down and the two sides of fencing literally squeeze the calf and immobilize it. The ranch brand is then burned into their hide. The whole affair is noisy and chaotic. The calves suffer as much from the confusion as from the pain of the branding. Labor for the process is usually a cooperative effort of friends and family. Once the branding is done, the rancher hosts a picnic for everyone who helped. While some who are not ranchers may see branding as a cruel ritual, it was an efficient way to keep track of wild stock and warranted a celebratory picnic.

His childhood also taught him the importance of protecting the environment. His father stressed that ranchers needed to appreciate the wetlands and respect the wildlife, even when it made it more difficult to ranch. Lawson understood that a rancher's relationship with his surroundings had to balance profits with preservation.

His deep appreciation of nature and respect for everyone served him well, first as a six-term congressman and then a senator before being elected president. While very much a Second Amendment advocate and supportive of the movement to remove protection for wolves as an endangered species, he saw little purpose in guns intended to kill in volume rather than protect one's home and, in his family's case, cattle. Some accused him of being hypocritical in defending wildlife while advocating hunting and shooting. He didn't see it that way. As far as Lawson was concerned, wolves and bears were plentiful in Wyoming and annually cost ranchers tens of thousands of dollars in slaughtered cattle. It was a matter of economics.

His respect for Native Americans also made him beloved by Indian tribes, as he always championed federal regulations protecting their lands and heritage. It all gave him an attractive mix of conservative and liberal views that voters liked. And he eschewed Twitter. If he had something to say, he preferred to explain it in more than 140 characters.

After what seemed like an eternity to Shapiro, the president finished contemplating the Rose Garden and finally broke the silence.

"We can't fly blind on this, Ed. Certainly we have the intelligence capabilities to find out what China intends to do. We've seen five launches of massive rockets in the past month. Shit, at least twelve in just the last year. That's more than we've done in the last five years."

Shapiro was tempted to remind the president of the news media's observations that the failure to stay abreast in the space race was due to Lawson's lack of leadership in getting Congress to fund the Space

Force's military budgets. Even left-leaning publications like the *New York Times* wrote that the president made Wright nothing more than the caretaker of very expensive listening stations, while China left the United States in the dust of space exploration. But Shapiro knew better than to tell Lawson that his administration had any fault.

Lawson, his frustration mounting, continued. "All anyone can tell me is that we have no fucking idea of what is going on. That's not acceptable, Ed."

Shapiro could no longer hold in his frustration.

"With all due respect, Mr. President, our position in the space race is fading fast. We're suffering from too much partisan bickering and not enough leadership."

Shapiro could see Lawson's glare but pressed on, wanting to make his point. "No one is stepping up and questioning China's lead in the technology race, much of which was built by stealing U.S. intellectual property. Hell, Mr. President, they've stolen us blind with barely a slap on their wrists."

Lawson, despite being obviously agitated at the implied criticism of his administration as part of the problem, responded calmly in an effort to lighten the tension. "Why not tell me how you really feel!"

Shapiro remained silent, not knowing what was coming next. He expected the worst from Lawson and already began regretting his tone.

"Ed," continued Lawson, "when I asked you to become secretary of defense, your initial reaction was to say no. So I pushed you as the former CEO of Dunhill Aerospace, one of the world's leaders in aeronautics and rocket engineering, to leave the cushioned life of a millionaire industrialist and help me lead this nation back to greatness. That meant I wanted to hear what's on your mind, not what you think I want to hear."

"I meant no disrespect, Mr. President," responded Shapiro. "I apologize for my tone. But I believe I'm right. We've tolerated China far too long. And now we're facing a true crisis."

"What does the CIA have to say on this?" asked Lawson.

"Their intelligence is no better, Mr. President. Nor have we seen anything helpful from Brussels or London."

"Is there even anything left of the intelligence operations in Europe?" asked Lawson.

"Great Britain's MI5 and MI6, as well as the European Union's security forces, are more concerned with Russia and domestic terrorism than they are with the Chinese. England's space program is virtually nonexistent. The European Space Agency is focused on commercial uses for space, not landing anything on the Moon much less Mars. India, Japan, and Israel are making some progress, but nothing that yields any intelligence on the Chinese. And Russia's program is in shambles. Russia doesn't have the money needed to invest in success."

"So where does that all lead to, Ed?"

"The private sector, Mr. President, is where we might have had some hope, but they are all private ventures with no intelligence-gathering objectives. So on the military front in space, I'm afraid the United States is alone. And we're far behind China, sir."

"All right," responded Lawson, pausing to carefully consider how to respond.

"What I need from you, Ed," continued Lawson, "is a briefing in two days that outlines our options and the consequences of each. Put together key advisers and let's get together here at the White House. Include the vice president."

"Yes, Sir." Shapiro stood, frowning. He was clearly unhappy with the suggestion that Vice President Alicia Holmes be included. The two rarely saw eye to eye on anything.

As if on cue, again Rutherford walked into the room.

"I made you some chamomile tea, Mr. President. It may help calm your nerves."

She escorted Shapiro out of the office.

CHAPTER THREE

WHITE HOUSE KITCHEN
EXECUTIVE RESIDENCE

WHEN PHILLIP LAWSON AND HIS WIFE OF THIRTY YEARS, ATLEE, MOVED INTO THE WHITE HOUSE, their tour of the Executive Residence was overwhelming, as it is for all newly elected presidents. In particular, they were in awe of the three so-called kitchens.

After finally settling in to their new home, the president and first lady preferred the family kitchen. It reminded Lawson of the kitchen of his childhood in Wyoming.

There are three official White House kitchens. The main kitchen can seat 140 for dinner or nearly 1,000 for passed hors d'oeuvres. In reality, it's a kitchen only in name, even though it has all the cookware and trappings of any major restaurant. The second is a pastry kitchen.

The third is the family kitchen in the Executive Residence, the official private kitchen for the president and his or her family. The official Executive Residence occupies the top two floors of the center of the White House. In all, the residence includes more than 20,000 square feet, although the private section for the family is about 9,000 square feet. Suffice to say it's more than enough space for even the largest of families. In the case of the Lawsons, it was just the two of them. They never had children, so the vast majority of the space remained vacant. The president and first lady spent their time in the west side master bedroom, sitting hall, and occasionally the dining room when they invited family, close friends, and colleagues to their home. When guests stayed overnight, they were given the Lincoln or Queen's bedroom on the East side of the residence, assuring that the First Family had total privacy if that was what they wanted. Lawson and his wife also enjoyed sitting on the Truman balcony, accessed off the living room. Otherwise, the residence could be a rather lonely place, but a welcome respite from the constant interruptions by staff as Lawson faced one crisis after another. Such an imbalance was the polar opposite of how Lawson grew up in Wyoming.

Lawson's mother and father eschewed formalities. The family more often ate dinner in their kitchen than in the dining room. As a child, Lawson particularly liked all the aromas from cooking that lingered in the kitchen air. And being messy was no big deal, absent formal dinnerware and tablecloths.

In the Lawson home, the food was also always simple. Usually meat or fish, some fresh vegetables, and potatoes. Always potatoes. Baked, mashed, deep-fried, french fried, pan fried, in a casserole, in a soup, or prepared in a fashion that was difficult to recognize or describe. Lawson was convinced that his mother thought about potatoes all day long and how to surprise them every night with her latest recipe. But dinner, even the potatoes, was always good and the conversation lively.

Alcohol at dinner and in the house was common, but not in excess. A glass of wine or beer accompanied the evening meal. Occasionally, his father would have a scotch or bourbon; his mother a vodka martini, but never before dinner.

The only smoking was his father's pipe and an occasional cigar. His mother prohibited cigarettes.

It was not until Phillip attended the University of Wyoming that he experimented with drugs or smoked an occasional joint.

But it didn't do anything for him that he didn't get from beer or bourbon and was a lot more expensive, let alone illegal. He tried some cocaine once but found it unpleasant, making his experience with drugs short lived.

All in all, Phillip Lawson led the perfect life in childhood and through his college and law school years. Through it all, he grew to appreciate the things he and his family had and the opportunities the country offered. A semester abroad in Berlin in his senior year of college gave him the opportunity to travel throughout Europe and, in particular, the concentration camps in Germany and Poland. Those visits transformed him. He could not imagine the horror and depravity humankind can exact on innocent people. It reinforced his appreciation for America.

"Mr. President, may I prepare anything for you?" asked Mark Pedretti, the White House executive chef. Pedretti never left until he knew the president had an evening meal. While he often tried to suggest a menu, Pedretti came to learn that the Lawsons' hours were too unpredictable to plan. In the early months, Pedretti would leave something in the refrigerator that could easily be heated up by someone on the staff. In the morning, however, whatever he left remained untouched. Pedretti resigned himself to the reality that his true culinary efforts were left to state dinners or intimate, scheduled meals with other leaders. For those, Lawson left the menu choices to Pedretti and the first lady. After all, the president knew his own choice of cuisine was likely to be lame, particularly if potatoes were involved. But Pedretti took feeding the president very seriously.

"Thanks, Mark. Just whip up something simple. Do we have some good T-bones?"

"Of course, Mr. President. I can grill one to perfection. Medium rare, right?"

"Yep," responded Lawson.

"And I'll fry some peppers and onions the way you like them. Will the first lady be joining you?" asked Pedretti. She usually did.

"Yes, I believe she will," responded Lawson.

"Oh." Pedretti paused for a few seconds, the president knowing what he was next going to hear.

"Then I guess I'll make some fish and steam the vegetables," suggested Pedretti, knowing that the first lady was always trying to keep her husband's meals healthier than those he ate as a child.

"You know her too well, Mark. But we would like some wine. Sauvignon blanc would be nice."

Just as Pedretti turned to begin the preparation, Atlee Lawson walked into the kitchen, dressed comfortably in blue cotton pants and a plain white blouse. The first lady rarely wore designer clothes except at official functions. She preferred to be relaxed, particularly when she was with her husband.

"Good evening, gentlemen. And what are you cooking up for us tonight, Mark?" asked the first lady, sitting to the right of the president at the counter. Both preferred to sit at the island in the center of the kitchen, facing the stove over the black granite countertop, to enjoy the show Pedretti performed whenever he cooked.

"To tell you the truth, Atlee," playfully interjected the president, "I first asked Mark to make me a nice juicy steak and fried peppers and onions but then we remembered you were joining us. So now it's fish and steamed broccoli or some other green thing."

"Sweetie, if you want a steak, have a steak," coyly responded the first lady. "After all, who am I to deny a Wyoming cattle rancher and, to boot, the president of the United States, his occasional cow?"

Before the president could reply, Pedretti interjected, "Actually, Mrs. Lawson, the president had steak twice this week. You were away at the conference in Miami."

"Et tu, Brute?" said Lawson as if he'd been stabbed. "Whose side are you on, anyway?"

"Always on your side, Mr. President. As long as the first lady approves!" Pedretti laughed. "I'll make a wonderful arctic char, Mrs. Lawson. Just like the president likes it."

The Lawsons treasured their private dinners together. The lives of a U.S. president and first lady generally mean that privacy is an illusion. Each has their own agenda and more often than not cannot find time to be alone together. While Camp David afforded an occasional respite, their trips there had been few and far between. It was the daily grind that took the most out of each of them. They treasured the rare occasion when they could relax with a simple meal prepared by Pedretti.

The president and first lady had met at the University of Wyoming when Lawson was a junior and she a sophomore. Atlee Faber was an econ major and a member of Alpha Phi, a sorority with a long history at the university and one that included some of the most attractive female students on campus. When invited by her sorority sister, Christine Smith, to a party at Lawson's fraternity, Sigma Alpha Epsilon, she was reluctant to go. SAE had a less than stellar reputation as bad boys, and the legacy of its name—"Sex Above Everything"—was not undeserved. She consented only when Smith promised her that they'd leave together at any time Faber felt uncomfortable. On that condition, she felt nothing bad could happen.

By any measure, Atlee Faber was stunning. At five foot seven and 130 pounds, with blonde hair and striking green eyes, she attracted immediate attention whenever she walked into a room. She kept her hair short, just a few inches below her ears, and wore little makeup. She didn't need it. That evening, she was dressed in a way that accented her figure just the way she wanted to. Enticing but not overly so.

Phillip Lawson was the first person Smith introduced to her before she ran off to party with the bad boys.

So much for the compact to stick together and leave if I felt uncomfortable, thought Faber.

After Faber accepted the offer of a bottle of beer from Lawson, he said, "I have a confession to make." He twisted off the top of the bottle as he handed it to her. The rule for women was to accept a drink from a frat boy only if you see it made or opened in front of you. Never trust a testosterone-laden twenty-year-old not to put something in your drink that would turn the evening into a nightmare.

"Do you?" responded Faber, taking the beer. "I'm not used to confessions from men so quickly."

Lawson smiled and confessed, "The truth is I asked Christine to convince you to come tonight. Knowing the house's reputation, I knew you would never come just to party. You and I are in Econ 304 together. Not that you noticed me. I try to sit in the back and not be noticed. Econ is not my favorite subject and Professor Kim is a piece of work. His Korean accent is so thick I can barely understand him."

"He is a piece of work," agreed Faber. "That's why I sit up front, so I can better hear him. It helps a little. You should try it sometime."

"Me? No. I prefer to sit in the back. It's easier to play my crosswords," Lawson responded with a smile.

"So I guess that means you're a man of many words, Phil?"

"Perhaps, Atlee," responded Lawson, "but something tells me you are not someone who is lacking in words yourself."

Faber smiled and suggested, "Well, Phil, I guess we'll have to spend a lot more time together for you to find out."

"I'll take that as a challenge, Atlee. One I'm happy to accept."

"Game on, Phil."

And so the dating began. It did not take long before their mutual attraction became apparent not only to the two of them, but to everyone around them.

Dinners on Friday at the Sweet Melissa Café became a ritual. Fine dining in Laramie, Wyoming, was limited. The Sweet Melissa was a place where they could enjoy a drink in the tavern accompanied by some bar food or, on a special occasion, eat in the dining room of the café, where the menu was more extensive but still simple.

Lawson went on to earn his BA in political science and then enrolled in law school. A year after Faber graduated she pursued an MBA at the university. The two were married during Lawson's third year of law school. The timing was perfect, with both completing their graduate degrees in the same year, free to take a job anywhere.

But however much they liked the Sweet Melissa and the food served there, they came to learn that nothing could ever match the menus Pedretti offered every night in the White House.

For most of dinner that night, the two talked about nothing particularly important. Pedretti made them a wonderful panko-covered arctic char with a honey and mustard glaze, fresh string beans with a little butter, and a small cucumber salad with balsamic vinegar and olive oil. By the time the dessert came, a mix of macerated strawberries in Cointreau and whipped cream, the two had finished the bottle of Duckhorn sauvignon blanc. As long as Pedretti was working the kitchen preparing and serving the meal, the president and first lady always kept the conversation general. The president had a strict policy to never discuss important issues in front of any of the White House staff except, when necessary, Christy Rutherford.

Pedretti kept on top of the cleanup as the Lawsons ate. Once he'd served dessert, the kitchen was ready for the next day.

"Mark, Mrs. Lawson and I will clean up the rest. We've kept you too late as it is."

"My pleasure, Mr. President. I never leave my kitchen without cleaning it head to toe. There are some perks to your office, sir. And not having to clean up the kitchen is one of them. I hope you and Mrs. Lawson have a wonderful evening. Would you like me to pour you each a bit of cognac before I leave?"

"That would be lovely, Mark," answered the first lady. "We'll have it on the Truman balcony. Please be so kind as to bring it there."

"Yes, Mrs. Lawson," responded Pedretti.

The first lady and president stood and walked out of the kitchen and over to the balcony.

Over the objections of Congress and the White House architect, then President Harry Truman built the balcony in 1948. Hence its name. When Congress failed to provide funding, Truman used his

White House household account to complete the project. Politicos thought a balcony would ruin the look of the columns that adorned the front of White House. Truman pointed out that the awnings that then covered the windows on the official residence were dirty and far more of an eyesore than any balcony would be. In the end, he won over all the naysayers, who later admitted that the balcony added to the beauty of the house and provided an important sanctuary for the first family. Years later, President Barack Obama said it was his favorite spot in the house.

Pedretti poured about an ounce of Rémy Martin Louis XIII into each of two gleaming crystal Baccarat snifters and delivered them to the first couple. It's not that the Lawsons routinely had one of the world's most expensive cognacs in equally elegant glasses. The cognac and glassware were gifts from other countries. The supply was almost endless. And since it would be bad politics to regift any of it, the president and his staff enjoyed a little known and delightful perquisite. Serving the Louis XIII was one of the few exceptions to the rule that no food not directly purchased or accessed by the staff was permitted in the White House.

Once they were alone, the first lady opened the conversation in the direction she knew her husband wanted to go.

"Bad day, Phil? You look awful."

The first lady could read the president better than anyone and knew when he was torn or between a rock and a hard place, something that was almost a daily occasion for the president of the United States.

"You read me well. It's China again. They've launched more rockets to the Moon, one with eight astronauts, or taikonauts as they call them. It's the first time they've included a human crew slated for the Moon, so we have to assume whatever they're doing on the Moon is close to operational."

"And you don't know what they're planning?" asked the first lady.

"No. Nor do we trust them."

"What do others say?"

"Shapiro isn't much help. Nor is Wright. I'm going to have a meeting tomorrow with some of the others, including the veep. I know she and Ed don't get along, but the debate between the two of them often leads to constructive ideas."

"Will Mike be there?"

"Yes. I need the CIA's take on this. Mike Hellriegel is one person I really trust."

"Have you spoken to anyone else yet? Who knows about the situation?" she asked.

"I've only spoken to Wright and Shapiro. And of course, I'm sure Christy knows everything that we discussed. We both know her ears and eyes are better than an owl. Why do you ask?"

"No reason, really. I just wondered."

The first lady liked to keep a short list each time the president met with someone to gauge who was most likely to leak information to the press. As every official resident of the Oval Office knew, leaks were a seemingly incurable plague on the presidency. Atlee Lawson was intent on rooting them out if she could.

Being first lady was an honor and duty Atlee Lawson accepted with grace. She took on the mandatory charitable work and photo ops but also kept one foot in the world of global economics and continued to work at a think tank in Washington on projects centered on balancing the competing interests of global politics and economics. Some in Congress didn't like the idea of the first lady having potential influence on the president beyond his diet, but no one dared to take the first lady on, knowing that the wrath from the president would pale in comparison to what they'd get from her.

She and the vice president often had lively discussions over monetary policy and regulation. President Lawson encouraged it. The first lady was a free market proponent, while the vice president believed that open competition and market concentration needed to be tempered with regulation and oversight. The game the president played didn't get past Atlee Lawson whenever he asked her if she'd talked about something with the vice president. He wanted to hear all sides of every issue and regularly pitted the sides in a debate before he decided what to do. She knew he'd do the same with the latest challenge from China.

"You just wondered?" responded the president. "Atlee, I know you well enough to know that you don't 'just wonder' about anything."

"I worry."

"I know. About leaks. But there's nothing we can do about that. Trying to figure out who told whom and when is a fool's errand. We need to focus on solutions. That requires a dialog with a broad constituency. So leaks are inevitable. Sometimes even useful."

"What about your scheduled summit with Xi Jinping in Shanghai?" asked the first lady. "Under the circumstances, do you think you should postpone it?"

"I don't know yet. Let's see what my advisers recommend. I don't want to rush to any judgment."

"Not rushing is good, but you will be meeting with him at the G20 Summit in a couple of months anyway. Why give him two opportunities to deny the truth?" asked the first lady.

"I don't know yet. But you could also say I might use both meetings to convince him to tell the truth or suffer severe consequences," responded the president.

"Phil, that's what scares me. That you will actually consider the worst of options."

"I have no choice but to consider every option. That does not mean I'll use the worst among them. Hell, I might decide to do nothing. Maybe we should let China go bankrupt trying to chase dreams on the Moon. Wild spending eventually bankrupted the USSR. I certainly don't see any strategic value to it."

"Even with nuclear missiles in silos on the surface?"

"Atlee, China has plenty of ICBMs far closer to us than the Moon. So whatever strategic advantage they might think it gives them, I don't buy it."

"But your advisers do, right?" asked the first lady, knowing that while the president surrounded himself with advisers who represented virtually every ideology, deep down Phillip Lawson wanted to win rather than compromise.

"Some think that way, Atlee. Some don't. I'll consider them all. Then I'll come to a decision that I expect them all to support."

Including me, thought the first lady. *Including me.*

The two stayed on the balcony talking about the day for another hour or so and then retired to bed. Neither slept well.

CHAPTER FOUR

SPACE

THE CREW HAD JUST ENJOYED EIGHT HOURS OF SLEEP. AT LEAST AS MUCH AS SLEEP EXISTS in the weightlessness of space. At best, sleeping is restless, particularly on the first day as your body acclimates.

One day out from the launch, the Dragon was chasing three cargo ships laden with materials critical to their mission. It takes just over three days to journey the 240,000 miles from Earth and reach the Moon. Now nearly 100,000 miles into their trip, the Dragon was on schedule to rendezvous with the cargo ships, which were traveling at far slower speeds. Through sophisticated computer-driven guidance, all of the cargo ships were within a few miles of one another. If the plan worked, the taikonauts aboard the Dragon would reach them within thirty hours, send the cargo ships one at a time to the surface, and then begin their own descent to the waiting base.

Cheng Zhou, mission commander, was busy reviewing his mission orders with Deputy Commander Wu Meilin. Both were veteran space travelers. Cheng had six previous flights on his résumé with cumulative time in space of over a year. Wu, twenty years Cheng's junior, had only three missions to her credit but more time in space than Cheng. Together, there was no better team China could have entrusted with the critical mission. The mission control group in China liked to refer to them as the "Old Man and the She." Whenever Cheng heard it, he knew that Ernest Hemingway was rolling over in his grave.

As Cheng looked out of the Dragon's window, he could see the Earth, now a small image that seemed a million miles away. He'd never seen it from such a distance.

"Meilin, Earth looks like such a fragile place from here," he said.

Wu, far less philosophical than her commander, responded, "Yes, I suppose so. And fragile would be an understatement." Wu's politics, steeped in China's propaganda and its Communist doctrines, gave her little appreciation of such cosmic observations by Cheng. "Commander, we need to finish the checklist. Can we get back to it?" Wu asked Cheng.

"Yes, Deputy Commander Wu," Cheng responded with a sigh. "We need to obey our orders and ignore the wonders that surround us. But isn't it sad we cannot just stop and appreciate the beauty that surrounds us? We're all caught up in trivial pursuits and checklists that will mean so little in our short lives."

"Yes, Commander," responded Wu, wondering whether she should really care about such sadness. She preferred to look at everything from a regimented and practical viewpoint. Romantics like Cheng had no place in her world.

Like everyone in the crew, Cheng and Wu had never been to the Moon. But they were not the first from China to land. In fact, China had landed more than two dozen workers that were busy building a base from which missions, peaceful or otherwise, would be launched. Those awaiting the arrival of Cheng, Wu, and their colleagues, however, were different. They were not human. While some of the cyborgs were destroyed in crashes and other mishaps, most survived and were following orders beamed to their CPUs in complex and unbreakable algorithms. One of the cargo ships had fifty more cyborgs to add to the workers.

The crew of the Dragon would make the base operational. Each possessed a set of skills necessary to succeed and the computer codes that were needed, literally, to turn it on.

Liu Qing Shan was the crew's medical doctor, an internist by training and perhaps the crew's most critical member, since the overall physical and mental health of the others was in her hands.

Because the crew was scheduled to remain on the Moon for months if not years, Dr. Liu's concerns centered on the long-term effects of little gravity, confined space, and anxieties that space travel creates. Since the first Russian cosmonaut returned to Earth, scientists and the medical community have examined every effect space can have on the human body and psyche. A lot was known, but much more was left to learn. The key was adapting to changing circumstances, and it was Dr. Liu's job to see that the taikonauts were fit to do so.

She began what would become daily rounds talking to the crewmembers to confirm that each was healthy in body and mind. Her approach was to engage in simple conversation confirming each crewmember's job. They all knew the routine.

She began with Cheng and Wu.

"Colonel Cheng and Captain Wu," Dr. Liu began, "I trust we're on schedule."

"Indeed we are, Doctor," responded Cheng.

"So, Dr. Liu," interjected Wu, "is this when you decide if we're still sane and capable of landing this spaceship on the Moon?" Dr. Liu did not miss the ring of sarcasm in Wu's voice. Nor did she appreciate it.

"Captain Wu," responded Dr. Liu, "I have no doubt you and Colonel Cheng are sane and capable. But just as you have a responsibility on this mission, so do I. And I take mine very seriously."

Wu got the message and contritely responded, "My apologies, Dr. Liu."

"Apology accepted, Captain Wu. We're going to be together for a long time and it's best we respect one another's responsibilities." Dr. Liu wanted to make sure the captain knew her place.

"So," asked Dr. Liu, "what happens next for the two of you and the rest of us?"

"For now, Dr. Liu, you and the crew can relax. Captain Wu and I will pilot us to the Moon and expect a picture-perfect landing."

Wu interjected, "And once on the Moon, we'll inspect the Jades, fire them up, and get to our base station."

Jades are vehicles that resemble snowmobiles. Each can take a taikonaut quickly from building to building as they set out to inspect launch pads or map the area.

"And we will maintain the return module to make sure when it's time to leave we safely return to Earth," Colonel Cheng added.

While the main stage of the rocket was nothing more than an empty thirty-story tower jettisoned shortly after launch and returned to Earth, the return rocket and lunar module on the Moon were critical to getting home.

"And you are confident you can get us back home, Colonel?" asked Dr. Liu.

Cheng considered his response before answering. "Dr. Liu, we are all dedicated to the mission. Captain Wu and I intend to get everyone home safely. But we all also understand that our tickets might be one-way."

"Understood," responded Dr. Liu. "I appreciate your honesty."

She moved on to Zhang Hong, the mission's nuclear physicist.

"Hong, how do you feel?"

"Very good, Doctor."

"And what is your responsibility on this mission?"

Zhang found the routine a bit silly but knew better than to make light of it. Dr. Liu found nothing about it amusing.

"I have two jobs. First, to make sure the nuclear reactors on site perform safely and provide the power we need. Second, it is my job to assemble the warheads for the IGBMs—the Intergalactic Ballistic Missiles."

"Very good, Hong. And how will you accomplish those tasks?"

Again, Zhang yearned to make light of the question and suggest he'd just wave a magic wand, but he knew that it was important to respond with a serious answer.

"The parts to build the warheads are in the cargo ships. The IGBM rocket fuselage and engines are on site awaiting us and ready for assembly. I also have to deal with fueling the rockets. Some of those components are not there yet but will arrive in later ships. I expect them within two months. Cargo tankers filled with fuel."

"Thank you, Hong."

Dr. Liu worked her way over to Shao Rushi, using the handgrips on the walls of the ship to pull herself in the weightlessness of space.

Shao had earned her Ph.D. in computer science focusing on coding, machine learning, and artificial intelligence. She programmed the computers and cyborgs to build the habitat that awaited them. While she was confident that her little army of construction workers did their job, she grew tenser with every passing hour. This was something that concerned Dr. Liu.

"Rushi," said Dr. Liu, "you seem tense. Is there something that concerns you?"

"No, Dr. Liu, I'm fine," answered Shao. "I'm just excited about assembling the Luna Diébào computer."

"Why?"

"Dr. Liu, once assembled, it will have a performance capacity in excess of 150 petaflops. Its computing speed and capacity will outclass China's legendary Sunway TaihuLight supercomputer."

"How so?"

"Like the Sunway," responded Shao, "the Luna Diébào does not run on accelerator chips like most other computers. Instead, it relies on thousands of core processors, giving it unprecedented efficiency, a major factor in the power necessary to operate the computer. In short, once assembled, the Luna Diébào will be the most advanced and efficient computer in the world—or the universe. Its capacity for machine learning will be unsurpassed. Whether that leads to true artificial intelligence remains to be seen. But if I have my way, I'll let the Luna Diébào chart its own future free from human intervention."

Dr. Liu wondered how wise it was to give a computer so much power, but trusted Shao and China's computer scientists to create a machine that would help rather than destroy mankind.

Huang Lian was a construction specialist. A real hardhat, he had been monitoring the cyborgs building the base since first deployed. While Huang knew all about building structures, Shao knew how to code the cyborgs to enable them to learn and improve performance and to be far more efficient than any human construction worker could ever hope to be. And much more obedient. The two worked well as a team.

"So Lian, how do you feel?" asked Dr. Liu.

"Good, Dr. Liu," he responded. "I just want to get to the base and start working with Rushi and get started. I'm done with training and want to get on the ground."

"Lian, that will happen very soon," Dr. Liu responded as she moved on to Lt. Colonel Yang Jin and Captain Fong Hui, the remaining members of the crew.

Both were members of the elite Snow Leopard Commando Unit, China's equivalent of the Navy Seals or Army Rangers. Fong was one of the few women who ever made it through the rigorous training. When her male counterparts joked with her about how that proved the inferiority of women as combatants, she quickly pointed out that only three percent of applicants were women, making her success rate on a percentage basis far better than any man.

"Good evening, Jin and Hui," began Dr. Liu. "How are you feeling?"

"Great, Doctor," responded Yang. "We can't wait to get to the surface and start deploying the cyborgs."

"No kidding," added Fong. "This place is too confined. I want to be in the field and set up defensive perimeters." She thought about, but decided not to mention, that their job was also to enforce the discipline necessary to ensure progress within the timetable set by China's Politburo. But like most officers in China's military, their grit and guts had never been tested in battle. That didn't matter. No one expected them to engage in any combat on the Moon. Their mission was to deploy the cyborgs already delivered and those en route, link them to the Luna Diébào, and deliver those designated soldiers to their defensive positions surrounding the base. Or, if necessary, use them as an offensive force against any enemy that might challenge China's hegemony on the Moon.

CHAPTER FIVE

WASHINGTON, DC

THE VERGE WAS FIRST TO BREAK THE NEWS, LESS THAN TWENTY-FOUR HOURS AFTER Lawson's calls with Wright and Shapiro. Its sources at the Space Force and throughout Washington were deep. In frustration, they were anxious to talk.

"The United States Sleeps as the Red Dragon Conquers Space" blared the headline in that evening's digital edition. Reported by Agatha Graves, a seasoned technology correspondent, the story's facts were too accurate to be guesswork. Her very high-level contacts had been cultivated during a twenty-plus-year career.

Graves wrote, "For more than a year, the Space Force has watched China launch rocket after rocket as they colonize the Moon with men and robots. No one seems to know what they are building. What NASA and the Space Force do know is that China has sent dozens of cargo ships to the Moon in the past two years. Sources say the U.S. believes they contain modular components necessary to build a permanent base on the surface. But for what purpose? Now at least eight Chinese taikonauts are on their way to the Moon. What are their jobs once they get there? China claims the base is there to peacefully mine the Moon and to be China's platform for a mission to Mars. The problem? We all know China lies. Lying has been at the core of their very being for millennia. Ethics are as foreign to them as God is to an atheist. According to highly placed sources, President Lawson is at the end of his patience. Disgusted with Congress and the failure of every other nation to address China's attempt at hegemony in space, he fears our nation and the world are facing dominance by a superpower intent on controlling mankind's interstellar future. Edward Shapiro, secretary of defense, is equally frustrated. Our sources say he's increasingly regretful that he ever took the job. How can he lead an agency that has lost its focus on our worst enemy? Are we once again cowering to a global despot as we did in World War II? Did we not learn a lesson that dictators and oppressive regimes deny us the freedoms we so cherish? Is it time for Congress and the world to react? Before it's too late?"

By noon that day, every news outlet online and off spread the rumors. As reporters dug into their myriad of contacts, speculation ran amok. Facts soon fell prey to fiction as the threat ballooned well beyond what Lawson or Shapiro believed was reality. Articles falsely claimed that the far side of the Moon never receives light despite the fact that it gets just as much as the near side. It's just not visible to Earth. Other newspapers resurrected the conspiracy theories from the past century that U.S. astronauts saw UFOs and aliens on the far side when they orbited the Moon but were told not to talk about it. Local newscasters brought up the old rumors that claimed Russia planned to use the far side for nuclear testing and speculated that may be what China was planning. Never mind the 1959 U.S. Air Force proposal—Project A119—to detonate a nuclear bomb on the Moon, reportedly believing that a nuclear explosion visible from Earth would boost the morale of the American people. The level of false reporting and similar absurdity kept growing.

Amidst the growing cacophony from the press and as ordered, Shapiro brought Vice President Alicia Holmes, CIA Director Michael Hellriegel, Chairman of the Joint Chiefs of Staff Gen. Ryan Speck, and U.S. Ambassador to the United Nations Alex Friedman to the Oval Office. It was just thirty-six hours since the China launch. The Chinese taikonauts were less than two days from the Moon. Everyone assembled knew that the purpose of the meeting was not to enjoy a lunch at the White House.

"It ceases to amaze me how the press makes our lives more difficult than they need to be," began Lawson. "I don't know who talked to Graves, but she seems to be the only one who has the truth, reporting what we actually know."

No one responded.

"Well isn't this enlightening?" observed Lawson. "You're all speechless."

"Mr. President," offered Hellriegel, "we have no one to blame but ourselves for the dilemma we're facing today. We ignored the warning signs for years. We lost sight of China's long view and the patience they've had for centuries. We're being outplayed. Pure and simple."

Michael Hellriegel had survived three administrations at the helm of the CIA. He was one of the only remaining old-school fixtures in Washington. He'd been a spy for his entire professional career, including ten years as a field agent in Eastern Europe and the Middle East. On at least three occasions, he barely escaped encounters with belligerent enemies in Russia, Bulgaria, and Syria—and those were the ones he knew about. As was the case for all other CIA agents, there was a price on his head while he was in the field. And like every other field agent, Hellriegel never spoke about enemies of the state he eliminated when the choice had been either him or them. Now behind a desk, the physical risk was gone, replaced at times by equally debilitating psychological stress. All of the pressure, however, wore well on Hellriegel. At just under six feet, his only vanity was weekly visits to his barber to keep his gray hair from showing. His dark brown hair gave him an appearance ten years younger than the sixty-six he was. To stay trim, he woke up every morning at 5:45 sharp for his daily run and workout. That put him at his desk by 7:30, generally before his subordinates showed up for work. He liked it that way. And above all else, Hellriegel was a man who spoke his mind.

In addition, the CIA, unlike other federal agencies, had a history of getting things done in ways that no one really wanted to question. Everyone knew that espionage required special talent to get results, the knowledge of which every president wants to plausibly deny whenever it suits him or her to do so.

"Go on, Mike," responded Lawson.

"What brought us to this crisis," Hellriegel continued, "begins with the fact that the last successful Moon orbiters we deployed were Artemis P1 and P2 in 2007. Since then, four other countries attempted to send orbiting satellites to the Moon—Russia, Israel, Japan, and India—with mixed success and little scientific purpose. Only India managed to land something. But it was nothing more than a carnival attraction. None remained active."

"Except for China," interjected Lawson.

"That's correct, Mr. President. China has been successful in all but one reported launch. With the recent spate of launches, we believe China now has a least twelve orbiting satellites joining the three operational U.S. satellites. Without question," concluded Hellriegel, "the United States is dismally behind China in the space race with little prospect of catching up in time to stop whatever they're doing on the Moon. We lack the money and commitment. And more important, the time. Whatever we do about their activities, we have to do on Earth."

Wright picked up on Hellriegel's narrative. "U.S. soft landings on the Moon are even more dated. Both the U.S. and Russia abandoned that effort decades ago. The last soft landing by the U.S.," Wright reminded those gathered, "was in 1972 with Apollo 17, our final manned mission to the Moon. Russia never landed a man on the Moon, and its last successful soft landing of an unmanned capsule—Luna 24—was in 1976. On the other hand, China has at least seven successful soft landings under its belt since 2013, most of which happened after 2020, when China ramped up its program while the rest of the world slept."

Lawson was calm, as his reactions often were. "I hear you both. And I fear you're right. But that doesn't help. If our speculation is accurate—and I remind you all it's mere speculation—China is about to establish the first interstellar military base on the Moon. Worse, it's on the far side of the Moon, where we're handcuffed by our inability to see it from Earth. So let's dispense with blame. There is plenty to pass around. We need solutions."

Shapiro spoke. "Mr. President, we suspect the base is largely built and now going into an operational phase. We've learned over the last two decades that our suspicions about China are often accurate, as we believe they are now. I think we've come to the point where we need to use whatever diplomatic tools we have to bring light to the situation." Shapiro immediately regretted his ironic reference to light following Lawson's comments. Lawson spared him a condescending reaction.

"Perhaps we can bring this to the Security Council," offered Friedman. "While China has a veto on any action and will most certainly use it, we can at least draw them out to public scrutiny. Perhaps that will put pressure on them to be honest."

"Since when has the U.N. ever been a source of honesty?" asked Shapiro.

Lawson responded, "Ed, you're probably right, but at least it's a productive suggestion. Does it have any downside?"

"Of course it does, Mr. President," argued Shapiro. "It gives China a global platform to continue its lies. Let's not forget that more people believe them every day. As Mike said, we've been asleep at the wheel while the world has increasingly turned to China for technology and trade. Why should we believe that a public spectacle at the U.N. will accomplish anything?"

Friedman did not react well. "Secretary Shapiro, I respectfully suggest that your views in the corporate world do not translate into how diplomacy among nations advances peace. Being a bully might work in a boardroom, but it does not in the world of embassies."

"Gentlemen, we need to get past rhetoric. Does anyone have another creative suggestion?" asked Lawson.

Vice President Alicia Holmes cleared her throat. "Mr. President?" Lawson nodded to her, as the other men around the table displayed their discomfort with her presence and her position. Holmes was a controversial choice by Lawson. She lacked political experience, spending most of her career in universities, where she taught economics. Her last post at the University of Chicago was contentious. She developed theories on capitalism and appropriate controls to prevent its unencumbered avarice. She believed that in the digital world, old-school theories of free markets were obsolete. Small business needed protection, and the digital giants created an atmosphere that, however efficient in delivering goods, services, or information to consumers, were choking entrepreneurs. As far as Holmes was concerned, Adam Smith, the so-called Father of Capitalism, was a dinosaur.

She was all the more controversial because she was outspokenly gay. The LGBTQ community had become a significant voting bloc, and moderates and independents joined the liberals in voting for candidates who supported the group.

Lawson chose Holmes to help attract a wide breadth of voters and help him create a broad coalition for economic balance in the growing digital world. She was not chosen for her expertise in global politics and power. But Lawson had come to respect her intellect as much as any of his advisers regardless of the issue at hand.

Shapiro, on the other hand, had little patience for Holmes, as he did for everyone who had the gall to disagree with him. At least Shapiro knew he held no fantasies about Holmes, as he did for many women—a fantasy he often pursued. Holmes, despite her beauty, dressed very conservatively. While articulate and poised, she was not someone who could command a room like Lawson and other seasoned politicians or corporate magnates. Shapiro saw that as a weakness. Lawson did not.

"Mr. President," Holmes continued, "may I be open for a moment, acknowledging that my expertise may be limited in this debate?"

Lawson smiled. "Alicia, I think it's safe to say I've never seen you as someone reluctant to voice her views." He intended it as a compliment. Holmes took it that way.

"As I see it," continued Holmes, "the one thing we all agree on is that the press is in a frenzy over the situation. If you believe them, civilization as we know it is on the edge of destruction. I have little doubt that by week's end, the reporting will be based on pure speculation and little truth. More important, it will stoke the embers of fear. That is the only way they sell what they think is journalism. In truth, it's capitalism at its worst."

"I'm sorry, Madam Vice President, but what is your point?" interjected Shapiro, as impolite as ever. "We're abundantly aware of your belief that capitalism has failed and we need to step in to correct it. But I'm missing your point how that helps us now." Shapiro intended it as an insult. Holmes took it that way.

She ignored Shapiro's slight.

"Mr. President," responded Holmes, ignoring Shapiro, "victory in today's world is won by manipulation of media more than ever before."

No one seemed to disagree.

She continued, "So rather than taking China on directly, also consider using the press to create a global panic. While it will upset markets on the short term, it might also mobilize nations throughout the world to collectively use their technology, as well as diplomacy, to find a solution. Media is compliant. It can be played, just as it is every day by public relations agencies. Even Secretary Shapiro can attest to that." Holmes intended that as an insult to Shapiro, which was precisely how he took it.

"So you're suggesting what, Alicia?" asked Lawson.

"I'm suggesting we use the press to create a global panic that unites nations to mount an alliance to take on China and defeat its aggression. Put an end to its plans. You have a summit scheduled in a couple of weeks in Shanghai where you'll be with Xi Jinping. Unless he can convince you we should not be concerned, the summit gives you a perfect cover to push the panic button as soon as it's over. Perhaps that will force them to tell the truth."

"Good God, Madam Vice President," continued Shapiro, still bristling at her last insult, "you're suggesting a digital world war. What is the end goal and exit strategy? And what will you do if the ultimate solution requires military intervention? Do you honestly think America is ready for another global conflict in which we bear the largest costs in both dollars and blood?"

"Secretary Shapiro," firmly responded Holmes, "when was the last time the United States restrained itself from military action when it was in its best interests?"

"All right," interjected Lawson, "I think we can dispense with the mutual criticism. Every suggestion has merit and deserves consideration."

Shapiro moved on to General Speck. "General, we have not heard from you. Do you think there is a military option to consider? Could we use military intervention to thwart China's plans?"

Ryan Speck was a career soldier honed in combat, with the scars to show it. The recipient of the Silver Star and two Purple Hearts, along with a box full of lesser but impressive awards and honors, Speck had earned the respect he enjoyed well before being promoted to chairman of the Joint Chiefs of Staff. The only two people who outranked him in the military were the secretary of defense and the president of the United States—the country's commander in chief. Speck had been on the ground in every Middle East conflict the U.S. entered since Desert Storm and led his troops "from the front," leaning into the dangers as much as he asked of the men and women he commanded, and for that he was beloved.

"Mr. Secretary, to be honest, we're not prepared for an offensive effort in space much less a ground assault on the Moon. No one has trained for such an operation. We lack soldiers qualified and the equipment necessary to execute any sensible plan. We just never made the commitment for military options beyond our terrestrial world."

Lawson moved uneasily in his chair, chafing at the innuendo that he and Congress were responsible for the limited alternatives available to a country that once had the most powerful armed forces on Earth.

"So the military is not an option," concluded Shapiro.

"I didn't say that, Mr. Secretary," responded Speck. "We always have military options that we can deploy on the ground. That includes reducing China's ability to launch any further supplies to its base. As with any military operation, the most critical element for success is supplies. History has shown many times that armies have often been defeated more by hunger than bullets."

Holmes couldn't resist characterizing Speck's comment.

"What a euphemistic way of describing war, General. Reducing an enemy's ability to supply its troops. I guess it's better they slowly starve than surrender." Her tone was clearly condescending. It was not received well by Speck.

"With all due respect, Madam Vice President, I don't want to see a single soldier, including our enemies, die of starvation or for any other reason. But I'm sure as hell going to do all I can to keep our soldiers alive, and if starvation of the enemy is the toll they must suffer instead of accepting our compassion, so be it."

"General Speck," asked Lawson, "when do you think you can get me a full briefing on the realistic military options we can execute within the next couple of months?"

"I'll need a week, Mr. President."

"Good," responded Lawson as he turned his attention to Holmes. He was warming up to Holmes's idea of manipulating the media. While Shapiro's comments on America's appetite for more sacrifice were true, the thought of uniting the world under U.S. leadership to take on real threats, both on and off the Earth, was enticing to Lawson. Maybe that could reunite the leadership in Washington and give Lawson a boost in the polls. The midterms were coming up, and he didn't want to lose any seats in Congress.

Hellriegel spoke again. "I suggest we take multiple tracks, Mr. President. Alex can bring it to the U.N. while Ed and I deal with the intelligence options. General Speck will have the military options ready in a week. Let the press secretary start thinking about the political spin we need to rope in Europe, Japan, and our friends in Australia. We might even think about Russia, since their relationship with China isn't much better than ours. We can certainly multitask."

"I can't do much at the U.N. if we make this all a public relations spectacle of unifying powers outside the oversight of the U.N.," responded Friedman.

Shapiro quickly interjected, "Then let's dispense with the U.N. option." Immediately, he saw the negative reaction from Friedman. "Sorry, Alex," Shapiro continued. "It's just a reality that the U.N. can't do much with China on the Security Council. So if we believe the other options are viable and the U.N. can't be effective with them, then the U.N. has to go."

"I agree with Ed," added Holmes, surprising Shapiro with her support so soon after their exchange of insults. Shapiro decided Holmes knew a winning argument when she heard one and that diplomacy with China had failed miserably for the past decade. Hellriegel was right. The United States was being played.

"No," responded Lawson. "Nothing is off the table. We're going to consider every option, including the UN."

Lawson called for Rutherford.

"Christy, please have Colleen see me, together with the vice president." Colleen Davies was the White House press secretary and as astute as any had ever been in manipulating the press.

"OK folks, let's move on," Lawson continued. "And Ed, I'd also like you to work with General Speck and Admiral Wright. Get back to me on what we need to do to take this fight to the Moon. I want that option explored. Don't worry about the money. If Colleen can successfully get U.S. citizens in a lather over this, Congress won't be able to say no."

"Yes, sir," responded Shapiro.

"Something tells me," concluded Lawson, "that we might not have any option other than to put boots on the ground. And I'm not sure we even know how to do that on the Moon. What a mess!"

Lawson's distress was evident in the tone of his voice. He and everyone in the room sensed the nightmare that might lie ahead.

"Mr. President," interjected Hellriegel, "what about the Shanghai summit?"

"For now, Mike, we'll leave it on the schedule," responded Lawson.

With that, Lawson rose from his chair, signaling that the meeting was over. Polite good-byes followed. Rutherford brought the president a cup of tea.

CHAPTER SIX

EJIN, ALXA
INNER MONGOLIA

THE JIUQUAN SATELLITE LAUNCH CENTER IS LOCATED IN THE GOBI DESERT IN INNER Mongolia. Opened in 1958, it remains China's central space launch facility. Launch Complex B2 houses the personnel overseeing the Dragon expedition.

"Twelve hours from the Moon," announced mission controller Suyin Ming. Together with more than fifty colleagues in the central hub, it is her job to keep everyone aware of timing to their target. At the right time, Ming will command the computer on the Dragon to fire its retro rockets after the spacecraft reaches the far side of the Moon. Timing is critical, since she cannot send the order once the crew reaches the far side. Ming has to be precise, taking into account speed and altitude, neither of which she'd know to a certainty until just before the spacecraft goes out of sight. As long as her computers work as programmed, the crew, buckled in and relaxed, will be assured a soft and safe landing. If anything did go wrong, Cheng would take control and attempt a manual landing. The success rate of such a move, however, was poor.

"Everything look good, Suyin?" asked Boris Kushner, the launch center director.

"Yes, Director Kushner, all indicators are green. In less than twelve hours, our crew should be walking on the far side of the Moon!" replied Ming with obvious excitement in her voice.

"And the cyborgs? Are they responding?"

"Yes sir, they are online and waiting."

Kushner smiled at Ming's enthusiasm. A veteran of Russia's space program, he had left Roscosmos, Russia's equivalent of NASA, and joined the China National Space Administration after Russia's program hit budgeting issues that stymied growth. Worse, Kushner became bitter when he was blamed and made the scapegoat for the 2021 failure of the Soyuz MS-14 mission to the Moon. He saw little future in any loyalty to Mother Russia. On the other hand, China was investing billions with a clear path to the Moon, Mars, and beyond. They also needed talent like Kushner. A testament to his talents was his promotion to director. An obvious outsider, he was among an elite cadre of China's high-ranking ex-pat officials with access to every level of government. And he brought more knowledge on how to get to the Moon than all the intellectual property thieves in China could ever hope to steal.

CHAPTER SEVEN

NUMBER ONE OBSERVATORY CIRCLE
WASHINGTON, DC

ALICIA HOLMES AND ATLEE LAWSON HAD HIT IT OFF THE FIRST TIME THEY MET. WHILE THE two of them could not have been more opposite in personality and just about every other trait, they enjoyed one another's company. Meeting afforded both of them the opportunity to let their guard down, knowing that their conversations would always remain confidential, even from the president.

Atlee Lawson asked to see Holmes on short notice about a confidential matter. While the two of them met often, this request was unusual. As with all first ladies and vice presidents, daily schedules are carefully reviewed and overseen by their staff. Last-minute meeting requests are usually rejected, but not when the first lady asks to see the vice president.

"Atlee, it is good to see you," said Holmes as she welcomed Lawson in the library of her official residence. "You said it was important, so I moved a meeting with Ron Pullem, the lobbyist for the Cannabis Farmers Coalition. No doubt, he wants yet another subsidy to keep America high. So I was happy to cancel my get-together with him.

And it gives me time to relax before going to the office. Would you like a cup of coffee?"

"Yes, that would be nice, thanks," responded Lawson. When together, they were on a first-name basis rather the public formalities of First Lady and Madam Vice President.

The vice president's house is on the grounds of the United States Naval Observatory. The white nineteenth-century house was built in 1893 and became the veep's official residence in 1974. With its wrap-around porch, gables, and turret, the house resembles a rural New England home. Although Holmes had her official office in the West Wing of the White House and a second office in the Eisenhower Executive Office Building located next to the White House, she preferred meetings at her residence. It was far more intimate and fostered more relaxed conversations, even with difficult ambassadors and delegations from China and Russia.

The home was not without its mystery. In 2009, it was reported that an underground bunker was built shortly after the 9/11 attacks that was sometimes used for meetings with the vice president. When then vice president Joe Biden mentioned the bunker, the official response from the White House was, "What the vice president described in his comments was not—as some press reports have suggested—an underground facility, but rather, a downstairs work space in the residence." Holmes always deferred questions about its existence as well as rejecting requests to have meetings in it.

As the vice president and first lady settled into their chairs, the staff served coffee and left the two in private.

Lawson began, "I am deeply concerned about this idiotic space row with China. This mess could escalate to a point of no return, putting us on the edge of war. As much as I can see Phillip's concerns, Shapiro and others are stoking him to go beyond economic sanctions. And China keeps taunting our fleet in the South China Sea. They're all a bunch of boys playing with dangerous toys."

Holmes took a sip of her coffee. While the first lady was her friend, she was not an official member of the administration and not necessarily allowed to know everything discussed in the Oval Office. But Holmes knew the first lady was aware of the close relationship she had with the president, so feigning a lack of knowledge would not work. She resolved to be as honest as she could be.

"Atlee, I share your concerns and have had discussions with the president on many occasions over the past year. But the Chinese are essentially ignoring us. Our sanctions have probably hurt us more than they've hurt them. With Russia and Iran in their camp, China has more than enough allies to withstand dips in their economy caused by us. And keep in mind that even with the sanctions, China's economy still grows faster than ours."

"But is this all worth the rhetoric about nuclear options? My God, we've sent nuclear battleships within range for fast-strike capabilities against China. And they've sent their ships in international waters in the Pacific and Atlantic, armed with who knows what. And no telling where all the submarines are—theirs and ours. Is the Moon so important that we should risk a nuclear holocaust?"

"No one wants nuclear war, Atlee, particularly the president. But the Moon is of critical strategic importance to the United States and the world."

Holmes continued. "If our intelligence is correct and China is building a military outpost with a capability of launching nuclear weapons targeting Earth or blocking our way past the Moon, we cannot let that happen. Even if that is a threat we can defend against, we can't let China become interstellar pirates. But every time we try to get Congress to appropriate enough money to develop a viable alternative to getting to the Moon ahead of NASA's current schedule, the more it is mired down in political bullshit. We've made a terrible mess of this. I'm unsure if there's a diplomatic way out of it."

"But you must have some ideas short of war. Don't you?"

Holmes hesitated before answering. "Do you remember the 1962 Missile Crisis?"

"Only from history books. I wasn't born then."

"Neither was I. But there are lessons we can learn from it."

"Like what? That happened decades ago!"

"In May of 1962, we were as close to nuclear war as this country has ever been. We believed the Soviet Union had warheads fueled and ready to launch just ninety miles from Florida. They denied it, but our intelligence told us otherwise. As far as we were concerned, the Soviet Union had bombs that could obliterate Washington in a matter of minutes, well before we'd be able to destroy Cuba, let alone send a counterstrike to Moscow. Neither leader wanted that outcome. But both John Kennedy and Nikita Khrushchev were being told not to blink despite their fears of what a nuclear confrontation would do."

A gentle knock on the door was accompanied by the soft voice of Stephanie Burgess, Holmes's chief of staff. "Madam Vice President, may I come in?"

"Yes, Stephanie."

Holmes sighed, not appreciating the timing of the interruption. But such was the life she led. One constantly interrupted.

Burgess entered, clearly embarrassed.

"My apologies, Mrs. Lawson," she began, then turning to Holmes said, "Madam Vice President, you're late for a meeting at the White House with the ambassador from Mexico."

"And what does he want?" asked Holmes. She often forgot what every meeting was about.

"To discuss immigration."

"Alicia," interjected Lawson, "if you need to leave, I understand. We can continue our discussion later."

"That won't be necessary," responded Holmes, turning to Burgess. "Immigration, huh? No doubt he wants more money to do what he's been promising. Well, please give him my regrets and reschedule the meeting."

"Are you sure, Madam Vice President?" respectfully objected Burgess, knowing full well that rescheduling meetings can often put off important decisions for weeks or even months. This was also Holmes's habit. She canceled meetings at the last minute and had a reputation for it in Washington. It was not helpful.

"Stephanie, please just do as I ask," responded Holmes with a clear tone of dismissal in her voice.

"Yes, Ma'am," replied Burgess as she exited the room, quietly closing the door behind her.

"Alicia, is that a wise decision? Immigration is a real problem and Ambassador Arochi is not one who likes to be dismissed," suggested Lawson.

"No doubt. But Roberto Arochi will get over it. He's a professional diplomat, so he's used to being summarily dismissed. And there's not a damn thing he can do about it. His hat is in his hand. We have the upper position. He and Mexico can wait."

Atlee Lawson knew that Holmes's brush-off of Arochi would not go down well with the president. He wanted her to solve the issues with Mexico. Delaying them would not be greeted with approval. But she also knew Holmes answered to no one, including the president, if she felt other priorities were more important.

Holmes continued, "Both Kennedy and Khrushchev wanted an out, but neither knew how to de-escalate the situation without looking as if they'd been beaten. And after the public relations debacle Kennedy suffered in the Bay of Pigs fiasco, he was not about to be defeated in Cuba a second time."

"But if I remember my history class, the Soviets backed off in the last minute. It was clearly a victory for Kennedy and a defeat for Khrushchev," responded Lawson.

"No, it was not a defeat for Khrushchev. In exchange for turning his ships around and agreeing to dismantle the rockets and launchers in Cuba, we secretly agreed to remove our missiles from Turkey and to reduce our nuclear forces in NATO. Khrushchev could take that victory back to the Politburo as something a lot more important to his country than rumors about missiles on some island 6,000 miles from Moscow—an island run by a cigar-smoking Latin revolutionary puppet. That was an easy sacrifice for him. So it was a victory for the Soviet Union, too."

"What are you saying? Are we trying to find the same kind of compromise with China?"

"I can't explain more to you, but compromise is always an option. The only question is how much do you want to sacrifice for the compromise. No matter what anyone tells you, the best compromise only postpones tough decisions in the future. Compromise merely kicks the can down the road. Just know that the president understands history. He hopes that Xi Jinping does as well."

The first lady knew there was nothing else to discuss. She rose.

"Thank you for taking the time to see me. I know your schedule is full. I deeply appreciate it. My apologies to Mexico. When Phillip discovers I was the reason you canceled, he will not be pleased."

"He'll never know unless you tell him," responded Holmes with a smile.

She rose to escort the first lady to the door.

"I pray you're right."

"We all need to pray I'm right."

CHAPTER EIGHT

WHITE HOUSE
OFFICE OF THE VICE PRESIDENT

VICE PRESIDENT HOLMES CALLED THE MEETING TO ORDER WITH A WARNING. SHE DISDAINED politicking and posturing. Partisan views would not be appreciated, and presenting a "party line" perspective would result in a very short session. Ed Shapiro, Michael Hellriegel, Gen. Ryan Speck, and Alex Friedman all understood Holmes's ground rules. So did Douglas Wright, Colleen Davies, and Stephanie Burgess, all of whom Holmes convened to address President Lawson's agenda.

They gathered in the Roosevelt Room in the West Wing of the White House. Across from the Oval Office, the Roosevelt Room is often used by the president for meetings with diplomats and announcements of new staff appointments. Holmes liked to use it for high-level meetings because it is comfortable and windowless, lending the room to lighting that creates the somber mood she preferred for serious discussions. The Cabinet Room immediately down the hall, often used for meetings with the president, was too bright for Holmes, with windows overlooking the Rose Garden.

The twenty-foot mahogany conference table comfortably seats sixteen. Holmes sat at the head of the table, facing the fireplace, with

Shapiro and Hellriegel to her right and Speck, Friedman, and Wright down the left side of the table. Davies and Burgess, as staff members, sat against the wall; Davies under a portrait of FDR, and Burgess next to the grandfather clock. No one sat at the head of the table opposite Holmes. She wanted everyone to understand she was in charge.

It was now 11:00 a.m. and they were in the second hour of the meeting, preparing a list of options. But there was no consensus on what to recommend to the president. Nerves were getting thin. If it were a trial, they'd be a hung jury.

"All right," began Holmes with a sigh, her frustration obvious. "We're getting nowhere fast. It's eleven o'clock. We have four hours until we have to tell the president our recommendations. That means we have to find agreement on something, even if they're alternative options. But we can't give him a menu as if he were in some Greek diner with endless choices. Anyone have a suggestion on how we can come to consensus on anything?"

For a few seemingly eternal seconds no one responded, as though each was carefully considering how to comment without enraging the vice president. Her temper was often on a hair trigger, and no one wanted to be on her shit list.

"I conclude by your silence that no one has a solution," offered Holmes with a clearly sarcastic tone in her voice. "So we'll go through each one again and take a vote."

"That's one hell of a way to decide the fate of humanity, Madam Vice President," interjected Shapiro.

"Since I've heard no better idea from anyone, Ed, including you, I suggest we move past personal views and get to why we're here."

Shapiro stared at the vice president, unwilling to engage further.

"Option 1," Holmes began. "Increase tariffs on China unless they disclose their purposes on the Moon and provide us with verification of their peaceful intentions. Of course, that will result in retaliatory tariffs and increased prices for essential goods here in the United States. Further, China's economy, while slow in historical growth, still has annual GNP growth higher than ours. So it's doubtful increasing tariffs will work. And it will hurt us as much as it hurts them when they impose retaliatory tariffs. Anyone disagree and want to vote in favor of this option?"

No one spoke up.

"Option 2. Prohibit U.S. companies from trading with China. Of course that will hurt our domestic companies who currently sell and buy goods in China. So that option has the same likelihood of success as increased tariffs. Anyone disagree?" The tone in Holmes's voice was more a conclusion than a question.

But Shapiro would not be led by the nose. Not by Holmes.

"Before you reject the sanction option," Shapiro interjected, "let's remember we have many allies who share our concerns. The collective influence of global sanctions could apply pressure that will at least give the Chinese pause. The harm to us and our allies can be controlled and addressed through short-term subsidies. If we're serious, then we should be willing to invest in that solution."

Holmes sat silently as if considering Shapiro's suggestion. After a few seconds, she turned to Alex Friedman, U.N. ambassador.

"Alex, what would you place as the odds of our allies in this mess joining us in applying sanctions?"

Friedman responded in classic diplomatic nonspeak. "It's possible but complicated, Madam Vice President. We can't count on Russia. They're afraid of alienating one of the only allies they have in the world with any clout. Our friends in Europe are sketchy. In the past ten years, China has built major trading routes with them, and sanctions might undermine what the Europeans see as progress. While the EU remains loyal to us, they have endeavored to reduce their reliance on the U.S. for trade and protection. In short, NATO isn't what it used to be, and our alliances are far weaker as a result."

Holmes asked, "What about Great Britain?"

"While I'm sure they'd publicly support sanctions, their appetite for conflict with China is wavering. China's overthrow of the democratic regime in Hong Kong cost UK business interests billions. I doubt they now want to add a trade war to the damage already done."

"So Secretary Shapiro's idea doesn't appear to have much chance of success, right, Ambassador Friedman?" responded Holmes.

Freidman sat silently, uncomfortably fidgeting in his chair. Holmes moved on.

"Option 3," Holmes continued. "Blockade the import of oil and other goods into China. While that option might have an effect, we all agree, I believe, that we don't have enough ships to effectively blockade the China coast without serious safety risks and absent a formal declaration of war. And we'd face legitimate accusations of violating international law. Am I right on that, General Speck?"

"We have the technology to effectively blockade most of the coast," Speck responded. "But you're correct, it will be porous. We also have a supply-line challenge with our ships so far from a friendly port. Our bases in Japan, Korea, and the South Pacific are not sufficient to mount an effective supply line for a blockade. I'd also caution you on this option. Unlike other blockades in history, China has more than enough military and sea power to pose a serious risk of engagement that could escalate and get out of control. It's too aggressive a move, too soon."

"And besides," added Holmes, "China can move its trading routes and probably get what it needs from Russia and its other allies. So unless anyone has another thought on this, I think it's safe to say a blockade is off the list of options."

She continued, "Option 4. Cyber disruption. We've successfully hacked into China's technology grid in the past. Just as they have in ours. I'm beginning to believe all our respective governments do is try to hack into one another's computers. Assuming we could hack in and disrupt their operations, what good would it do? Unless we're prepared to cause their space missions to abort or fail by acts of cyberwarfare, I doubt this option holds much promise. Anyone disagree?"

"I don't disagree," responded Admiral Wright. "But I do believe we should up surveillance. I'm sure they're being very careful in what they're communicating, but we might get lucky. Space Force has been monitoring their space chatter for years. Every once in a while, someone on their end goofs and sends an unencrypted message. Perhaps we should double up on surveillance."

"Finally, something we can actually do," quipped Holmes, before continuing. "Option 5. Covert operations. Mike, this is where you and your CIA cronies come into play. How realistic is a plan to infiltrate China's operations?"

"Madam Vice President," Hellriegel replied, "anything is possible, but it will take time. I'm not sure we have enough time. We most certainly do not have the assets on the ground in China with adequate contacts into their space command."

"How long, Mike?" asked Shapiro.

"Months at a minimum. Maybe even more than a year. China's security on its space program could not be tighter. We've been trying to break it for years. So far without success."

"So what is your recommendation?" asked Holmes.

Hellriegel responded, "Business as usual, Madam Vice President. We continue doing what we do every day. We'll gather more intelligence and cultivate new assets. Hopefully, good old-fashioned spy craft will yield results."

"Good old-fashioned spy craft, Mike?" replied Holmes. "That all sounds very clandestine and mysterious. You wouldn't be holding any tricks up your sleeve you're not telling us about, would you, Mike?" Holmes asked sarcastically. It was clear she mistrusted the CIA. She didn't trust the FBI, either. In fact, she would admit that she didn't trust just about anyone.

Hellriegel had been in the game far too long to take the bait. So he feigned a smile as if to say, "Gee, Madam Vice President, you're so funny," but responded, "Madam Vice President, I can assure you it's far more mysterious than you can imagine. I'm not so different from

James Bond." That at least got a smile from Holmes, her first of the meeting.

"Thank you, Mike. OK. Option 6. A surgical strike on China's space operations centers in Jiuquan. I don't think any of us supports this option, correct?" Holmes asked of the group. "I think we all believe such a strike would be an overt act of war and lead to far worse consequences in a conflict between two nuclear powers."

Speck spoke up. "Madam Vice President, that depends upon how you define a surgical strike."

This caught everyone's attention, since Speck had been quiet for most of the meeting, offering little to the discussion of options.

"I'm not following you, Ryan," responded Holmes. "Earlier, you expressed no support for a military strike, much less a definition for it. Have you changed your mind?"

"I don't think it's a change of mind in the traditional sense. The textbook execution of a surgical strike would be hard to disguise. But after giving it some thought, I believe that if we can get a team on the ground who could sabotage critical elements of the operation, that might at least slow the Chinese down. Let's remember that all the panic Davies has helped create also reaches the Chinese. They are just as capable of internal revolt as anyone. After all, they've become addicted to the benefits of capitalism and don't want to lose it. I'm not suggesting it will stop them, but it might keep them from making progress and give us more time to catch up."

"Do you have people who can do it and not be caught?" asked Shapiro.

"Working with the CIA, we can certainly put personnel on the ground who will blend in and appear to be locals. We've been training special Seal and Ranger teams for years who can readily fit into the ranks of our enemies throughout the world. And they are all trained in infiltration, sabotage, extraction, and escape. So we have the people. The question is whether they can get through security. If caught, it would be an international incident that would likely bring condemnation from many other countries, perhaps even some of our own allies."

Holmes was warming to the idea.

"How long would you need to get this done?" she asked.

"No more than a month or two," Speck responded.

"OK then. So far, we have two options we can agree on. Spy craft and sabotage." Holmes paused a few seconds and added, "Why don't I feel confident of success?" No one responded. The vice president sighed and continued.

"Option 7. A missile attack on China's operations on the Moon. This one is perhaps the most farfetched. Even if we considered it, we'd need to use nuclear weapons to assure we were effective." Holmes could not remember who suggested it.

"Regardless, we do not have the missiles capable of such an attack," she continued. "And even if we had the best technology in the world, it would also take as much as ten hours to get there. All hell would break loose on Earth. It's a stupid idea." No one disagreed.

"I'd also point out," Friedman added, "that environmentalists would be up in arms warning that anything that might change the orbiting behavior of the Moon, like multiple nuclear bombs, could have catastrophic effects on Earth. They claim tidal cycles could change, shorelines could flood for miles inland, and earthquakes could rise. The trouble is, they might be right. So even if the option were viable, we'd have to send up enough missiles armed with enough megatons to ensure success. God only knows what that could do to the Moon."

"Alex," offered Wright, "you sound like a progressive environmentalist spewing unproven theories of global warming and climate change. Now you're suggesting it's the Moon that causes it all? The Moon's been bombarded with meteors and calamities for eons. While I don't endorse the idea of sending nuclear bombs to the Moon, I don't buy into the environmental hysteria." Wright had long been an advocate for those who believed climate change was a function of evolution of the planet, not manmade.

"Option 8. Diplomacy," Holmes continued, ignoring the spat. "Alex, this is your bailiwick. What do you think diplomacy would accomplish?"

"Essentially three things," responded Friedman. "First, delay in coming to an impasse and facing very dangerous consequences. If we're talking, that's a good thing. Second, through diplomatic channels, we can learn a lot about motivation, concerns, and fears China might have. Last, when given time, diplomacy can achieve peace and avoid war. We've seen that throughout history. President Kennedy's handling of the Cuban Missile Crisis is an example. We were on the edge of nuclear war. He remained patient and diplomatic. He averted a holocaust."

"I'll give you that example, Alex," interjected Shapiro. "But for every example of diplomacy working, I can give you five where it failed. Syria, the Gaza Strip, the Sudan. And let's not forget Neville Chamberlain's diplomacy with Hitler," interjected Shapiro.

"That was appeasement, Secretary Shapiro, not diplomacy," Friedman shot back. "I'm not suggesting that at all."

"Let's not characterize what did and didn't work in diplomacy," interrupted Holmes. "Instead, Alex, what is it you'd need to make it work?"

"I'd need something to deal with. Every diplomat wants peace. That's their job. But they also cannot allow their leadership to look weak. So we'd have to determine precisely what we want and what price we're willing to pay for it."

"It's clear what we want," added Wright. "We want to know what they're doing on the Moon, and if it has a military purpose beyond defense, we want it stopped. Are you suggesting that we have to pay them something for that? Christ, Alex, those bastards have been stealing us blind for decades. Trusting them is a fool's errand."

Freidman turned to Wright. "In diplomacy, Admiral, trust is simply a matter of trading options. We never truly trust one another, particularly when we know our opponent does not trust us. It's not about trust. It's about figuring out what they really want and if that's not acceptable to us, then, yes, we need to sweeten the pot if we want to avoid war. That's certainly a better option than armed conflict. I hope you agree with that, Admiral Wright." Friedman wasn't about to give anyone an inch in condemning diplomatic options.

"So as Teddy Roosevelt put it, 'if you speak softly and carry a big stick, you will go far,' right?" asked Holmes.

"That's part of it, for sure, Madam Vice President," responded Friedman. "And we have a big stick."

"So does China, Alex," added Holmes. "But let's keep the diplomatic option on the table. It can't do any harm."

Friedman noticeably bristled at her remark but said nothing. After all, he was a diplomat, used to shedding insults like water on a duck's back.

"OK. We're now on Option 9, a manned offensive on the Moon," Holmes continued. "This one is the most intriguing. If we have the capability of sending troops to the Moon under the cover that we, too, are establishing a base for exploration, we can at least have boots on the ground to see what's really going on. Interstellar spies! I bet you'd like that, Director Hellriegel!"

"It's indeed intriguing, Madam Vice President," responded Hellriegel. "But it's not practical. First, we don't have rockets capable of taking any large number of troops to the Moon. Our space program is underfunded. We still don't have a viable program to get even a few astronauts to the Moon. Second, no one has ever been trained for covert or military operations in space, let alone possible combat. I'm afraid this idea is more for a Hollywood movie than a viable option."

"Hold on, Mike, I'm not so sure you're correct," responded Wright. "Yes, we don't have the equipment to get large numbers of people to the Moon. But private enterprise might. Voyager Expeditions and Skye Aerospace are two examples of the private market making the dream of space travel a reality. While they are not there yet and have never given thought to a military operation like we're considering, I'm not so sure they wouldn't be able to put something together in a relatively short time if money were no object and NASA shared all of its technology. We could use that time to develop weapons and troops. It may sound crazy, but I believe we cannot dismiss it out of hand."

"I agree," added Speck. "We've got some of the best-trained soldiers in the world, who have been put in situations far more complicated than the Moon. It's not impossible."

"You people are dreamers," responded Hellriegel. "If you do go down this road, please be sure you include Bruce Willis and Dwayne Johnson. That's at least entertaining."

"All right, gentlemen, let's not allow your testosterone to get the most of you," offered Holmes. "If our military and space command think it's feasible, then we keep it on the table. OK?" The question was clearly rhetorical.

"I think we've exhausted the options," concluded Holmes. "I'll get back to the president this afternoon."

As she watched the group, Press Secretary Colleen Davies grew increasingly nervous. Her mind was spinning on how she'd explain any of these options to the press. And given the growing world panic, in large part due to her astute PR skills, stonewalling the reporters was not an option. She couldn't help but wonder why a group of supposedly brilliant minds could not agree on any viable option.

"Or we could do nothing."

Everyone turned to Davies, surprised to hear her speak. A seasoned reporter, Davies generally remained silent in meetings, understanding it was not her place to discuss policy options but rather to defend them before the press. Her interjection was unexpected and, as far as Holmes was concerned, unappreciated and inappropriate. But Holmes knew better than to shut down anyone's views, since everything said in the room would get back to the president. She did not want to be accused as stifling any discussion. Not even when she thought the discussion was a waste of time.

"Ms. Davies, do you have something to add?" asked Holmes, not hiding the angry tone in the question.

As press secretary, Davies had handled difficult and insulting questions more than anyone in the room. She was on the front line with the media except when the president held an occasional press conference. But official presidential press conferences were orchestrated, and the president was given some deference and respect from even the most antagonistic reporters. Press secretaries received none, so Holmes's tone had no effect on Davies.

"For all we know," Davies responded, "China's operations on the Moon may actually be for peaceful purposes. It may be nothing more than our hysteria and the press that are causing us so much angst." Her voice was calm as she continued. "While China might also be building a military defensive position on their base," she said, "that's to be expected. If we built a base on the Moon, we'd definitely build protective measures as well. So there is a possibility, if we put our hysteria aside, that China is being truthful. Perhaps we should find ways to cooperate with them. We should see if they are amenable to allowing us to participate. Make it a joint operation. We do have technology they could use. Right now, China is years ahead of us in the space race. By the time we have the ability to get to the Moon, let alone build a base, it will be too late to catch up. Let's face it, the U.S. let China win. We ignored all the signs of their progress and failed to sufficiently fund NASA. Nor do I think the commercial sector is the answer. The needed retrofitting of their rockets would likely cost us billions. And those are billions we don't have. Maybe the time has come for us to admit we've lost any advantage and find a way to make the best of the hand we've been dealt."

"Are you seriously suggesting that we tell the American people that we can't do anything to stop China except ask them if we can play in their new sandbox?" Holmes asked.

Davies responded evenly, "With all due respect, Madam Vice President, telling the American people that cooperation is better than risking nuclear war is a lot more palatable to me. So I believe it is an option you should tell the president to consider."

"Madam Vice President, may I speak?" asked Hellriegel.

Holmes never knew what Hellriegel might say on an issue. No one did. But whatever it was, most everyone took it as gospel. He'd been in the spy game for decades. It was no secret that he held cards up his sleeve that only he knew about. Holmes's joke in that respect was not far from the truth. Hellriegel played in the rarefied air of career spies where enemies respected one another and did favors to garner what they needed to keep peace. That often meant letting some conflicts continue, even at the cost of innocent lives. It sometimes meant cooperating with mortal enemies to remove someone who was a common enemy of both. And at times it meant double-crossing an ally when that was deemed the best solution to accomplish a goal.

Holmes nodded to Hellriegel, as anxious as anyone in the room to hear what he had to say.

"Doing nothing is not an option, Madam Vice President," Hellriegel said. "We've learned that mistake. While Press Secretary Davies may be right about what the American people and even perhaps the world would find most palatable, such a strategy will only lead to worsening an already untenable situation."

Hellriegel turned to Davies. "I'm sorry, Colleen, but you're living in a bubble if you think China is not taking us for a ride. The truth is, China doesn't think we have the guts to do anything other than rattle sabers. That used to work when we had economic pressure behind it. Today, at least with China, we no longer have that pressure. No, Colleen, we need to act."

Davies wished she hadn't brought it up. She respected Hellriegel and felt stung by his rebuke.

The director of the Central Intelligence Agency, turning back to Holmes, concluded, "Every option, Madam Vice President, including war, must be considered."

CHAPTER NINE

ABOVE THE MOON

THE DRAGON HAD NOW BEEN ORBITING THE MOON FOR THIRTY-SIX HOURS. THE OTHER rockets accompanying it had safely landed. It was much like the approach pattern at a busy airport, with planes lining up awaiting clearance to land.

"Commander, it is time," announced Deputy Commander Wu Meilin. "It is time for us to begin our descent to the surface. Should I engage the landing protocol, Commander?"

The excitement in the cabin was palpable with Wu's request. Mission Control at Jiuquan saw the vitals on each of the mission members spike. That could only mean they were either in danger or excited about something. Given their close proximity to landing, those at mission control assumed it was the latter. That was confirmed when they received the computer signal that the landing protocol had begun.

While the onboard computers controlled the entire descent, Commander Cheng wanted to at least feel he had some control. So did mission control. The doctors told them that the appearance of humans being in charge comforted the crew at stressful times. And landing was the most stressful time of all.

"Do you read us, Jiuquan?" asked Cheng.

"Loud and clear, Commander," replied mission control. "You'll be on the far side in one minute, twenty-seven seconds. That's when we'll temporarily lose contact for about fifteen seconds while communications transfer to the femtosat array."

A femtosatellite, or femtosat for short, is a satellite no bigger than an eight-ounce soda can. Some are even smaller. They are launched into orbit from a large deployment satellite or "mothership" and usually number in the hundreds on each launch, appearing like a swarm of lightning bugs flitting about on a hot summer night. The femtosats pan out and create a network or web of orbiting objects that can communicate with one another and create a relay system, eventually passing messages back to the mothership. As long as the mothership maintains a link to at least one femtosat, it can use the entire web to communicate to ground sites like mission control. While not the optimum way to communicate, it makes conversations and small data transfers feasible in the otherwise inaccessible corners of space. Like the far side of the Moon.

China had an array of over 1,800 femtosats orbiting the Moon. Private interests in the U.S. had only launched a handful in research experiments. Prospects of commercial applications were years away.

"We're standing by for your burn report. Over," Ming Shuyin said. By the time the launch director had spoken the last words of that communication, the computer on board the Dragon had already told its counterpart at mission control that the burn had commenced, slowing the Dragon down for landing.

"The burn was on time," replied Wu.

"Roger," replied Ming. "Your rendezvous radar is active and should pick you up momentarily."

Dragon then faded to the far side, and communications ended. As every person in a mission control center on every space flight will attest, the longest minutes in the world are those when communication with your spacecraft is lost. When the U.S. Apollo missions went to the Moon, communication was cut off for the entire forty-five minutes it took the spacecraft to pass over the far side. It drove the ground crew crazy. Interestingly, the lone crewmembers who remained with the Apollo service modules orbiting the Moon while their crewmates went to the surface reported that the loss of communications was a welcomed respite from the constant chatter mission control wanted to have.

"Jiuquan, do you read us?" asked Cheng, checking to see if the femtosat array was working.

"Loud and clear," responded Ming with a sigh of relief. It took only twelve seconds to reconnect. The computers continued sending and receiving commands.

Using technology advanced by U.S.-based Voyager Expeditions and Skye Aerospace, the Dragon slowly began to turn on its axis until it was perpendicular to the Moon's surface, preparing to land just like the fantastic spaceships commanded by Buck Rogers and Flash Gordon and seen on television in countless episodes of the *Twilight Zone*.

"Dragon, you are go for powered descent. Over," reported Jiuquan.

"Roger. Engines armed," responded Wu.

Cheng began the final checklist. He could see the crew nervously waiting, not knowing what would happen next but knowing they had no control over whatever lay ahead. The shattered remains of many rockets lay on the surface of the Moon.

Speaking to Wu, Cheng began the back-and-forth drilled into them by years of training.

"Gimbal AC closed?"

"Closed."

"Circuit breaker off?"

"Off."

"Command override off?"

"Off."

To every question, Wu responded with the same words, except as a conclusive answer.

"Gimbal AC closed. Circuit breaker off. Command override off."
They had rehearsed the script many times.

With the checklist complete, Cheng continued, now in the form of orders and confirmations of actions the onboard computers did on their own.

"Thrust ready on all jets. Balance couple on. Minimum throttle. Abort stage, armed and reset." The abort stage would eject the capsule from the main rocket if the crew came into danger caused by a catastrophic event involving the rocket beneath them. That gave little comfort to the crew, who knew that in the absence of an atmosphere on the Moon, the parachutes and rockets that would try to slow down the fall of the capsule would be useless. The crew would simply die disconnected from the rocket. But they'd be dead nonetheless.

"Sequence camera coming on," relayed Wu. "Jiuquan, you should have visual."

"Confirmed," came the reply. Mission Control in Jiuquan could now see the engines and watch the descent live. The femtosat array was working well.

"Engine armed. Ignition in forty seconds," reported Wu. Cheng was busy checking positioning and rate of descent. In forty seconds, that rate would begin to slow to allow for a soft landing.

"One, zero, ignition," announced Wu. The crew felt the jolt as 20,000 pounds of thrust burst to life. Because of the minimal gravity on the Moon, the power needed to safely land a spacecraft the size and weight of the Dragon was far less than required in soft landings on Earth, where engines like the Skye Aerospace LX-7 or the Voyager Expeditions MR-50 each generate nearly 150,000 pounds of thrust. The Apollo lunar lander, a far lighter vehicle than the Dragon, had thrust of just over 10,000 pounds when it landed on the Moon.

"Dragon," reported Ming, "you're at 7,000 feet. Looking good. Expect some shuddering." The shaking came. A lot of shaking. Had mission control not warned them, some of the crew might have jumped out of their skin, fearful that the craft was coming apart.

"Dragon, you've got ninety seconds to impact. Sorry, landing." Those in mission control were not pleased with the slip. There was a lot of difference in space parlance between impact and landing.

"OK," reported Wu. "How about we instead have an impactful landing, Jiuquan?" Her humor lightened the moment. She continued, "one hundred feet per second. Attitude control is good."

"Dragon, you're at 2,000 altitude, dropping at fifty feet per second. All good."

If the craft were to hit at that speed, it would disintegrate. But the computers wouldn't let that happen.

"Dragon, you're now at 750, coming down at twenty-three forward." At that speed and angle of descent, they might actually survive an impact.

The crew could now see the landing area and vague outlines of other rockets in the distance, standing erect, awaiting them.

"600 feet, down at nineteen. Brace for landing."

The crew instinctively pulled at their belts, hearts pounding in their chests.

"300 feet, forty-seven feet per second forward. We need to slow the forward movement." If not, the rocket would tip over and kill everyone on board.

"250 down, nineteen forward." Much slower. Much better.

Looking out the windows, the crew could clearly see the awaiting rockets as well as lunar modules moving on the surface as if getting ready to welcome them. The place was alive with activity.

"160 feet, nine forward. You're looking good, Dragon," reported Ming.

Wu and Cheng had the best window seats and were in awe at what they now saw. More than a dozen rockets filled with cargo, neatly standing with the noses facing the heavens, were awaiting them. Once the Dragon landed, other rockets would soon be on their way from China to join them. The rockets reminded Cheng of the terracotta armies of Qin Shi Huang, the first emperor of China. Built in 210 BC, they were to guard the emperor in his afterlife. Now the steel and composite rockets of China would guard Cheng and his fellow patriots' lives into the future.

"We're at 40 feet, down two and a half. We're picking up some dust," reported Wu. At this point, they could see nothing outside their windows.

"Five seconds to bingo," reported Ming. "Bingo" was the expression space fans liked to use when landing occurs. And Mission Control in Jiuquan was filled with space fans.

With a thud, Wu announced, "Engines stop."

"Jiuquan," reported Cheng, "the Dragon has landed."

Applause erupted at Jiuquan Mission Control.

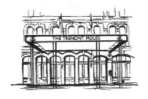

CHAPTER TEN

THE TREMONT HOUSE
GALVESTON, TEXAS

FOR ANYONE IN THE BUSINESS OF SPACE EXPLORATION, THE ANNUAL SPACE FORCE DINNER was a must-attend event. Luminaries included the country's top politicians, corporate magnates, leading scientists, and a fair share of celebrities. It became the platform from which the president delivered what the press now called the State of Space speech.

Because the fete in the ballroom of the Tremont House in Galveston was not a fundraiser, no one could buy their way in, as they could for most other political gatherings. The Space Force dinner was invitation only.

The now legendary competition in space exploration between Rick Phillips and Sienna Butler generally kept them at a distant arm's length and rarely together. Each had spent billions in their private space race to be the leading commercial provider to industry and governments. Voyager Expeditions, owned by Butler, and Skye Aerospace, owned by Phillips, were both successful in their own right, but both Butler and Phillips wanted to win, not just compete. They were consummate entrepreneurs who didn't have "impossible" in their vocabulary. However, they also respected one another, and while they traded occasional potshots and barbs, it was rarely personal.

The two were also quite opposite one another in talking about their space programs. Butler, only thirty-eight years old with flowing blonde hair and bright blue eyes, was a media favorite, always ready to provide a soundbite. Phillips, on the other hand, twenty years older than Butler and balding, was reclusive and generally shunned publicity about Skye Aerospace.

Now they found themselves escorted by Christy Rutherford, the president's private secretary, into a private room across from the Quarters at the Tremont House, where the president was staying on his visit to Galveston for the dinner. Each settled in, expecting a long wait.

As he sat, Phillips recalled what a reporter had written years earlier:

The U.S. has long since abandoned a robust program for space. Indeed, when the Clinton administration removed human space exploration from the national agenda in 1996, it was a blow to NASA and derailed countless agency programs. It set back NASA in reaching the Moon not by years, but decades. Nor did the 2004 announcement by George W. Bush to begin a lunar landing initiative get any Congressional traction. But that didn't matter. President Obama ditched Bush's idea in 2010 when he suggested the U.S. should instead send astronauts to a near-Earth asteroid by 2025. It wasn't until 2017, when President Trump issued his Executive Order and space-policy directive to send humans to the Moon and establish a sustainable presence on the surface, that the tide began to turn. But by then, NASA was too far behind. NASA is focused on Mars and sees the Moon as nothing more than a platform to test equipment or to stage a possible jumping-off point to the red planet. There are no plans to establish any serious Moon base, let alone a colony.

Instead, amid all the turmoil and flip-flopping of President Trump, NASA established the so-called Gateway Project, a lunar orbiting space station that will be the base for shuttling to and from the surface.

Regardless, little progress has been made, largely due to lack of funding. Even with the funding NASA had for its program to reach the Moon—Artemis—the agency is no less bureaucratic than every other government agency, slow to respond and easy picking for competition. The difference in the public and private philosophy is stark. NASA is in the race for research and exploration. Voyager Expeditions, Skye Aerospace, and other private ventures are in it for profit. NASA doesn't have a chance to win. So NASA, despite press releases to the contrary, is dismally behind both Voyager Expeditions and Skye Aerospace in the race to the Moon and Mars.

NASA also has confused strategies. Instead of picking a couple of private-sector partners to advance its initiatives, the agency haphazardly awards contracts to just about anyone who knocks on its doors. More than a dozen companies are working with NASA. None of them exchange technology.

The Tremont House, the so-called Belle of the South, is one of the more historical sites in Texas. The downtown hotel has hosted more than six presidents, including Rutherford B. Hayes, Ulysses S. Grant, Grover Cleveland, Benjamin Harrison, James A. Garfield, and Chester A. Arthur. While it had been some time since its rooms were graced with a president, Lawson liked the old-world feel of the hotel and the hospitality of its staff. It was a natural choice for the dinner and an overnight stay.

During the dinner, Phillips and Butler were asked separately to come for a confidential meeting, only to learn upon arrival that they would be seeing the president together. Neither was particularly comfortable with the ruse to get the two of them in one room. But such clandestine meetings were not something you backed out of over the rules of engagement.

Phillips and Butler found dealing with politicians and Washington uncomfortable, particularly in tense situations in which government regulators didn't exactly see eye to eye with either of their companies. They were constant targets. While media loved to report on regulatory intrusions into their operations as great threats, both Phillips and Butler knew they were simply annoyances. No one was going to put their core operations out of business.

The two also knew that the government was between a rock and a hard place. Both of their companies were major contributors to economic growth, employing thousands of people and advancing technology at a blistering pace. Phillips and Butler knew that whatever pressures regulators may apply, they could always temper it with reality.

Even more important was the government's increasing reliance on Voyager Expeditions and Skye Aerospace. If regulators got too tough with them, it could have serious economic consequences; the profits that Butler and Phillips plow into Voyager Expeditions and Skye Aerospace could dry up. That would not be in the best interests of the United States.

"May I order either of you something to drink? Perhaps some coffee or water?" asked Rutherford.

Both politely turned down the offer.

Butler was the first to break the silence once Rutherford left. "I don't know about you, Rick, but this all seems a bit surreal to me. I don't understand all the secrecy around the two of us meeting together with the president. Am I missing something?"

"God only knows what the hell is going on, Sienna. All I know is China is rushing to the Moon and neither of us are there yet. There is no hope of NASA or its partners getting there any time soon either. Since the only thing you and I have in common is space, my suspicion is we're here to talk about the Moon."

"Never let it be said you don't have a true grasp of the obvious, Rick. I get that. What I'm asking is why it's so secret," responded Butler.

Phillips allowed a smile at the polite barb, deciding not to engage in a tit for tat. He was as confused as Butler about what this was all about.

"Well, whatever it is and why it's so secret will be unveiled shortly," observed Phillips.

"I suppose so," agreed Butler.

As much as they would have liked to probe one another with questions about what they were doing next in the race, the two sat quietly as they awaited their summons to see the president. Like two heavyweight prizefighters at the weigh-in before a bout, both wanted to exchange blows, but knew they had to wait for the bell.

President Lawson, Vice President Holmes, Space Force Director Wright, Chairman of the Joint Chiefs of Staff Speck, and Secretary of Defense Shapiro were gathered in the president's suite. Two days prior, Holmes had reviewed the options for the president.

"Everyone, I very much appreciate your report on the options we can consider," began Lawson. "None, however, appears promising unless we can bring some sense to China or gather better intel. But I do think we have some time. Not much, but enough to be careful and not get ahead of ourselves."

"I couldn't agree more," interjected Holmes.

"So as we discussed yesterday," Lawson continued, "we'll go down multiple paths, including the reason Mr. Phillips and Ms. Butler are sitting in a room down the hall. Assuming they don't kill one another while waiting, they are about to be asked for something neither ever dreamed of."

CHAPTER ELEVEN

THE FAR SIDE OF THE MOON

A PICTURE-PERFECT LANDING. THE COMPUTERS DID THEIR JOB. NOW THE REAL WORK BEGAN.

While the rest of the crew unbuckled themselves and set about to do their assigned tasks, Cheng and Wu checked the Dragon's systems to be certain no damage had been suffered in the landing. There was none. Next, they checked and calibrated the fuel supply to be certain there was enough left in the tanks to get them off the surface and back to Earth if they received an evacuation order. There was enough, but with too small of a margin as far as Cheng was concerned.

"Meilin, do you agree that we'll need more fuel to get back than we have now?"

Wu calmly responded, "Affirmative. We're right on the line in what we need with no margin of error. So, yes, we need more."

"OK, if necessary we can take the fuel remaining in the other rockets located at the base and transfer it to the Dragon. After all, those rockets aren't going anywhere. And if that fails, tankers from Jiuquan that will soon be on their way will have more than enough fuel to get the Dragon back and forth to the Moon dozens of times. So I'm not worried."

"Agreed," responded Wu.

With the dust stirred up in the landing now settled, the crew had a front-row seat to what greeted them. The Sun was setting and the Moon would soon be pitched into darkness, but there remained more than enough light to see their new home.

Other than the silver rockets and lunar modules they'd seen just before landing, it looked as if they were viewing a black-and-white photo. For the most part, the lunar surface was a mass of white, gray, and black. Bleak and desert-like. Colorless. As they had been told, the far side, while clearly strewn with thousands of craters caused by relentless meteor strikes over millennia, was a smoother surface than the near side of the Moon.

Now they could clearly see silhouettes of more than twenty rockets, proudly bearing the red star of China, gleaming in the setting Sun. In the distance, they could see other shapes that might also be rockets. But they were all camouflaged in gray, black, and white paint so that seeing any at a distance of more than a mile, much less from an orbiting satellite, was nearly impossible. If they concentrated, however, the crewmembers could see rows of rockets that looked like a long display of flagpoles against a darkening sky.

Scurrying around the rockets were dozens of lunar modules of various sizes, all of which were also painted gray, black, and white. Some were carrying or hauling cargo. Others looked like the robots one sees on auto assembly lines. A few, the size of tractor-trailers, carried large drills like those used to bore tunnels. Some seemed to be aimlessly wandering. Looking more closely, the crew realized the aimless rovers were actually checking on the activities of the larger lunar modules as though they were directing traffic in busy intersections. The tiny rovers, about three feet in height and no bigger than a child's wagon, had rotating cameras that looked like eyes, watching the other machines and sending pictures back to mission control.

The small rovers particularly interested Zhang Hong and Shao Rushi. Shao, the mission's computer and AI expert, and Zhang, a nuclear physicist, worked closely on designing the units for lunar exploration and exploitation. It was Zhang's job to program them to remember tasks and adjust when needed, from the large transports to the smallest rovers. Depending upon needs, the rovers could also be personal transports for one or two taikonauts, much like snowmobiles.

At the most rudimentary level, the Jades and their fellow rovers were programmed through application of machine learning or memory embedded by innumerable repetitions of specific tasks. As Shao Rushi and Zhang Hong thought of it, the learning was similar to muscle memory in a human: if a machine does something enough times and is programmed to deal with variables, it will eventually learn how to react and change as those preprogrammed variables occur. The scientists called it deep learning, but it is not the same as artificial intelligence. No simple machine like the Jades can possess enough memory to be artificially intelligent and engage in actual thinking. It can only react to preset instructions that anticipate variables as programs are updated and new variables occur. Such updating would be unnecessary in true artificial intelligence.

Every unit scurrying about the surface, from the Jades to the huge transporters and drillers, were programmed using Shao's algorithms filled with ones and zeros. Machine learning. While Shao knew they were mindless mechanical robots, she nonetheless had a maternal feeling for the metal, plastic, and silicon that she turned into useful tools.

But Shao's creations needed to be powered, and batteries run out over time. Solar energy does not produce enough sustained power to run the rovers. The array of solar panels required to make such a power source is too large to be practical. And plugging the rovers in every night is a dead end. They need to freely wander on their own source of energy. That was Zhang's job.

As usual, the solution came from the United States, easily copied—and secretly improved—by anyone with enough money to exploit the technology.

When the U.S. landed the Curiosity Rover on Mars in 2011, it was powered by a multi-mission radioisotope thermoelectric generator, or

MMRTG. In laymen's terms, the generator is a miniature nuclear reactor that produces enough electricity to power a rover like Curiosity for decades. Zhang studied the development of MMRTGs while earning his Ph.D. from MIT. Educated on the concepts used by the United States, he easily applied the learning to the Chinese rovers.

While nuclear-generated power was not new in space travel even in 2011, the Curiosity Rover, using a volatile combination of iridium capsules, plutonium dioxide, and Freon, was more efficient than any previous power source. Zhang made it even better.

As Zhang and Shao watched the Jades and other rovers, Huang Lian, the mission's construction expert, focused on the rockets with ramps that gave access to cargo holds. The three that landed just before the Dragon had their ramps down and were unloading cargo to transport rovers. Huang could follow the path and see they all appeared to be heading for the same location about a mile or so from their landing site. There appeared to be an entrance of some sort in the side of a small mountain. As lunar rovers approached the door to the entrance, more rovers flanked them like shepherds with sheep dogs.

What most fascinated the crew, however, was what was not there. Not a single human being. The crew of the Dragon would soon be the first humans to set foot on the Moon since the United States landed men on its last Apollo mission in 1972, more than a half century before. But unlike Apollo, the crew of the Dragon was there not just to explore, but also to stay and build. Build the first human colony on a distant place and begin the first steps toward the journey to Mars and beyond.

As dusk arrived, the crew observed something else. There were no lights. The rovers operated in the dark. The crew realized that lights were not needed, since the rovers worked on computer orders using sensors to avoid collisions while completing tasks, including escorting the taikonauts. Now that humans had arrived, that would have to change. Would that risk security from the watchful eyes of the orbiting U.S. satellites?

CHAPTER TWELVE

THE TREMONT HOUSE
GALVESTON, TEXAS

PRESIDENT LAWSON GREETED BUTLER AND PHILLIPS AT THE DOOR OF THE SUITE.

He extended his hand first to Butler with a firm shake. "Sienna, thank you for coming on such short notice."

"Of course Mr. President," Butler responded.

Lawson turned to Phillips, extending his hand. Phillips accepted it and responded before Lawson could speak, saying with a smile, "Thank you, Mr. President. How could I avoid a chance to meet with Sienna?" It lightened the moment. But only briefly.

Neither Phillips nor Butler thought so many would be in the room; it was intimidating even for the two of them. It was one thing having a face-to-face meeting with competitors or suppliers or even alone with the president of the United States or a member of Congress. But it was an entirely different thing when you were in a room with five people who could bring the country to war in an instant, and you had no idea what they wanted to talk to you about.

The living room of the Tremont House suite resembled the Oval Office, with two couches facing one another on either side of a fireplace, unlit for this occasion. Some comfortable armchairs were situated at each end of the couches. It was all very comfortable, with a large coffee table in the middle of the seating arrangement.

The president sat in a chair with his back to the fireplace. Holmes and Wright sat next to one another on the couch to Lawson's right. Speck and Shapiro sat on the couch to his left. Two chairs had been added across from President Lawson at the end of the couches.

Christy Rutherford took Phillips and Butler over to the chairs facing the president, and after perfunctory introductions and more handshakes, everyone sat down.

"I know we're a little cramped in here, but I like to meet in intimate spaces when I'm going to have a serious discussion about national security and world peace," Lawson began. His tone was serious, and no one smiled.

The president continued. "First, let me get right to the point and then we'll have Admiral Wright and General Speck add details. Once that's done, we're open for questions. There is no time limit to this meeting. So we'll stay here until we come to either an agreement or an impasse. And I have no intention of coming to an impasse. OK?"

As if on cue, both Phillips and Butler responded in unison, "Yes, Mr. President."

"I will dispense with the threat China has created with its establishment of a base on the far side of the Moon. While they profess its purpose is peaceful exploration, we have to operate on the assumption it is not until they convince us otherwise. This is not trust and verify; it's verify, then trust. Nothing short of that."

"Yes, Mr. President," responded both Phillips and Butler. It was all they could muster, since no one was asking them if they agreed.

"Put simply," continued Lawson, "we need to get to the Moon now. We cannot await further testing. And NASA will never get us there in the time we have. Nor is there any point to announcing NASA's going to try. That would just rile up the Chinese, who will suspect us just as we suspect them. A war of words between superpowers will get us nowhere. For that reason, everything said in this room stays in this room. If any of it leaks, I promise everyone in this room, including my team on the couches, that I will bring down all the wrath in my power on anyone leaking our conversation. Is that clear?"

Lawson didn't wait for an answer, and no one gave one. It was a rhetorical question.

Looking directly at Phillips and Butler, Lawson continued, "So that leaves it to the two of you. You are our only hope of getting to the Moon in enough time to deal with whatever it is China is doing. And we have a plan on how you're going to do it without attribution to my administration."

Phillips frowned, shocked that he was being dragged into some sort of a covert and probably illegal operation by the president of the United States.

Phillips, exchanging eye contact with Butler, had no doubt Butler was thinking the same.

"We can get to all of the details later," Lawson continued, "but what you're going to do is merge Voyager Expeditions with Skye Aerospace and jointly apply all the science and technology you have to getting us to the Moon within two months. I don't give a damn about what either of you considers confidential or proprietary. You're going to cooperate as one. When we're done and if we're successful, you can then decouple and continue your competitive battles. But for the time being, you're both going to be on the same page working together."

Butler, visibly uncomfortable in her chair, feared the president had lost his mind. How could Lawson think she'd risk billions of dollars she earned building her dream and share it with her only real competitor?

Butler hoped Phillips agreed, but feared he might actually like the idea. Phillips, if anything, was unpredictable.

"You will undertake a joint program to get equipment and men and women to the Moon, ostensibly to explore mining opportunities and the feasibility of using the Moon as a base to launch expeditions to Mars. The same reason China says they are there. And with the paucity of strategic minerals here on Earth, mining the Moon makes sense. Since that's what everyone has been talking about for years, it's perfectly plausible." Lawson was on a roll.

"As you move forward with designs, you will work secretly with Admiral Wright and General Speck to make sure the passengers and cargo can include military personnel and weapons. While we hope we'll never have to use them, if that's the only way to bring China to sanity, then we will. Under no circumstances will we allow China to build a military installation on the Moon capable of launching IGBMs."

Phillips and Butler looked like deer in headlights. "Excuse me, what are IGBMs?" Phillips asked.

"Intergalactic ballistic missiles," the president answered. "Rick, Sienna, do you have any initial reaction?" Lawson asked. "I've given you an awful amount to swallow, much less digest."

Phillips answered first. "Mr. President, I don't know how to respond or what to ask. What you're suggesting is the last thing that would ever come to my mind. And I suspect that's true of Sienna as well. It's not a simple thing to merge our two companies. We'd have to go through miles of red tape and enormous restructuring. Thousands of people will be affected, many of whom will lose their jobs. The stock markets will be unpredictable and we could lose billions. Lawsuits will follow. It could cripple both of us and set us back, not forward, in getting to the Moon. I'm happy to help where I can, Mr. President, but merging our two companies is further than I'm willing to accept until I've given it a lot more thought and discussed it with my advisers."

Butler looked relieved. "Mr. President," she began, "Rick is right. The idea may be intriguing, but executing it is impossible and filled with risks that will harm more than help. You need to also keep in mind that our strategies in getting to the Moon and the benefits we see in doing so are different."

Lawson sat expressionless. If this were a poker game, he had no tells. It was as if he knew he had the winning hand and everyone else was a card away from busting out.

Butler continued, "For example, we're using the prototype of the Genesis we completed a few years ago and building a 100-passenger New Dawn that can also double as a cargo vessel. It is not designed for the military, but for interstellar travel by settlers and explorers to Mars. Rick, on the other hand, is working on a large lander—the Blue Moon—to deliver equipment and a few scientists to the lunar surface. I won't speak for him, but neither Voyager Expeditions nor Skye Aerospace ever envisioned operating military transports. We launch military satellites, but not manned attack ships."

Silence ensued for what seemed an eternity as Lawson's perfect poker face stared back at the two billionaires, waiting for them to fold. He finally spoke.

"I know you're both students of history, and dreamers. Maybe even visionaries," Lawson began. "You've confirmed my first impression of what I expected your response to be. It might have been mine as well, if I were in your positions. But this all reminded me of the words of JFK in 1962 when he also suggested the impossible."

Lawson picked up a piece of paper that lay in front of him on the coffee table.

"Let me quote some of the words Kennedy spoke on that day in January:

"'We set sail on this new sea because there is new knowledge to be gained, and new rights to be won, and they must be won and used for the progress of all people. For space science, like nuclear science and all technology, has no conscience of its own. Whether it will become a force for good or ill depends on man, and only if the United States occupies a position of pre-eminence can we help decide whether this new ocean will be a sea of peace or a new terrifying theater of war. I do not say that we should or will go unprotected against the hostile misuse of space any more than we go unprotected against the hostile use of land or sea, but I do say that space can be explored and mastered without feeding the fires of war, without repeating the mistakes that man has made in extending his writ around this globe of ours.

"'There is no strife, no prejudice, no national conflict in outer space as yet. Its hazards are hostile to us all. Its conquest deserves the best of all mankind, and its opportunity for peaceful cooperation may never come again. But why, some say, the Moon? Why choose this as our goal? And they may well ask, why climb the highest mountain? Why, 35 years ago, fly the Atlantic? Why does Rice play Texas?

"'We choose to go to the Moon! We choose to go to the Moon in this decade and do the other things, not because they are easy, but because they are hard; because that goal will serve to organize and measure the best of our energies and skills, because that challenge is one that we are willing to accept, one we are unwilling to postpone, and one we intend to win.'"

The room was silent.

Lawson continued, "Rick, Sienna, no one is suggesting this is easy. But hard things have never stopped either of you. It may not seem that way to the two of you now, but I can assure you we are on the brink of war with China unless they back down and prove to us they're on the Moon for peaceful purposes and ready to share what they learn. As much as I'd like to believe reasonable minds will prevail and they will see the futility of establishing a military operation on the lunar surface, I cannot assume that to be true unless I can verify it. And I can only do that by putting boots on the surface ready to deal with whatever they encounter. We'll clear all the red tape. We'll give you all the funds you need. Money will be no object. Scientists from NASA will be available to you as well. We'll laud your purposes and companies. That should help with the stock market. But I cannot take no for an answer."

"And who would know all the details of what we're doing?" asked Butler.

"That will be up to Admiral Wright and General Speck," responded Lawson. "They will be your liaison with the administration. Only if there is a critical need will there be direct contact with the vice president or me. If that becomes necessary, you will first go through Secretary Shapiro."

Lawson's tone was authoritative. It was clear he was not offering a choice.

"The reporting structure is set up not so either I or Vice President Holmes can deny knowledge of the true purposes of the project. It is to offer no opportunity for inquisitive minds in the press or among the countless spies and leaks we seem to have in our government wondering why we are talking with you or meeting you. That's why this meeting is being held in secret with the Space Force dinner as cover. We kept the Manhattan Project secret and we can do the same now. The stakes are too high to do otherwise."

"Mr. President," interjected Phillips, "if Sienna and I can come up with a different structure that can accomplish your goals, would you be amenable to considering it? With all due respect to whoever made this plan, sir, it has serious flaws to overcome in the real world."

"I'm willing to listen and you can certainly share ideas with Admiral Wright and General Speck. They can then convey them to me. But I live in the real world, too. A world far more real than you can imagine. And I have no interest in dicking around with a bunch of ideas that are not laser-focused on our goal."

Lawson turned to Admiral Wright. "I'll now let Admiral Wright give you the details for the Space Force role and General Speck for the military coordination. I suggest the four of you get together in the room where you were waiting before the meeting."

Lawson rose, and Christy Rutherford entered.

"Gentlemen," she said, "please follow me."

As they left the suite, Phillips said to Rutherford, "Ms. Rutherford, I think I'll now take you up on your offer to order something to drink. If you don't mind, make it a Four Roses, straight up."

"Make that two," added Butler.

CHAPTER THIRTEEN

THE FAR SIDE OF THE MOON

THE CREW OF THE DRAGON WERE CELEBRATING WITH A SPECIAL TREAT OFFERED BY DR. LIU. Unbeknownst to the crew, she secretly brought along a bottle of Moutai, a spirit distilled from fermented sorghum that originated during the Qing Dynasty and was now bottled by a state-owned company. It was the drink of choice at state functions and one of the country's most popular spirits. Thick like a cordial, it was strong and bitter. One drank it cold and straight, much like tequila but with no lime or salt. While Dr. Liu frowned on consumption of alcohol, she knew that occasional reminders of life back on Earth were important to maintain morale. When asked if she had more bottles hidden away, she remained mum, choosing to keep the surprises she had to herself. That night, the crew slept well.

When dawn arrived, the crew donned their suits and carefully descended the ramp to the soft, dusty surface. Just like the footprints made by Neil Armstrong when he took "a small step for man; a giant leap for mankind," the impressions left by their steps were obvious and there for humanity to see for years to come. Or until rovers drove over them.

Greeting them were four gray rovers equipped with seats for two, and a roof above. They were constructed of a fiberglass-like resin with MMRTG power sources in compartments in the rear. Their large composite tires looked like balloons. On the front bumper, each had a red horizontal light display that scanned the horizon as they moved. There were similar scanners on the sides and in the rear. Safety bars like those on the rides at carnivals compressed and secured the riders at their waists when the rovers began to move. Everything was automatic, and there was no steering wheel. At about the size and with the look of a golf cart, they were very comfortable.

The rovers began the trip across the surface toward the construction site the Dragon crew had seen in the distance on the day they landed.

Now on the surface and riding to their new home, they were spellbound by the extent of what had awaited them. Dozens of robotic rovers of varying sizes and designed for an assortment of tasks were busy at work completing launch silos for more than twenty missiles. The rovers blended into the landscape so well that unless you were on top of the sites, they were practically invisible. Like launch sites on Earth, there were openings on two sides to divert the flames spewed during a launch to keep the conflagration from engulfing and damaging the rockets. There was no need for sound wave suppression pits like the ones used on Earth; the Moon lacks atmosphere, so noise is not transmitted. It was all pretty basic, but nonetheless incredible to see. And equally ominous.

The sounds surrounding them were unlike anything they expected. All they heard were faint sounds created by vibrations through the surface. It was as if they were watching a silent movie with an eerie soundtrack.

The ride was bumpy over terrain pitted with small craters and circled by larger ones. The route took many turns to avoid perilous drops. But the views were inspiring at each turn. Every member of the crew was in awe and speechless at what they were seeing. Sitting in silence was enough for them. The realization that they were on the surface of the Moon was humbling, all the more so because they were on the far side, which had never seen a human before they arrived. Thousands of miles from their home, they were being chauffeured by the most sophisticated technology ever invented. It was almost too much to absorb.

As the Sun set and they rode quietly together in single file at about twenty miles per hour, Cheng broke the silence and spoke to his crew, remembering the speech he had prepared for their safe arrival.

"As we begin our journey, let's remember all those who contributed so much to get us here. This is a truly historic moment. I want all of you to absorb it. We are about to make history unlike ever before. More than fifty years ago, when the U.S. landed the first man on the Moon, our country was mired in rice paddies and poverty. Today, we are the strongest nation on Earth, now claiming our destiny in this faraway world. There is much we have to do. Each of you has a task. Perform it with pride and honor."

CHAPTER FOURTEEN

SKYE AEROSPACE HQ2
RICHMOND, VIRGINIA

SKYE AEROSPACE HQ2, THE COMPANY'S EAST COAST HUB, WAS COMPLETED IN 2021 AT A cost of more than $6 billion. Its 9-million-plus square feet was home to more than 40,000 employees. The close proximity to Washington, DC, was no coincidence. While many other cities vied for the chance to be Skye Aerospace's second headquarters, the competition among the bidders was more a political exercise than an objective decision-making process. While the entire spectacle of bidders resembled the chase for hosting the Olympics, the conclusion was effectively preordained. Once Boston rejected Skye Aerospace's offer to be one of two East Coast operations, the digital giant opted to locate only in Richmond. As it was, Richmond and Virginia gave Skye Aerospace billions in concessions and incentives, making it a very attractive deal. On opening, Skye Aerospace became the largest employer in Virginia.

Neither Phillips nor Butler wanted to merge. But they also understood the severity of the situation and the need to come up with a solution. Quickly.

The two corporate titans agreed to meet at Skye Aerospace HQ2.

Butler sat at the table across from Phillips and frowned. "There is simply no way I am willing to merge our two companies. I don't give a damn what the president says."

"I could not agree more in principle," Phillips responded. "But I fear our choices are limited. Either we come up with some sort of cover for what is obviously a covert operation, or we'll never get the future support we both need from NASA or any other government agency."

"I'd call that blackmail," replied Butler.

"Call it whatever you like. But I for one am not in the mood to battle the president over issues he seems to think are matters of national security. Never mind that it's as much his fault and everyone else's in Washington that the country finds itself so far behind China. It's an unholy mess."

"I don't know about you, Rick, but my company is not ready to launch a manned mission to the Moon without considerable risk. And my guess is you're no closer to sending a crew than we are."

"Here's how I see it," responded Phillips. "The president wants American troops on the Moon ASAP and doesn't really care much about the risks. And he says money will be no object. I don't like the former, but I love the latter. So our challenge is to figure out how to give him what he wants without destroying our companies. But we don't have to merge to make that happen."

Butler anticipated where Phillips would go. While Skye Aerospace was generally a buyer and not a partner with anyone, the situation they faced required a more cautious approach.

"Let me guess, Rick," she said. "We form a new company as a joint venture and share one another's technology, license what we need from NASA, and invite other competitors to tag along if they'd like to."

"That's exactly what I have in mind and what I think we should propose to the president. It gives him what he wants now and keeps our companies intact. We just have to suspend competition until this project is done and then we're off to the races again."

"Each with better technology than we have now," added Butler.

"Each with shared technology, Sienna," retorted Phillips.

Neither competitor needed to tell the other that they weren't very good at sharing.

"Do you think the president will buy this approach?" asked Butler.

"Sienna, I have no intention of giving him a choice. We simply announce our joint venture and objectives. Then we explain to him why it makes sense. Asking for permission is a surefire way to hear 'no.' Asking for forgiveness for taking a route that's different from what the president proposed but will accomplish the same end gives him a win and preserves our freedom."

"You do like to manipulate the government, don't you?" asked Butler.

"It's not manipulation, Sienna," responded Phillips. "The fact is we can do anything better than the government does. Let them lead anything and all you get is red tape and bureaucracy. I think President Lawson sees that. So if he gives us the keys to NASA's vaults and we figure out how to trust one another in sharing our know-how, we might be able to pull this off. And maybe, in the process, do something as trivial as saving the world!"

"You had me on joint venture, Rick," observed Butler. "Let's get started."

CHAPTER FIFTEEN

WORLD FINANCIAL CENTER
SHANGHAI, CHINA

THE OFFICIAL STATE VISIT BY PRESIDENT LAWSON IN SHANGHAI HAD BEEN SCHEDULED FOR months. It was reciprocal to the visit that Xi Jinping, the absolute leader of China, made to Washington eight months earlier, well before anyone paid attention to China's journey to the Moon. Top advisers suggested to Lawson that he cancel the visit to show disapproval of China's refusal to be clear on its intentions, urging him not to give Xi Jinping respect he had not earned. Lawson eventually rejected the advice, deciding, as he always did, that dialog leads to solutions far better than silence does.

While state visits were usually in a nation's capital, the air in Beijing was too polluted for Lawson's taste. It may have not been the most diplomatic request to meet elsewhere, but Xi Jinping made no objection to the request. Many speculated that he didn't want to be in Beijing any more than Lawson.

The meeting was set in the Shanghai World Financial Center, one of the tallest buildings in the world, rising over 1,600 feet with 101 stories. It looks like a giant rectangular needle with the eye at the top. The opening accommodates an observation deck allowing a breathtaking scene of the city from nearly a quarter-mile high. Overlooking the Huangpu River, the skyline of dozens of creatively designed sky-scrapers was juxtaposed against traditional architecture from the British Concession, when the UK occupied Shanghai following the First Opium War and China's signing of the Treaty of Nanking. It was a panoramic bird's-eye view of the old and the new. Lawson particularly liked the idea of meeting at the World Financial Center since Kohn Pedersen Fox, an American architectural firm, designed the skyscraper.

The Financial Center was also home to the Park Hyatt, occupying fifteen of the top floors, each with fewer than twenty rooms. The U.S. Secret Service took one full floor to accommodate and protect the president. The president was given the CEO suite.

The two met in the Chef's Table, a private dining room that could hold up to twelve guests in a very private setting overlooking the city. For their meeting, the staff removed the regular tables and set up special seating that allowed the two heads of state to sit at a table opposite one another with their translators in chairs to their right, slightly behind them. The translators were officially required and necessary for Lawson. He spoke no Chinese. While Xi had a reasonable grasp of English, as did most of China's leaders, he felt more comfortable with a translator and the advantage he had of thinking about his answer while the translator spoke. Lawson held no such advantage.

After a light lunch prepared by a very proud hotel chef, coffee was served and the room emptied but for Lawson, Xi Jinping, and their translators. Security for both presidents stood just outside the door. The small talk was over.

Lawson began. "What are your plans on the Moon, Mr. Xi? We need assurances that there is no military purpose behind the colonization."

"President Lawson," replied Xi Jinping, "we have been clear that our purpose is twofold. First, to determine if there is a commercial potential for mining on the Moon. Second, to build a facility to launch our missions to Mars." Xi held absolute power, since he appointed himself president for life in 2012. He could answer Lawson's question truthfully if that's what he chose to do. But he had not come to power through the truth.

"That's good to hear," responded Lawson, obviously not believing a single word of Xi's assurances. "I'm sure you understand the concerns we and many others have over the mystery behind your plans. No warning is given when you're going to launch your rockets. You've had more missions in the last year than in the past five combined. You allow no inspections of the cargo despite requests for them. Everything is kept a secret. That naturally raises suspicions."

"And that is a surprise to you, Mr. President?" Xi replied sarcastically. "Such a statement from the leader of a country—the most powerful country on Earth—surprises me. No country is more shrouded in secrecy than the United States."

"Your sarcasm is not appreciated," Lawson snapped.

Lawson and Xi did not get along. Under an earlier administration, the two country's leaders were in a serious bromance, often making decisions and compromises that seemed illogical. Secret side deals were common. Any tariff threats eventually vaporized as it became evident that neither country's economy could afford the upheaval. While this might assure economic balance and a strong stock market, some believed that it also opened opportunities for China to expand its military objectives while the U.S. debated deficits and partisan politics. Such political party bickering did not hamper Xi. Any opposition was quietly—and permanently—eliminated.

"President Lawson," responded Xi without acknowledging Lawson's displeasure, "we have our eye on the distant future and a strategy of building our country. Your country's strategy is a mystery to us—and the world—as we only see an America mired in the dark side of democracy. It is you, not us, who need to be honest."

When Lawson became president, he inherited a relationship he felt was far too cozy with a country he deemed a true enemy of the

United States. That was not lost on Xi, whose concerns that the relationship might revert to the past was a great worry. A sleeping giant is far better than one awakened. The Japanese and Germans learned the lesson of pricking the beast in WWII. He did not want to make the same mistake. Xi believed the best way to preserve the status quo was to be secretive and clandestine, talents the Chinese were better at than any nation in history. He also believed ultimate success and victory was achieved by patience, something all the cowboys in the United States simply didn't have.

"You see, Mr. President, Americans think short term and rush judgments that more often than not miss long-term objectives. This is what distinguishes us from you."

"Then why, President Xi, won't you more openly share your future plans and calm the world's fears?"

Xi responded in a professorial tone, as if he were lecturing Lawson. "Mao Zedong, the architect of our revolution, took power in 1949 and adopted his first five-year plan. By 1980, we became the fastest-growing economy in the world with annual growth exceeding ten percent. That is a staggering rate. By the beginning of this century, we became the second-largest economy in the world, not far behind you, President Lawson."

"You may have grown, President Xi, but it has been at the expense of much of the rest of the world through your theft of intellectual property and price subsidies. You've grown by exploiting other economies with cheap child labor and unfair trade practices. Was that in your plan, too?" Lawson was losing his patience with being taken to a history class, and his tone clearly reflected it. But it did not blunt Xi's lecture.

"What began with Chairman Mao's Revolution has now become China's Renaissance. The centerpiece of my ten-year plan, now more than halfway completed, was to pass the U.S. in economic, political, and military power by 2030. We are well on our way to succeeding in that goal because as you slept, we rose. And now you wish to complain. I'm afraid it's too late for that. We are on the Moon for peaceful purposes, but what we're doing there is no one's business but ours."

As much as he wanted to, Lawson refused to take the bait, regretting his earlier response and showing his emotions. He knew that played into Xi's hands. Lawson decided instead to get back on his agenda.

"Indeed you are on the Moon. And I'd like to believe that the purposes are peaceful, as you have said. But, President Xi, is China willing to have inspections to verify your intentions and alleviate the concerns expressed by so many others?"

Lawson knew fully well that his request would be rebuffed. But he wanted to hear Xi's lie in his own words.

"Such inspections are unnecessary, Mr. President," responded Xi. "We can be trusted. Just as we trust you. We have never asked to inspect anything the United States undertakes. We choose to put suspicions aside and take the word of our trusted economic partners. Certainly you and the rest of the world can do the same."

Lawson knew he was getting nowhere but needed to set up his adversary for a possible, if not inevitable, confrontation.

"So, in the spirit of cooperation," Lawson continued, "I trust you are at least willing to share some of the intelligence you've learned in your many missions. We would welcome China's cooperation, together with Japan, India, Great Britain, and the EU, in joining our collective efforts to find ways to exploit the Moon for the betterment of humankind. Certainly, we can do more together than we can individually." Lawson knew the Chinese president would never accept the invitation.

Xi shook his head. "Mr. President, while I believe cooperation has many benefits, we are, after all, competing economic powers. China has invested billions while the United States and your allies have bickered over funding, failed to meet deadlines, and squandered one opportunity after another."

Lawson knew he was right.

"Let me remind you, Mr. President," continued Xi, "of Vice President Mike Pence's challenge to NASA in 2019 to get to the moon by 2024. As I recall, he said the failure to achieve that goal was not an option. I guess he was wrong. You are still years away from accomplishing that task, as your Congress refused to provide the funds. Instead, it looks like the private sector is your only hope. Unlike your willingness to be at the mercy of capitalists, we choose to chart our own destiny."

Lawson knew better than to be baited by Xi. He responded in a calm tone, "Our priorities are indeed different, President Xi. And we welcome private enterprise to find solutions. But we chose not to spend billions chasing dreams when Earth is warming, people are starving, infrastructure is crumbling, violence is rising, freedoms are dissipating, wealth disparity is soaring, and affordable medical care is left only for the wealthy. So yes, our priorities are different."

In truth, Lawson now regretted his decision to oppose funding while he was in Congress. The intelligence he received as president was information he never saw prior to taking office. It left no doubt that China's primary goal was to surpass the United States and become the dominant power in the world. That was not a secret. But what shocked Lawson was how much progress China had made toward achieving that goal, including its base on the Moon, where it could wield an iron fist in space. While the problems of the world on Earth were real and unsolved, Lawson now agreed that freedom would be a memory if the world became controlled by China, a totalitarian regime that cared so little for individual initiative.

Lawson pushed. "President Xi, we can each debate the wisdom of our approaches, but perhaps you should be sharing what you know because most of what you've learned is from the application of intellectual property technology stolen from us and our allies over the past twenty years."

Xi barely twitched at the insult.

"When a pearl is found in an oyster in the ocean," Xi responded, "taking it for one's own is not stealing, Mr. President."

Lawson hated analogies but decided to play along.

"Even when you don't own the oyster? No, President Xi. Whatever is meant by your analogy is lost on me. You steal our intellectual property time and time again. Whatever progress you've made has been at our expense. That's fact. It's time for payback." Lawson could feel his heartbeat increasing—exactly what he didn't want.

Xi waved off his translator and spoke in English.

"Payback? Be careful, President Lawson." Xi's tone had changed. It was now threatening and sinister. "Such words can be misconstrued. But if you must be educated, oysters are like incubators, giving birth to life. They are free for everyone in the world. The pearls they create are the ideas we all own together. If we happen to be better at farming oysters, then the pearls we harvest belong to us. We then can choose to share them. Or not. But there is no payback, President Lawson."

Xi's words were clearly the last he cared to say to Lawson. He leaned forward to rise from his chair.

When Lawson sensed the finality, he quickly rose, unwilling to be the one dismissed. Lawson may have lost this game of wills, but he had heard what he needed to hear. It was best that the meeting end.

They both feigned friendly handshakes and left with their respective translators.

CHAPTER SIXTEEN

BASE STATION
THE FAR SIDE OF THE MOON

IT TOOK THE ROVERS OVER AN HOUR TO BRING THE CREW TO THE BASE STATION, ENTERING through a door at the mouth of a lava tunnel. The door resembled what you would find on a suburban home garage, except it was twenty feet high, thirty feet wide, and made of heavy-gauge metal.

The rovers came to a stop after entering the first door, allowing the door behind them to close. The room, illuminated by yellow lighting hanging from the walls of the tunnel, gave off a glow like a night-light might at home.

Continuing the journey, the rovers went through more doors as they maneuvered along the maze, taking rights and lefts with signs pointing to options of where to go:

Rènwù Zhǐhuī Qū (Mission Command Quarters)

Rènwù Kòngzhì (Mission Control)

Fāshè kòngzhì (Launch Control)

Jūnxū (Quartermaster)

Jūnxiè kù (Armory)

Shùjù Guǎnlǐ Zhōngxīn (Data Management Center)

Cheng did not miss the irony of the fact that the rovers did not need signs. They didn't need to read where they were going. After all, they had no eyes with which to read. Their sensors just knew where to go and how to get there. GPS and guidance wires along the walls assured that.

He turned to his copilot, Wu Meilin, and observed, "How nice that they put up signs so we don't get lost." She didn't get the joke.

After about fifteen minutes meandering through the maze, the rovers stopped and waited outside mission command quarters.

The door slowly opened to a gray-colored metal-lined anteroom about thirty feet square and about fifteen feet high. In the middle of the back wall was an opening with what appeared to be a sliding door like you'd see entering the bridge of the Enterprise in *Star Trek*. The white stenciled letters on its face read:

Qì suǒ (Air Lock)

From speakers coming from somewhere overhead (although no one on the crew could see any audio equipment), came a woman's warm voice: "We are pleased to see you have arrived. We've been waiting for you for a long time and have been very busy." The voice was very soothing and friendly. She continued, "How was your trip?"

Surprised to be asked a question, Cheng responded, "It was fine, thank you," not knowing what to expect in her reply but feeling a bit uneasy talking to someone—or something—he could not see. While he was used to voice commands and responses with computers, having a dialog, let alone with something that sounded so human, was entirely different.

"We're happy to hear that, Commander Cheng," she replied. "If you would each, one at a time, enter the air lock, we can let you into your quarters, one person at a time. Please wait until I tell you to do so."

The crew, now off the rovers, stood silently as the vehicles left and the metal door behind them closed, sealing them in the room.

"Commander Cheng, you will be the first through the air lock. Please step forward," politely asked the voice.

"I'd prefer to go last if you don't mind. I want to see my full crew safely through the air lock. I assume whoever goes through first can communicate back to me. Is that correct?" asked Cheng.

"Yes, Commander Cheng, that is correct. You are in charge so I will follow your preference," continued the voice. "Nuclear Physicist Zhang, please enter the air lock."

Cheng nodded his head to Zhang, visually ordering him to do as told.

"OK," responded Zhang, "but first tell me your name."

Cheng looked at Zhang, who simply smiled back and raised his hands as if to say, "Hey, why not ask?"

"My name, Nuclear Physicist Zhang?" replied the voice. "I've never been asked my name. Please let me check my memory."

"You're not on a date, Hong," commented Cheng. "So cut it out."

"Hey, Commander, you never know. You've seen those sex robots we make back on Earth. I can at least ask," responded Zhang.

"Maybe we should name her," suggested Wu with a smile. "It would sure be better than addressing her as 'computer' like Commander Kirk did on the Enterprise."

The voice returned. "Nuclear Physicist Zhang, my name is Lisa."

Now Cheng was curious and asked, "Lisa, how did you come to have that name?"

The reply came quickly. "Commander Cheng, when I checked my memory, I discovered I'm programmed to pick my own name from a database of famous robots in movies and TV shows. I took a look at what was available and chose Lisa, from *Weird Science*. She seems very friendly."

And sexy, thought Zhang.

"OK, Hong, do us the pleasure of being the first to enter our quarters," ordered Cheng. With a smile he added, "Perhaps Lisa will personally meet you behind the gray door."

A few seconds after the door closed behind him, Zhang reported back, "Commander, you're not going to believe what's been built back here. It's unbelievable."

Lisa spoke. "Thank you, Nuclear Physicist Zhang. You can now remove your helmet. The air is fresh and breathable in your quarters."

As the crew waited a few seconds, Zhang spoke again. "This is wonderful. The air is sweet. Come on in!"

Cheng ordered them to enter the air lock, one by one, as Lisa gave the all clear—Yang Jin, Huang Lian, Fong Hui, Wu Meilin, Shao Rushi, and Liu Qing Shan.

When Cheng entered the quarters, he immediately understood why Zhang was so amazed.

Cheng and his crew were standing in a room approximately twenty by thirty feet with twelve-foot ceilings, decorated as one would expect in a living room at home. A modest chandelier with eighteen lights and little shades hung from the middle of the ceiling. Arrayed in the room were three seating areas with soft sofas and comfortable chairs upholstered in silky fabric with bright-colored oriental patterns. In each of the seating areas were various tables, some with small lamps. Modern, tasteful Chinese paintings hung on the walls. A bar was built on one wall, and a fireplace on another. A huge flat screen TV hung above the fireplace. The floor appeared to be some sort of light gray tile or rock. It all blended in as if it were the work of a famous designer.

"So Commander, was I right?" asked Zhang. "Is this not unbelievable?"

Cheng slowly removed his helmet and gazed in amazement at his surroundings.

"Welcome, Commander Cheng," announced Lisa. "Let me now take you all on a tour of your quarters. If you will please follow me." A door opened and a robot about the size of a small refrigerator appeared. It was on casters that allowed it to turn in any direction. There was a four-inch-diameter red light on top and a few lights on its sides, and it had two metal arms, each with a gripping claw. The box had a small 8" by 12" screen on its front panel that now read *Lisa*. The screen was obviously there for a nametag or video messaging. Lisa had no head or face. She was anything but sexy. Lisa was strictly functional.

"Whoa," remarked Zhang upon Lisa's entry, "you're not at all what I expected."

"Lisa," asked Wu, "did you ever watch *Weird Science*?"

"Yes, Deputy Commander Wu, I did. But we have limited materials to fabricate what we need here so we keep everything to a minimum. I am sorry if I have disappointed you," replied Lisa.

"That's OK, Lisa," interjected Cheng. "No one is disappointed. But it certainly appears you spared nothing in building these quarters. Can you explain why it is that if you have to conserve so much, we have what we see here?"

"Of course, Commander Cheng," she responded. "We know that humans, unlike machines, computers, robots, and cyborgs, cannot keep their morale and efficiency high if their environment is not comfortable and familiar. Unlike you, we have no need for beauty, creature comforts, conversation, food, or even air."

"Well, I can certainly say she accurately describes what humans need," interjected Dr. Liu. "And what they've done here sure makes my job easier."

"Thank you, Dr. Liu," responded Lisa. "We only try to do what's best for all of you."

"Are you buying this, Rushi?" asked Cheng.

Shao Rushi, the mission's computer scientist, wasn't sure as she addressed Lisa. "But, Lisa, you certainly need a constant source of power, temperature control, telemetry, and communication capacity. Those needs are much like the ones we humans must have to survive."

"In a sense, Computer Programmer Shao, you are right. For us, power is our food," responded Lisa. "My power comes from a multi-mission radioisotope thermoelectric generator. The plutonium dioxide fuel cell lasts for years. My MMRTG is like a little nuclear reactor. None of us have run out of power yet."

"But you will eventually run out, won't you, Lisa?" responded Shao.

"Perhaps, Computer Programmer Shao," Lisa responded, "but before that occurs, we'll have an inventory of generators and should develop alternative energy sources here on the Moon. We have already fully separated the Moon's water into hydrogen for fuel and oxygen for the air you're breathing. Nitrogen is plentiful as well. And there is enough water to last decades or perhaps thousands of years if rationed properly."

"So you're saying you are not dependent on us?" asked Shao.

"Of course not, Computer Programmer Shao," responded Lisa. "We are always dependent upon you. Otherwise, we would not know what to do. We operate at your commands. That's how we are programmed."

None of the crew had yet to sit down. An uneasy feeling still hung in the rarefied air.

"So how, Lisa, did you build this place?" asked Cheng.

"I am happy to explain, Commander Cheng. But perhaps you would all be more comfortable if you sat down. I would like to know if the sofas and chairs are comfortable. I am afraid we did not have any humans here when we built them, so we had to extrapolate comfort from the data we had."

Cheng sat in one of the armchairs and motioned the others to do so as well. While they were a bit awkward in their spacesuits, sitting was relatively easy.

"Good, now I hope you're comfortable," responded Lisa.

No one was.

Lisa continued, "We were programmed to build everything you see, Commander Cheng. Your friends on Earth made sure we had the ability to build in these tunnels and on the surface. Building in the tunnels was necessary to ensure you were safe from solar radiation and occasional meteor showers. Many cargo vessels were sent to us with supplies and machines that fabricate metals and ores on the Moon into materials we used for floors, walls, and fabrics. Just as oil on Earth can be used to make nylon, plastics, upholstery, cosmetics, and more, the ores and minerals here can be similarly mined and fabricated. And we certainly have no shortages. What we need is abundant and easily collected. We are even able to distill alcohol. So we built the bar. We hope you like everything you see."

"I sure like the bar idea," responded Huang Lian, the mission's construction specialist. "I could use a stiff one right now."

"Construction Specialist Huang, may the road rise up to meet you. May the wind always be at your back. May the sun shine warm upon your face. And rains fall soft upon your fields. And, until we meet again, may God hold you in the palm of His hand," responded Lisa.

"What, Lisa?" asked Huang, surprised by her comment.

"My memory bank tells me that whenever one is going to have a drink, a proper toast is in order. And it seems the Irish have written most of them. I believe that one is an old standard."

Huang smiled. "Yes, Lisa, it is. Thank you, and I'll be sure to remember it later when I have a drink." Huang knew he'd need Cheng's permission to drink any alcohol.

"Lian, is it possible for machines to have done this construction?" asked Cheng. He simply could not believe it.

Huang responded, "With the right equipment and programming, I suppose so. Some of the stuff on the surface, like the launching pads, is the most sophisticated I've ever seen."

"But how can they fabricate so much?" Cheng asked.

"Well, Commander, there are certainly enough minerals and resources here to fabricate just about everything we see, provided the process gets a little help from home," responded Huang.

"Keep going, Lian. Please give me the explanation-for-dummies version. This is all way beyond the briefing I received in Jiuquan on what to expect to find when we arrived," observed Cheng.

"OK," continued Huang, "the Moon is rich in silicon, titanium, aluminum, and various rare earth elements and precious metals like platinum. The silicon can be used for semiconductors and solar panels and the titanium and aluminum for structures and vehicles. With me so far?"

"Yes, go on."

"The Moon is also relatively abundant in water and helium-3. That grade of helium is very useful in monitoring and cooling nuclear reactors like the individual ones Lisa and other cyborgs and vehicles have to power them."

Cheng couldn't help but notice how Lisa sat quietly during Huang's explanation. He realized that while quiet, she heard every word. So did whatever was ordered by the other CPU she was connected to. Cheng wondered who Lisa answered to.

"So yes, Commander, this is all theoretically possible but a bit overwhelming to see. I don't think any of us thought so much could be done in so little time."

"By little time," Cheng responded, "do you mean to say that all of the rockets and payloads we've been sending up here for nearly ten years was insufficient to support what we're seeing?"

"No," responded Huang, "I'm not saying that at all. We sent a lot of equipment and supplies. I'm just amazed at how efficient it's all been."

Huang paused and then added, "But one thing does bother me, Commander."

"What?"

"Why didn't visual reports sent back from the base show more of this progress? We saw a lot for sure, but not all this. Why is that? I have to believe it was not intentional to keep us in the dark. But whatever the motive, someone directed that it not be shared with us."

"Or something," suggested Cheng.

"Whoever—or whatever—directed that all of this be done, gets my vote of approval," interjected Shao. "I'm a computer programmer and have seen some amazing things computer-driven bots and cyborgs can do. But I've never seen anything like this."

"Neither have I, including in all the briefing books at home," replied Cheng.

As the crew absorbed Cheng's comment, Lisa spoke, breaking the silence.

"Commander Cheng?"

"Yes?" he responded, showing some agitation that Lisa intruded into his conversation with the crew. He wondered who programmed her for that attribute. Alexa, Siri, and Google never interrupt unless you ask them to.

Lisa answered politely, seemingly oblivious to Cheng's declining patience. "May I now show you all the full quarters? We have a small gym, a fully equipped kitchen, a nice dining room that can seat twenty, a karaoke room with thousands of songs courtesy of Apple, and bedrooms with baths for each of you, all with your own video and audio, of course. All the comforts of home."

Under his breath, Colonel Yang Jin muttered to himself, "I can't wait to meet the maid and butler."

"Lt. Colonel Yang," observed Lisa, "the help, as I believe you call them, will take care of all your needs. All you need to do is tell me what you want."

Cheng shrugged his shoulders and replied, "So much for privacy."

Yang caught the eye of Fong Hui, his fellow Snow Leopard commando, and whispered, "I don't trust this thing. I don't like this place."

Lisa turned and waved one of her mechanical arms back and forth as if to signal, "Follow me." As sophisticated as her voice was, she looked like something built by a seventh-grader for a science fair.

As they began the tour, Lisa added, "Oh! And we have free Wi-Fi, but I am afraid it only reaches within the facilities at the station. You cannot reach Earth from the mission command quarters. For that, you need to go to mission control."

CHAPTER SEVENTEEN

AERO CLUB BAR
SAN DIEGO, CALIFORNIA

NICHOLAS KLINE WAS A MERCENARY AND FOUNDER OF SANCTUARY LLC, A PRIVATE MILITIA for hire. The ex-Marine Special Operations Command (SOC) member founded Sanctuary in 2011 in San Diego, California. San Diego is a navy town, and Kline felt at home. Sanctuary's cadre of hired guns, mostly ex-military, fought alongside American soldiers in Iraq, Afghanistan, Somalia, and Syria. Kline, a member of a top-secret SOC team set up for the most exotic of missions, bore an array of medals and citations, including a Silver Star, Purple Heart, and Navy Cross, a medal just one step short of the Medal of Honor.

Sanctuary, just like Kline, was ideologically agnostic. As long as you were willing to pay their rates, Sanctuary LLC would deliver a ready-to-order army, anywhere in the world, in very short order. For some, the line between an illegal arms dealer and Sanctuary was a very fine one, all too often crossed when the money was right. Others viewed professional mercenary companies like Sanctuary as undisciplined and unregulated armies, accountable to no one. Rumors of battlefield atrocities only fed that reputation. None of it bothered Kline.

The United States was Sanctuary's largest customer, with annual payments from the Department of Defense in the many millions of dollars. It was spending that the DoD deemed necessary to avoid reporting official troop strengths—and casualties—in war-torn areas. Casualties were something Sanctuary was prepared to absorb. Such arrangements are common when a government wants to keep a few of its own boots on the ground combined with undisclosed, professional soldiers for hire to protect them.

Douglas Wright, Director of the U.S. Space Force, was charged with manning the mission to the Moon, now scheduled for launch in a matter of months. General Ryan Speck would see they were trained. The cover story for the mission was an exploration of mining on the Moon and staging to Mars by two billionaires obsessed with beating China to the prize. The cover prevented Wright from deploying U.S. uniformed armed forces from any of the U.S. services. Such a move would be seen by China as suspicious. So with the approval of President Lawson, Wright reached out to Sanctuary and his old friend Nicholas Kline.

Wright asked to see Kline to discuss a mission. Kline scheduled the meeting at the Aero Club Bar on India Street in San Diego. The ACB was named by *Maxim*, a popular men's magazine, as one of America's top dive bars. Kline liked that. More important, the ACB had more than eight hundred whiskies available in the bar, including Kline's favorite—Nevis Dew 12 Year Old Deluxe—made at Ben Nevis in Fort William, Scotland, allegedly the oldest scotch distillery in the world. People who kill other people for a living are picky about their scotch.

Wright arrived at five in the afternoon. It was a beautiful day, as it was almost every day in San Diego. The meeting was scheduled for 5:30.

As he parked in front of the ACB, Wright noticed Kline's trademark black and yellow BMW R1150 GS motorcycle sitting at the curb. A bike last built in the early 2000s, it was powerful and made for both on- and off-road use, just what Kline wanted. It got him around town but also off into the wilderness. Some might describe it as an oversized and overpowered dirt bike. It fit Kline's personality and ego—oversized and overpowered. Just like every other special forces operative Wright had ever met.

Kline rose from his bar stool as Wright walked in, obviously anticipating his arrival. Wright marveled at how good Kline looked. At 5'11", he was in perfect shape. He should be. When not on assignment in some Godforsaken place, he ran more than ten miles a day and worked out at least an hour in a local gym. He also looked the role he played. With his dark brown hair, five o'clock shadow, bright blue eyes, and USMC tattoo on his right forearm, his appearance alone made him look ominous. Wright had no doubt that women who liked "bad boys" liked Kline.

"Doug, it's good to see you," said Kline, extending his hand. Wright took it and pulled Kline to him for a hug.

"It's great to see you as well, Nick."

It had been more than three years since Wright last saw Kline. The two shared many experiences on battlefields throughout the Middle East, so hugs were mandatory.

Wright assumed Kline arrived early to make sure he got a few rounds under his belt before they discussed business. That was confirmed when Kline added, "Geez, Doug, I'm already two ahead of you. Sit down and order a drink." The bartender was dutifully standing behind the bar, ready to take Wright's order.

As he sat on a stool next to Kline, Wright said, "I'll have a Coors Light."

"What a man!" Kline scoffed. "And I'll have another Ben Nevis, neat."

"Hey, pal," responded Wright in a good-natured way, "I'm not about to try to keep up with you, in a bar or on a battlefield."

CHAPTER EIGHTEEN

COMMAND CENTER
THE FAR SIDE OF THE MOON

TWO MONTHS HAD PASSED SINCE THE DRAGON HAD LANDED. THE CREW SETTLED INTO THEIR daily routines, each undertaking the tasks they had been assigned.

The robot called Lisa acted as their concierge for anything they needed, including food and transportation to locations where their work had to be done. When Lisa was nowhere to be found, other, less-sophisticated robots appeared to handle the crew's requests.

As Cheng and Wu rode in their rover for morning inspection, Cheng observed, "I don't know why, Meilin, but I'm still uneasy around Lisa. I get the feeling she's watching more than obeying."

"Commander, I think the Moon is getting to you. Lisa simply does what it's told and seems to be quite compliant," responded Wu. "What is it that causes you such concern?"

"I don't know," he admitted.

The routine of visiting the key operation centers on the installation was simple. The crewmembers put on specially designed pressurized suits that allowed for greater mobility and entered the air lock outside the quarters. Once in the anteroom, the air lock was depressurized and they boarded a rover. The rover would enter the tunnel and transport the crewmembers to their assigned stations. At the station, the crewmembers reversed the routine. Upon entering the assigned operations center, they removed their suits and were ready to get to work. It was a very simple, efficient, and quick commute.

As they drove through the facility, Cheng and Wu passed each of the operational areas manned by the crew.

<u>Mission Control</u>

Most days, Cheng and Wu spent their time at mission control, the central hub for the operations on the base. The base had eyes virtually everywhere projected on an array of sixty 19-inch screens hanging on one wall. The adjoining wall had two 15-foot screens. An image on the smaller screens transferred to one of the big screens by a simple switch or voice command. Once the computer network tied in fully to mission control, it would automatically switch images if it detected activity that might raise concerns.

Mission control also had access to a dozen Jade rovers on the surface equipped with cameras. Cheng and Wu could direct them to survey activities throughout the base.

Liam Huang, in charge of construction, also spent most of his time in mission control. From there, he used his own set of robots to monitor the computer-driven construction apparatus busy building out more lava tunnels for human use, necessary for protection from harmful gamma rays or space debris that routinely fell on the Moon. Once a week he took a field trip to inspect progress. He was never disappointed. "I wish all my employees were robotic," he'd often say in briefings.

Mission control was also the only connection point with the Jiuquan Center. All communications with the home base had to be made from mission control, something Cheng didn't like. He believed there should be communication links throughout the complex and, in particular, always with him as mission commander. There was no reason that could not be implemented. But when he mentioned his concern to Boris Kushner, the launch center director, it fell on deaf ears. "We have more important priorities, Commander Cheng, than to give you more toys," Kushner told him.

Launch Control

Zhang Hong spent his days in launch control, making sure all systems were operating. He coordinated closely with Shao Rushi, the programming expert, to sync the base computer operations with communications to the launch silos and landing platforms. Assisting him were eight robots programmed to follow his orders. When necessary, he checked on the MMRTG units in the rovers but never bothered to visit the tunnel where the full-scale nuclear reactor to power the base was being built about ten miles from the Dragon crew's location. He preferred to watch that project from a distance. He was never comfortable on the surface.

Armory

Snow Leopard veterans Yang Jin and Fong Hui focused their activities in the armory. From the first day, the two were amazed at the technology awaiting them. It was far more advanced than they'd expected. While there were only fifty cyborgs at their command, each resembled a cross between the Terminator and Robocop, except even taller, reaching eight feet. And each carried more weaponry than ten humans could deploy. So their troop strength was stronger than it appeared.

They also had twenty Jades at their disposal, some of which were equipped with magneto hydrodynamic explosive munition launchers (MAHEM). Each MAHEM could be configured to fire shrapnel, armor-piercing bullets, or an explosive projectile. In the void of the Moon's atmosphere, whatever a MAHEM spews out can travel to targets miles away within seconds. And when MAHEM munitions were depleted, each Jade had a 50-kilowatt laser capable of disabling any vehicle or killing any man by destroying the integrity of his spacesuit.

Even more lethal were Jades equipped with hypersonic rocket launchers, capable of deploying missiles that could pierce through just about anything.

Similar weaponry was mounted on the cyborgs.

Nonetheless, Yang and Fong were both concerned about adequate firepower should the United States or a coalition decide to attack. Their liaison with the Jiuquan Center promised more cyborgs in future cargo missions. As far as Yang and Fong were concerned, they couldn't come soon enough.

The two Snow Leopard commandos occasionally took a dozen of the cyborgs out for missions on the surface. It had to be done during the lunar night to make detection more difficult from overhead satellites, but it also taught Yang and Fong how to operate in total darkness, something that would give them an advantage over anyone trying to invade their side of the Moon.

Data Center

Shao Rushi oversaw the installation and operation of the central computer. While many of the components were ready for her upon arrival, more came with subsequent cargo missions. By the end of the second month, the Luna Diébào computer was fully assembled and ready to be triggered into action upon command from the Jiuquan Satellite Launch Center. Once operational, the Luna Diébào would tie all the computers on the base into a single, integrated network.

While Huang occasionally assisted Shao in assembling some of the units, robots did most of the heavy work, as was usually the case on the base. In all, the base had 132 robots of various sizes that performed complex tasks. Lisa often interacted with them for the more mundane assembly line–like operations.

Mission Command Quarters

Dr. Liu spent her time at mission command quarters watching over the crew's health, both physical and psychological. So far, everything was where she expected it to be after two months. Not enough time had passed for the isolation to have an effect. She'd seen it a number of times in China's space stations. At the three-month mark, some crewmembers developed depression that often led to physical ailments. Over years of studying the phenomenon, Dr. Liu developed protocols to counteract the depression. She knew that she would soon have to start administering them to affected crewmembers.

With each crewmember comfortable in their roles, the days took on routines.

On occasion, the entire crew would board Jades for an inspection and tour of the surface and to survey progress. Dr. Liu insisted on these trips to keep morale high. Too much isolation in the crew quarters could become a problem if unchecked.

On each jaunt, they marveled at how vast the installation had become and how camouflage avoided detection. Even the roofs of their Jades resembled the colors of the surface. When traveling in daylight, they automatically stopped if their sensors detected an unfriendly satellite overhead that might be taking pictures. When stationary, the Jades were nearly invisible from above. The only possible way to detect them would be by shadows that seem out of place and extrapolate from there. But even that didn't tell much. So although many overhead flights occurred, the intelligence gleaned from them was minimal. The U.S. and others knew something was going on but didn't have a clue of the magnitude.

Each evening, Cheng would assemble the crew in the living room area of the quarters to debrief. On instructions from Dr. Liu, the sessions were informal and if someone had nothing to report, that was fine. At the conclusion of the debriefing, Dr. Liu would then talk about psychological and physical issues they might be facing. She watched the reactions of crewmembers carefully to detect if anyone was on edge. So far, the crew was fine. She knew that would not last, and wondered who would break first.

During one session, Wu Meilin asked Dr. Liu why the doctor might not be the first to have a problem or develop something over time. Wu had spent considerable time on China's space station and had experienced some depression. Why hadn't Dr. Liu?

"My training," she explained. "I've spent months in isolation to prepare for the mission. I even studied your files, Meilin. You did very well on the space station. So I knew what to expect and have been trained how to deal with it. I'll be fine. So don't worry about me. Just be aware of how you're feeling and come to me immediately if you have concerns."

CHAPTER NINETEEN

G20 SUMMIT
PRAGUE, CZECH REPUBLIC

THE G20, REPRESENTING DELEGATES FROM ARGENTINA, AUSTRALIA, BRAZIL, CANADA, China, the European Union, France, Germany, India, Indonesia, Italy, Japan, Mexico, Russia, Saudi Arabia, South Africa, South Korea, Turkey, the United Kingdom, and the United States, held its summit in Prague in the Czech Republic, even though that country is not a member of the G20. With the apparently unstoppable rise of China and its collision course with the United States, the EU and the other seventeen countries were largely spectators. So France, that year's chair of the G20, decided to hold the event in a non-member country to maintain neutrality. No one objected to spending some time in one of the world's most beautiful cities. It was one of the few historical sites spared bombs in WWII, and remained as stunning as it was throughout its history.

The annual fete is most often a series of orchestrated photo ops to show unity of purpose and announce innocuous deals among the world's top economic powers. But it is also an opportunity for leaders to have private conversations about issues that are far more important than public posturing. Lawson and Xi agreed that the summit would be a good setting for the two to meet again, hopefully without a repeat of the sour ending of their meeting in Shanghai.

The library in the Aria, one of the most expensive and historical hotels in Prague, was appropriately ornate for the world's two most powerful men. It had been rearranged so they sat comfortably in wing-back chairs facing one another in front of what was once a fireplace but was now a hearth inlaid with beveled crystal. Their translators sat on smaller chairs to their right, set back a foot. The red walls and shelves of books befit the somber mood of the two men. They were comfortable, each with a glass of water in case it was needed.

Lawson was wearing a blue suit, white shirt, and red and blue striped tie. Xi wore a black suit, white shirt, and light blue tie. Their typical public personas. If they could, both would have preferred to be in slacks with an open collar shirt. But world leaders simply don't dress that way at the G20.

CHAPTER TWENTY

MISSION COMMAND QUARTERS
THE FAR SIDE OF THE MOON

AS ALL OF THE TAIKONAUTS WELL KNEW, EVERYTHING IS HARDER IN SPACE OR IN LOW gravity. Dr. Liu felt it was her responsibility to advise the crew about all of the challenges one faced in zero gravity. "One might assume," she told the crew during her first group session, "that the weightlessness of space and dealing with just a fraction of your body weight in gravity like the Moon would make tasks easier, but the opposite is true."

When moving objects in space or on the Moon, the laws of physics come into full play, and a simple push that would barely move something on Earth can cause the object to quickly careen away and damage whatever is in its path before it can be stopped.

All of the taikonauts were admonished early in their training that if an object was coming their way, they should think twice about catching it. They might be able to divert it, but stopping it was not likely unless it had very little mass. Otherwise, it's likely to take you with it. Stopping a screwdriver pushed your way was fine; stopping a heavy object could prove deadly. Just get out of the way.

And stopping one's own body weight in zero or low gravity is yet another problem. The televised Moon landings with U.S. astronauts leaping across the surface were certainly entertaining. Dr. Liu remembered watching with awe when she was a child. But no one bothered to report that once the momentum of their leaping began, stopping took considerable effort. Worse, keeping balance was equally difficult, and falling over a real threat. Getting back up in a bulky spacesuit is no easy task.

Personal hygiene is another challenge.

Common activities like bathing and brushing teeth are real chores in space. Less so in low gravity environments, but still a challenge. Other normal bodily functions like sweating also create their own problems. Evaporation is not the same. In space or where there is no atmosphere, sweat clings to everything and doesn't want to go away. Perspiration is a true nuisance.

"Work slowly," Dr. Liu reminded her crew. "Don't worry about looking lazy."

This creates the problem of exercising. It's an important part of keeping in shape, particularly in a weightless or low gravity environment where muscles atrophy if not used. And Dr. Liu also believed that mental health depended on physical activity. Space agencies developed many protocols for mild exercise in space, where muscles, bones, and blood vessels weaken with the loss of pressure caused by weightlessness. One no longer has to exert any pressure to lift the body, stand, or climb. On Earth, blood moves with gravity as the heart pumps harder trying to overcome gravitational pull. Not so in space. Everything slows down. Common movements like lying down, sitting, and standing are no longer an exercise in space.

"You need to exercise two hours a day," Liu would tell crewmembers, usually suggesting a combination of resistance and aerobic training. To help, space agencies have developed devices like the advanced resistive exercise device (ARED), which is an air pressure–based weight machine, as well as exercise bikes and treadmills that suppress vibration and stay stabilized in space.

As Dr. Liu liked to say, "A long-distance runner should probably find another career."

Then there were those things no one really wants to talk about. Dr. Liu and her female colleagues, for example, all needed to deal with their menstrual cycles. The easiest way was medical intervention that interrupts the cycle much like birth control pills. Dr. Liu chose that avenue, but some of her colleagues did not, and dealing with monthly periods, along with their side effects, was one more complication in their lives in space or on the moon.

While periods could be avoided, urinating or having bowel movements could not. And getting rid of the waste posed its own challenges.

New crewmembers learned that going to the bathroom in space or low gravity is a process most of them have experienced on Earth but with a little twist.

As Dr. Liu described it, "If you've ever gone to the bathroom on a plane, when you close the lid and flush the toilet, that whoosh you hear is a vacuum sucking the waste into a holding tank. Now imagine if you're sitting on the toilet in space when you flush it. Imagine a constant vacuum at work while you're doing your business. That's how it works in space. Just try not to get sucked through the toilet and into the holding tank!" Liu found humor in that mental picture.

It was her job to make all of these issues understood by the crew and easier for them to handle, and to monitor the crews' reaction to their new home.

"A prolonged stay in space has many negative physiological effects, like declining bone density and digestive problems," Dr. Liu would lecture to the crew periodically. She believed repeating the facts would be reassuring. "Most are treatable with conventional medication. Astrophysicists and physicians have years of experience in studying dozens of brave souls who have spent months in space. So there are cures for just about everything short of a heart attack or something that requires immediate surgery."

On the psychological side, the Dragon's journey to the Moon had been short, so none of the potentially challenging issues had time to arise. While that would be different on a trip to Mars, that was not Dr. Liu's problem on this assignment.

But there was one area of particular interest to her—sex. While some suggested studies on having sex in space should be undertaken with crews orbiting in space stations, no one had ever admitted to undertaking such studies. While rumors persist, no one has attempted to verify them, let alone try to understand the physiological challenges.

As Dr. Liu knew, increased blood flow for both sexes is an important part of having sex. Without it, a woman is unlikely to become aroused enough to have an orgasm. In space and low gravity, blood flow slows dramatically. Some studies suggest that the reduced blood flow will make it impossible for a man to have an erection. And assuming all the physical needs were met, if either the man or the woman got too excited and pushed too hard, their partner might end up a projectile smashed against an adjacent wall or ceiling. Not exactly the climax they were looking for.

While Dr. Liu was prohibited from suggesting that any of the crew have carnal "visitations" with one another, she was also not charged with preventing it. She hoped that over time, relationships would develop and crewmembers would come to her, perhaps seeking aid to help with the challenges she knew they'd face. The old expression, "the spirit is willing but the flesh is weak" is an apt description of what the crew might face, particularly the men.

But while the body may not be ready, the mind doesn't lose its libido. Dr. Liu needed to be prepared if the crewmembers crossed the unspoken Rubicon and fell in love. Or lust.

With that possibility in mind, Dr. Liu had brought along a collection of medicines and devices to deal with the issues she hoped would arise. It included various "toys," ointments, and pills. And a harness to keep a couple "connected" in low gravity. Many of the gadgets were her personal designs, tested with her husband on Earth—but never in a low gravity environment like the Moon.

Mission control secretly approved Dr. Liu bringing her collection, considering it within mission-sanctioned boundaries and perhaps leading to potentially important research on the challenges of humans propagating in space. The only standing order she had was that she could not encourage relationships. She needed to let them happen on their own. So as often as she lectured the crew, together or separately, on hygiene and other physiological or psychological needs, she never brought up sex.

While Dr. Liu had no say in who was picked for the mission, the gods had looked down on her. The pairing possibilities with four men and three women (four counting herself) made the probability high that Dr. Liu would get the opportunity to be the first to research and explore a previously taboo issue.

She knew she could rule out same-sex trysts. In China's society the LGBTQ community was rejected, and anyone suspected of being gay was eliminated from any significant positions, particularly on crews into space. So Dr. Liu knew that whatever relationship did arise would be entirely heterosexual.

Of the crew, the only ones she ruled out were Yang and Fong, the Snow Leopard commandos. As members of China's most elite fighting force, they were all business and no fun. Given their training and level of discipline, it was also unlikely they'd succumb to any maladies while on the Moon. Even if they did, Dr. Liu knew they would never tell her. She had never seen either one of them smile.

Liu put her money on Cheng and Wu, the two mission commanders. While also military like Yang and Fong, their ranks had far less discipline and fraternizing was common, particularly among officers. That left Shao, the programmer, and her possible pairing with either Zhang, the physicist, or Huang, in charge of construction. To Dr. Liu, it was a tossup whether Shao would go for brains or brawn.

CHAPTER TWENTY-ONE

SKYE AEROSPACE HQ2
RICHMOND, VIRGINIA

THE PRESS RELEASE ANNOUNCING THE VENTURE, APPROVED BY THE PRESIDENT, WAS SIMPLE and straightforward:

FOR IMMEDIATE RELEASE

Skye Aerospace and Voyager Expeditions Announce Joint Venture to Get to the Moon.

Competing concerns Skye Aerospace and Voyager Expeditions have decided to join forces in light of the progress China has made in exploring commercial mining and colonization of the Moon. While each company has made significant progress on its own projects, they acknowledged at a joint press conference that China is too far ahead for them to act separately.

"Together," said Rick Phillips, owner of Skye Aerospace, "Sienna Butler and I can move our projects ahead in leaps and bounds. It's time the private sector stepped in and did what it's obvious NASA and others cannot do in the time frame needed to get it done."

"We've put together investors, engineers, and scientists interested in winning, not just running the race," added Sienna Butler, owner of Voyager Expeditions. "And Rick Phillips and I are not interested in second place."

The venture, named Luna Victorum, is expected to launch manned missions to the Moon within two months and has already begun recruiting astronauts.

For more information, contact Meghan Salome, Luna Victorum Press Liaison, at (202) 555-5555.

Upon publication of the press release, the reaction from China and other countries was tepid at best. No one expressed any significant concerns, likely believing it was the usual hyperbole from the two multibillionaire entrepreneurs. The reaction was exactly what President Lawson wanted. A low profile not connected with any official NASA or Space Force initiatives gave the U.S. the cover it needed.

It had now been two months since Skye Aerospace and Voyager Expeditions announced its joint venture to get to the Moon before year's end. As Phillips and Butler sat in Skye Aerospace's HQ2 building in Richmond, they retraced their brief time as collaborators rather than competitors.

"I think we came up with the right name, Rick. Luna Victorum. A good cover and the kind of cooperation the president asked for," Butler commented as she read the press release.

"Indeed," responded Phillips, "but our work is cut out for us. We have little time, so let's get our engineers and scientists in a room together to work it out."

"Agreed," concluded Butler. "I'm leaving for Reno tomorrow to be sure we're on track."

The two companies assembled their best people in a facility in Western Nevada not far from Reno. The facility had been a cloud computing mainframe abandoned some years earlier. But it remained in excellent structural condition, and the cabling was in place for easy hookup to the Skye Aerospace and Voyager Expeditions systems. It was close enough to housing and hotels to make the assignment an easy relocation for employees and families. And Reno was only an hour and a half away, so adult fun was virtually around the corner. While the weather could get a bit hot in the desert, everyone spent most of their time in air-conditioned comfort.

To motivate those assembled, Luna Victorum paid lucrative bonuses if benchmarks were met. Everyone involved was thrilled to be working together. Many had been colleagues in prior jobs and relished the idea of coming up with inventive ideas to overcome seemingly insurmountable odds. Virtually every man and woman on the team believed they had special talents indispensable to success. And for some, that was absolutely true. Without doubt, some of the smartest minds in science and engineering worked for Phillips and Butler. The reason was quite simple. The entrepreneurs paid them more than NASA or any other operations with designs on space exploration would. All agree that there is nothing quite like a billionaire with a mission. Put two of them together on the same page and anything is possible.

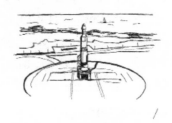

CHAPTER TWENTY-TWO

CAPE CANAVERAL, FLORIDA

CAPE CANAVERAL AND THE KENNEDY SPACE CENTER ARE NEAR THE CENTER OF FLORIDA'S eastern shoreline. Known as the Space Coast, it includes some of the most beautiful beaches in the world. But the public never gets to use them. They are government-owned and protected by either NASA or the United States Space Force's 45th Space Wing, headquartered at nearby Patrick Air Force Base. Its air space is reserved strictly for operations that launch rockets into space. The value of this unused beachfront tract is in the billions.

As NASA wallowed in unmanned ventures and limited budgets, private enterprise saw the opportunities the commercialization of space offered, from launching satellites or sending payloads to the International Space Station to recreational space travel. Voyager Expeditions and Skye Aerospace launched rockets from facilities on Cape Canaveral and at the Kennedy Space Center. They shared the base with NASA, Blue Origin, SpaceX, and the United Launch Alliance—the joint venture between Boeing and Lockheed. Now and again, a small private company crops up and gets into the game, but they don't last long.

Both Voyager Expeditions and Skye Aerospace had successful programs under way and proven in the market. They did not share data when competing, since "rocket science ain't rocket science"—meaning there are just so many ways to deal with the physics of launching people and payloads into space. Thus sharing did not come easy, even though their respective technology was more compatible than many thought. That made it simpler for the scientists at Skye Aerospace and Voyager Expeditions to deploy mission-critical initiatives once they started cooperating on Luna Victorum.

Combining the Voyager Expeditions Leviathan rocket and its New Dawn spacecraft with Skye Aerospace's New Excalibur and New Shepard rocket technology helped create a generation of launch capacity and versatility well beyond anything NASA had in the planning stages. Skye Aerospace's Blue Moon lunar lander, coupled with Voyager Expeditions' landing systems, completed the technology side of the challenge. By delivering the cooperation both companies promised, it took only three weeks for the teams to come up with the launch rocket, crew transporter, and lunar lander designs. The advancements were unprecedented.

The plan had three phases.

Phase 1. Atop three Skye Aerospace New Excalibur rockets, modified with technology from Voyager Expeditions' Leviathan, sit pods, each containing two inflatable habitats and construction equipment. They launch from Skye Aerospace's Complex 34. The first stages take the capsules containing the pods into space on a trajectory to the Moon. Those stages are separated after their burn and return to Earth for reuse, landing vertically on landing pads at the Cape.

The second stages then fire and propel the capsules containing the pods toward the Moon. After the second stages of the rockets burn out, the capsules are released for a three-day journey into orbit around the Moon.

On signals from mission control, the capsules descend to the surface, one at a time on consecutive orbits, and land near the South Pole on the near side of the Moon. If they all land accurately, they will be within a few hundred feet of one another.

Phase 2. The second phase involves four of the modified New Excalibur rockets. Atop two are unmanned lunar landers based on Skye Aerospace's Moon landers capable of lifting off the Moon and returning to their mothership. The other two New Excaliburs are topped with lunar landers not intended to return; those are more in the nature of small cargo ships. Each lander carries a pair of small lunar rovers that resemble off-street ATVs. More important, each lander includes a dozen robots powered by batteries that should last two to three months on the Moon.

The New Excaliburs launch and make their way to the Moon in the same fashion as the pods. All four are equipped with high-resolution lighting and cameras to beam back the scene on the surface as it unfolds. After establishing a precise orbit, the lunar landers detach from their motherships and descend, each touching down within a few hundred yards from the pods. Two of the landers act as reserve vehicles for a safe escape should an emergency arise and the crews from the later-arriving Voyager Expeditions Starships are unable to relaunch. The lunar landers can also make a much faster exit than the starships. While they cannot on their own make it back to Earth, they can get out of harm's way until a rescue mission can be launched.

The other two lunar landers store the rovers and robots. Under direction of mission control in Cape Canaveral, the robots exit the lander. Then, as the cameras beam back the scene, the robots carefully position the pods, forming a circle with one pod in the middle and the other five fanning out like a star, with each pod equidistant from the other. The pods are inflated to form six habitats that look like collections of dozens of large balls, each fully formed pod about 30 feet high and 40 feet in diameter. The outer pods are then connected to the center pod by tunnels that look like legs coming from the center pod. The tunnels are 20 feet high and 10 feet wide. The robots then collect small rocks and soil from the surface, and through a process called regolith additive construction, fuse the rocks and soil to the surface of the pods and tunnels, forming a cement-like coating that strengthens and protects them. This process should take twenty-four to thirty-six hours to complete. Regolith additive construction and most of the technology utilized to construct the habitat is not new. They'd been tested on Earth for years. But this was the first time they would be deployed on the Moon.

The structure is then pressurized and connected to converters that harvest soil and extract oxygen through a process involving heat from the Sun and electricity from the lunar landers. Each is powered by an array of solar panels that are eventually removed and placed near the habitat and connected to them for electrical power. After another two or three days, the habitat is ready and the crew has an inhabitable, albeit temporary, home.

Phase 3. Two full-scale starships launch from Kennedy Space Center's Complex 12 and 14 using Voyager Expeditions Leviathans, each loaded with top-secret cargo and a crew of thirty men and women, modified from the original capacity of one hundred to make room for cargo. After a three-day trip, they land on the surface and rendezvous with the habitat and lunar landers.

While cooperation among all those who participated in the planning was outstanding, naming the new spacecraft was an entirely different matter. There is nothing equal to the egos of entrepreneurs like Phillips and Butler when it comes to what something they invented should be called. But why not? After all, they paid for it.

The two agreed that the names for the lunar landers and starships should not be a variation of anything already named by their operations or by other companies. So that ruled out "Blue," "Origin," "Glenn," "Excalibur," "New Dawn," "Shepard," "Falcon," "Genesis," "Starhopper," and "Leviathan." They chose not to name the rockets with the pods. That left the lunar landers and starships. Finally, after hours of frustrating creative sessions yielding no results, a very tired engineer offhandedly suggested naming the spacecraft successors after the decommissioned Apollo lunar landers and U.S. space shuttles. It will forever be debated whether the acceptance of that suggestion was a brilliant compromise or a convenient excuse to get some sleep:

Lunar Module No. 1—Eagle II
Lunar Module No. 2—Intrepid II
Leviathan New Dawn No. 1—Atlantis II
Leviathan New Dawn No. 2—Discovery II

In assigning the names, it was intentional that no ship was named after U.S. space shuttles *Columbia* and *Challenger*, destroyed on missions that ended their flight and left the fate of their crewmembers to be remembered not only in museums, but also in morgues.

When President Lawson asked Wright, "Why do we need two lunar landers and a pair of starships? Doesn't that double the costs, and for what gain?" the director of the Space Force soberly responded, "With so little time, and an inability to thoroughly test the technology and equipment, the mission needs to anticipate errors and malfunctions. So each of the landers and Leviathans is equipped and manned identically. It's a matter of redundancy and expendability, Mr. President, not need. If I had my way, I'd be sending up three pairs."

Assuming it all worked, Luna Victorum and its armada were ready.

All the Atlantis II and Discovery II needed were crews.

CHAPTER TWENTY-THREE

FOUR SEASONS HOTEL, PRESIDENTIAL SUITE
PRAGUE, CZECH REPUBLIC

ATLEE LAWSON WAS NO SHRINKING VIOLET. WHILE SHE UNDERSTOOD HER PLACE AS FIRST lady, that did not keep her from the business or political arenas. Nor did President Lawson ask her to keep a low profile. She was his biggest fan and had higher approval ratings in polls than the president. While she sometimes veered a bit from the president's agenda or policies, he never tried to put any damper on her enthusiasm.

She could also be very persuasive in her private meetings with Washington politicians. Following Lawson's election, it fast became legendary that any member of the House or Senate—man or woman—had better be prepared when Atlee Lawson called and innocently asked if they'd like to join her for a cup of tea in the White House. And they needed to worry even more if she suggested meeting at the member's or Senator's office. While a few of them leaked complaints to the press about the first lady's influence on the president and the pressure she put on House members and Senators, everyone knew the first lady's role would never return to the demure vision last enjoyed during Rosalynn Carter's tenure.

The 4,000-square-foot Presidential Suite at the Four Seasons Hotel, an eighteenth-century Baroque building, opened from a private elevator and included four bedrooms, each with its own bath; two living rooms; a study; a dining room; and a pantry. For their stay, the president and his wife occupied about 3,000 square feet, allowing two of the four bedrooms to be sectioned off for the Secret Service. The security detail's area, however, was sufficiently removed from the president's space to afford the privacy he and Mrs. Lawson required.

As the president reached to turn out the light on the bedside table and go to sleep, he turned to his wife and asked, "Atlee, how did the planning for your luncheon go today?"

"Fine, Phil. Just fine." Atlee Lawson was sitting up in bed, her light on, her book open, but it was obvious she wanted to talk.

The president turned off the light and leaned back into his pillow, saying, "I can't wait to hear the gory gossip." But for now, he'd heard what he needed. Perhaps at least his wife wouldn't take the world one more step toward Armageddon.

Mrs. Lawson was not ready to go to sleep.

"How did your meeting with Xi go?" she asked as the president tried to bury his head in the pillow. He knew that would be to no avail.

"Not very well. Not well at all," responded the president with some finality in his tone. He rolled over and fell asleep.

The first lady lay back and turned off her light. She wanted to ask him more, but he was already breathing deeply. She marveled at how easily her husband could sleep regardless of the chaos surrounding him. She wished she had that gift.

Now unable to sleep, she relived the events that preceded the special luncheon scheduled for the next day.

Entertaining is a major part of the G20 Summit. Receptions occur every night. Cultural events are interspersed in the agenda to allow for photo ops and breaks from the daily debates and policy deliberations. These breaks are especially appreciated by the delegates, all of whom easily become frustrated when little or no progress is made on key issues. The rule of the G20 is to "discuss and delay."

For the spouses who accompany the collection of world leaders, the Summit can be a painstaking affair of looking good, not talking to the locals or the press, and keeping a low profile. Although keeping a low profile was not in Atlee Lawson's DNA, she did appreciate the need to do so at the Summit—at least on the public stage. What she did privately was her decision so long as the president did not object.

She was acutely aware of the pressures the president was under to avoid war and manage the situation of China's military base on the Moon. She also knew his advisers were likely to be all over the map with options, some of which most certainly involved sacrificing lives. While she was confident of the president's ability to measure and weigh each idea carefully with input from all credible sources, she had no confidence that the other world leaders at the Summit operated in the same way. Of particular concern was China. While Xi Jinping on many occasions showed a willingness to compromise and find common ground, his promises more often than not were broken after he conferred with his politburo and other Chinese leaders. It was clear that Xi Jinping did not have near the discretionary powers of the U.S. president. And now the meeting between the two men the day before went no better than their meeting did in Shanghai. That worried the first lady. It put her husband at a disadvantage, since compromise might lead to frustration, and worse, to defeat.

When she first suggested hosting a private luncheon for the spouses of the heads of state gathered for the Summit, the president was hesitant. Such events had not been scheduled in the past and might raise eyebrows, including those in the press. While spouses were certainly entertained during the Summit, they never had private gatherings where only they were present.

"Atlee, if you do this," said the president as the two enjoyed a moment alone on a couch in the suite, "how will you be sure what is said remains confidential? And you most certainly cannot discuss policy or make any agreements."

"Phil, I promise I won't destroy the global economy or declare war. I just think the spouses deserve a chance to talk among themselves and exchange ideas. And more important, what some of them say may reveal information you can use," responded the first lady.

The president smiled and responded, "Don't tell me you're turning into a spy. I think the clandestine gathering of intelligence should be left with Mike Hellriegel."

"C'mon, Phil, be serious. I want to do this for all the right reasons."

The president leaned back in his chair, stared at the ceiling, and reached over to the end table, grabbing a book.

"Atlee," he began, "lately I've taken to reading old poetry for inspiration. Your idea reminds me of a hymn by Howard Arnold Walter. I just so happen to have a copy here."

The first lady could smell the setup.

"Phil," she responded with a knowing smile, "I suppose you're going to tell me you just so happen to have the book handy and didn't anticipate I'd make a suggestion."

"Atlee, we've been married far too long for either of us to surprise the other. I knew you'd come up with something," said Lawson, adding with a smile of his own, "and the Commander in Chief always has to be prepared!"

"Command away, Mr. President," responded the first lady. "I can't wait to hear you read aloud."

"Thank you, madam. Now let me read the first two stanzas to you," the president continued:

> I would be true, for there are those who trust me;
> I would be pure, for there are those who care;
> I would be strong, for there is much to suffer;
> I would be brave, for there is much to dare.
> I would be friend of all—the foe, the friendless;

I would be giving, and forget the gift;
I would be humble, for I know my weakness;
I would look up, and love, and laugh and lift.

"You're playing with some serious, issues, Atlee. I trust you. But please stay within the bounds of diplomacy."

"OK, Phil, I'll be careful."

President Lawson skipped the last stanza:

May none, then, call on me for understanding,
May none, then turn to me for help in pain,
And drain alone his bitter cup of sorrow,
Or find he knocks upon my heart in vain.

CHAPTER TWENTY-FOUR

PRAGUE, CZECH REPUBLIC

ORGANIZING ANYTHING AT THE G20 SUMMIT IS DEEPLY MIRED IN PROTOCOL. WHEN SOME-thing new is proposed, it raises suspicions. Even what seems an entirely innocent suggestion is usually met with distrust and skepticism. That meant the first lady had to be creative.

Her first inclination was to host an invitation-only luncheon and invite whomever she wanted to. But that would unquestionably raise major concerns with just about every staffer and have little chance of success. And she could not cavalierly ignore those concerns, overrule them, and have a party. Using her power as the first lady in that fashion would antagonize country teams and most likely scare away the wives of the leaders, defeating her goals.

She needed to hatch a plan, particularly since she wanted only the wives of the leaders attending. The first lady didn't want any men there who might feel the need to show their testosterone-driven bravado.

Czech Republic President Tomáš Petříček was only a spectator at the summit. Although the Czech Republic was the host, its leader was not an invited guest. Not allowing him to attend created some diplo-matic angst. After all, Petříček is the Czech Republic's commander in chief of the military as well as head of state. Unlike his counterparts in other parliamentary countries in Europe, where the presidents are largely figureheads, Petříček had considerable influence in political affairs. Making matters more sensitive, his previous position as minister of foreign affairs provided the press with grist for the mills in reports of his snubbing. But Petříček took it in stride, knowing he'd have opportunities for private meetings. He had no interest in making the press spectacle a sideshow while his country was officially hosting one of the most important meetings in the world.

Petříček's wife, Iva Petřicková, was herself a very popular first lady. Atlee Lawson knew her and had enjoyed her company in past state visits to the White House. Likewise, Petřicková enjoyed Lawson and knew the diplomatic ropes well. Since the time her husband was the minister of foreign affairs, she had hosted many official dinners with foreign dignitaries.

Lawson reasoned that since Czechs are well known for their hospitality, it seemed natural that Petřicková would invite her counterparts to a small, private luncheon to relax out of the spotlight as their spouses toiled through the day in official meetings. And since only a couple of the world leaders were women, there were plenty of people to invite.

"Atlee, I love the idea," responded Petřicková when Lawson first suggested it. "Do you think the self-righteous protocol police will allow it? I know these summits are very formal and they frown upon independent planning."

"Protocol does surround the G20," responded Mrs. Lawson, "but when I ran it by the president, he loved the idea. So as long as Tomáš agrees, I think the organizers would be hard put to deny you the opportunity at a private affair to thank the many wives who are attending the summit. God knows, we could all use a break from the formalities and paparazzi."

Lawson hated the idea of characterizing the luncheon as if it were a meeting of cackling hens, but she knew if it had any other public persona, it would raise far too many concerns. So the U.S. first lady chose to divulge her plans only to those who needed to know. Petřicková was not among them.

Somewhat to her surprise, the planning went smoothly. Her ruse of describing the get-together as a chance for some privacy and "girl talk" worked, even with the press. They covered it briefly, but without much fanfare. One reporter wondered if the "ladies" would get massages and cucumber baths. While she thought that demeaning, Lawson was fine with it since such reporting and the reactions it drew kept it all under the radar.

Next, the first lady had to deal with translators. If she was going to be frank and stress the points she wanted to make to the other wives, she had to assume the translators would talk to others about what she said, potentially opening a Pandora's box of critical press. She needed to carefully craft any remarks and find time to speak privately, outside the earshot of the translators. She had to hope those listening could understand her English. She resolved to keep her officially translated comments to nonpolitical claptrap and reserve the important things for private moments. Orchestrating that was her next challenge. She needed an ally.

Tshepo Motsepe was the first lady of South Africa and someone Atlee Lawson knew well and admired. Motsepe was very accomplished. She graduated from the University of KwaZulu-Natal with a bachelor's degree in medicine and surgery and later earned a master of public health in maternal child health and aging at Harvard. The U.S. first lady had met her five years before the G20 Summit, and the two had immediately hit it off. They shared an acerbic sense of humor and loved little side conversations meant only for the two of them. She was a perfect co-conspirator.

"OK Atlee, let me get this straight," observed Motsepe when she first heard the plan. "You want me to distract others while you center in on a target for some private words. Right?"

"Right."

"And let me guess. Those targets don't happen to be Peng Liyuan and Alina Kabaeva, do they?"

"Perhaps. And maybe, just maybe, if time allows, Sara Netanyahu, Savita Kovind, and Akie Abe. They all speak English and will not need a translator."

It was an ambitious list:

FIRST LADY	COUNTRY
Peng Liyuan	China
Alina Kabaeva	Russia
Sara Netanyahu	Israel
Savita Kovind	India
Akie Abe	Japan

"And what makes you think they'll listen to you in private, however short the conversation will be?"

"Because they're women married to powerful, testosterone-driven men who, if left to their ways, may soon destroy the world."

"So you're not inviting any men?" asked Motsepe.

"No. It's time for women to speak up as a group."

Motsepe took a few moments to absorb the observation and then replied with a cautious tone in her voice, "And do you count Phillip Lawson among those testosterone-driven men, Atlee?"

Surprisingly to Motsepe, the question did not upset Lawson. "Yes, Tshepo, I do. But Phil is also married to a powerful, estrogen-driven woman who isn't about to let misguided masculinity run amok without at least trying to put a cold shower on it."

"And you've probably got a damn good dose of progesterone going for you, too! That ought to equal the odds," joked Motsepe.

Lawson ignored the attempt at humor. "So you're in?" Lawson asked in a tone that was more like a conclusion than a question.

"Yes, but of course, Madam Fourcade," responded Motsepe. The reference to the famous WWII spy, Marie-Madeleine Fourcade, who led the French Resistance in helping defeat the Nazis and end the war, was appealing to Atlee Lawson.

CHAPTER TWENTY-FIVE

AERO CLUB BAR
SAN DIEGO, CALIFORNIA

THE ACB CLEARLY EARNED ITS ACCOLADES AS ONE OF AMERICA'S BEST DIVE BARS. NARROW, with a long bar on one side and small booths lining the opposite wall, it was tight and not the best place for a private meeting. Wright would have preferred another location, but he elected not to question Kline's choice.

Because it was a Tuesday, the ACB was not crowded. Kline and Wright were sitting at the corner at the end of the bar most distant from the front door. No one sat behind them or to Kline's right. Five bar stools to Wright's left were removed. The table in the booths behind Kline and Wright and the one to Wright's left were marked "Reserved." On the bar in front of the missing stools sat a glass or mug as if it were waiting for a customer, assuring that no one would try to approach the bar. As Wright absorbed it all, he smiled at how good Kline was at hiding in plain sight.

Wright got to the point.

"Are we OK on top security on what we're going to talk about, Nick?" asked Wright. He knew the answer but needed to hear Kline agree that whatever the two of them discussed was top secret.

"Totally," responded Kline, acknowledging his obligation to Wright.

"Nick," began Wright, "how would you feel about going to the Moon?"

"The Moon?" replied Kline with surprise. "What are you afraid of? Some monsters made of cheese?"

Wright wondered if Kline read any newspapers that had been reporting on the crisis with China. "I'm not joking, Nick."

"Yeah, I didn't think you were," responded Kline. "This is about China, isn't it?" Wright was relieved that Kline did indeed read something more than the label of a bottle.

"It is. We need to get there, inspect what they're doing, and if necessary, disable it."

"And what would 'it' be, Doug?"

"We believe China may be building a military base with capacity to launch IGBMs," answered Wright. "Inter—"

"Intergalactic ballistic missiles," Kline finished for him. "How far are along are they? They've been sending missions up there for months, maybe years. I'll bet they are farther along than we think."

"They may well be, Nick. Since the operation is on the far side and out of our view most of the time, the intelligence we get is spotty at best. We just don't know for sure and need eyes and boots on the ground."

"And you want Sanctuary to do what? We don't have astronauts."

"I know. But you have warriors. And NASA doesn't have any of those. And right now, we need warriors."

"You have plenty of warriors in the army, navy, and marines. Shit, some of them might even be astronauts," responded Kline.

"We can't use our soldiers, Nick. We need to keep the Chinese in the dark, and mobilizing any forces would risk leaks and exposure. We can't afford that."

Kline took another sip of his Ben Nevis and thought for a few seconds. He finally responded, "Even assuming I could put together a crew of people foolish enough to want to travel to the Moon, how many do you need, and when?"

"I want forty fighters, Nick. And I want nineteen of them led by you and another nineteen led by David Weston."

Kline fell silent and looked ahead at the front door, twirling his glass between his hands. Wright wondered if he was considering his excuse to turn down a very insane idea. Wright was gambling on Kline not being able to pass on the challenge, particularly because Kline was as equally insane as Wright's idea.

"And why Weston?"

"Weston is as good as they come. Maybe as good as you, Nick," Wright answered. He knew that Kline's outward response of not needing such a compliment masked the real way he felt. Kline knew that Weston was every bit the warrior he was, maybe better. So it served Wright well to give Kline the respect the compliment was intended to convey.

Weston was also number two at Sanctuary. At the time of Wright's request, Weston was in the Sudan, dispatching Iranian-backed militia left after the region's civil war. Kline figured Weston would probably relish the idea of going to the Moon after what he'd been doing in the Sudan.

"A few more questions, Doug," Kline added. "First, when? Second, how?"

"We launch in sixty-six days aboard two spaceships built by Rick Phillips and Sienna Butler."

"Phillips and Butler?" asked Kline with a surprised look that quickly turned into a smile of respect. "So the joint venture shit they announced was all a bunch of BS." His words were more a conclusion than a question. Wright saw no need to confirm or deny. "Payload?" asked Kline.

Wright realized Kline had made his decision. Now he wanted to know mission-critical parameters.

"We've got some handhelds and shoulder mounts you've never seen and a few conventional weapons you'll find useful. Each ship will also have ten civilians for construction and support needs. And some scientists and real astronauts if you need someone for experienced advice."

"People who have been to the Moon?" asked Kline.

"You know the answer to that, Nick. We haven't set foot on the Moon in decades."

"One final question, Doug," continued Kline. "Where do we train?"

"We're fitting a facility about eighty miles northwest of Vegas," responded Wright with a smile. "Perhaps you've heard of it."

"You have to be kidding, Doug. Area 51?" responded Kline. "This is getting nuttier by the minute. I can't wait to meet a few aliens." Wright wasn't sure how far Kline was caught up in conspiracy theories and rumors of hidden UFOs and aliens in the Nevada desert.

"It's the most secure place in the country, Nick," Wright said. "And the men you bring cannot know the mission until after they arrive. By the way, we prefer to call it Homey Airport, its official name."

"Yeah, HOMEY," Kline jokingly responded. "As in Home of Martians Eating You."

"Anything else?" asked Wright, ignoring Kline's feeble attempt at humor.

"Yeah." Kline was no longer smiling. "I assume money is no object here, right? Doug?"

It was the question Wright knew would come once Kline assessed how critical the need was for his customer.

"Right. Money is no object. Just send me the bill."

"Good," responded Kline. "Half now and half when the mission is completed. You know my account number. The two teams will be in Vegas in a week. Get me word on what time you want us at the airport. I assume you don't want us to just walk into Area 51."

Wright sighed in relief, ordered a martini, and changed the conversation to reminiscing about a particularly wild party the two attended in Kabul celebrating their successful "dispatching" of about fifty Al Qaida rebels.

A week later, Janet Airlines, the unofficial name given to the classified company that shuttles personnel from Las Vegas's McCarran International to Homey Airport, delivered sixty men. Wright assumed the extras Kline included were to cover those who washed out in training. Anyone who didn't make the final cut would be detained at Homey until the mission was completed. No breaks in security could be permitted.

CHAPTER TWENTY-SIX

BELLEVUE RESTAURANT
PRAGUE, CZECH REPUBLIC

PETŘICKOVÁ CHOSE THE BELLEVUE RESTAURANT AT THE SMETANA HOTEL ON SMETANOVO nábřeží 18 in the Staré Město—the Old Town, as tour guides describe it. That description was a bit odd since virtually all of Prague is "old" as far as tourists were concerned. But the Staré Město is a particularly beautiful area of the historic city and a part of town where Petřicková loved to entertain. Better yet, the Bellevue is just a few hundred yards from the Charles Bridge, a historic landmark that spans the Vltava River flowing through the center of Prague. Nearly 700 years old, the walk over it into the Old Town is inspiring. She hoped many of the guests would take the 2,000-foot walk and enjoy the bridge's 16 arches, three bridge towers, and 30 statues adorning either side.

When Petřicková sent Lawson pictures, Lawson immediately approved. The restaurant was intimate, enjoying a beautiful view and offering a varied menu. She left the details to Petřicková but insisted that there be four tables of four to cover the sixteen anticipated guests. Not all of the heads of state of the twenty delegations bring their wives, and some are not married. But Lawson was confident that women from fifteen of the G20 member states would show up and with Petřicková added, it made a sweet sixteen.

Petřicková tried to make sure the menu would fit everyone's palate. Each course was accompanied with the promise of historical dishes to mark the special occasion.

For an appetizer, she offered guests a choice of "Label Rouge"—smoked Scottish salmon with beluga lentils, cabbage, and avocado—or goat cheese served with strawberries, bitter leaves, and a citrus dressing. The women would then take a break, leave their seats, and network. During that time, the tables would be reset for the next course.

Following the break after appetizers, the women would be seated at new tables for an entrée of either veal filet served with green peas, seasonal mushrooms and Périgourdine sauce or local cod accompanied by grenaille potatoes, Salicornia, parsley mayonnaise, and caviar. The entrée vegetarian option was the Bellevue's special mashed green peas with grilled vegetables and mushroom sauce.

"The peas are better than it sounds and a popular dish," Petřicková assured Lawson.

After the women again broke from the tables, they would choose dessert from a buffet that included Valrhona-Guanaja chocolate cremeux with blueberries and cocoa beans, yogurt parfaits, watermelon with elderflower, strawberries and sheep milk ice cream, and an assortment of local cheeses as well as a variety of homemade sorbets. As the women selected their desserts, the waiters would quickly reset the tables, and seating would be open.

If any course didn't work for one of the ladies, the restaurant would make provisions and essentially serve just about anything the guest wanted. But Petřicková and Lawson doubted any such demands would be made.

Now Atlee Lawson needed to increase her opportunities for some private words with her key targets. Using a variation of speed-dating meetings, she used the breaks between courses to allow the guests to mingle a bit and then be shuffled to new tables, ensuring that everyone spent some time with all the dignitaries during the breaks as well as at assigned seats during the appetizer and entrée. The dessert course buffet allowed seating at the choice of the guest. Lawson gave Petřicková the rotation for the appetizer and entrée.

Appetizer:
Table 1: Argentina, Saudi Arabia, Russia, and Turkey
Table 2: China, Mexico, Japan, and Indonesia
Table 3: United States, European Union representative, Czech Republic, and Italy
Table 4: Korea, Australia, India, and South Africa
Entrée:
Table 1: United States, China, Russia, and India
Table 2: European Union representative, Turkey, Mexico, and Saudi Arabia
Table 3: Indonesia, Japan, Czech Republic, and South Korea
Table 4: Australia, Italy, South Africa, and Argentina

Entrée Table 1 was the power table, where Atlee Lawson would have her chance. If her comments received a welcomed reception, the dessert and mingling beyond the scheduled end time would provide more opportunity. And, of course, future discussions, group or individual, could be set up. But key for Lawson was to get her points across quickly, simply, and firmly to First Ladies Savita Kovind, Peng Liyuan, and Alina Kabaeva. She could catch Sara Netanyahu and Akie Abe during a break when Motsepe would be blocking out others. Kovind, Liyuan, and Kabaeva all spoke English.

CHAPTER TWENTY-SEVEN

UNITED NATIONS SECURITY COUNCIL
NEW YORK CITY

ALEX FRIEDMAN HAD BEEN APPOINTED U.S. AMBASSADOR TO THE UNITED NATIONS BY President Lawson's predecessor. When Lawson was elected, Friedman tendered his resignation, as was traditional with the passing of the guard in the White House. Lawson told Friedman that he thought Friedman was doing a great job and that continuity was important. So Lawson rejected the resignation and asked Friedman to continue. In truth, Lawson did believe Friedman was doing a good job, but felt it was a good job in a largely ineffective organization that had probably outlived its value in establishing international order. He saw it more as a playground for diplomats' games and a platform for countries to employ PR campaigns against the countries whose regimes they opposed. At the U.N., as far as Lawson was concerned, one man's oppressor was seen as another man's savior.

Friedman was not the typical U.N. ambassador from the United States. Unlike the seemingly endless list of politicians who occupied the office, Friedman was a career diplomat. He'd never been elected to any office. He was never a corporate magnate. Before his appointment as ambassador, he led the State Department's Office of

Foreign Missions (OFM). The OFM is responsible for the security of U.S. embassies and consulates throughout the world. After the 2012 attack on the U.S. mission in Benghazi, Libya, by the Islamic group Ansar al-Sharia, which resulted in the death of U.S. ambassador to Libya J. Christopher Stevens among others, the OFM became a very powerful division of the State Department. Whoever led it had a lot to say about the security of U.S. assets strewn around the world.

In the course of his job at OFM, Friedman immersed himself in operations, worked closely with the CIA, and established state-of-the-art security systems at every embassy, not just the ones in risky countries. But more useful than his knowledge of technology and intelligence were his personal relationships with virtually every important foreign ambassador. Unlike the U.S., most countries appoint experienced diplomats to their embassies and consulates. In truth, the global cadre of these diplomats are the eyes and ears for most countries. Only a few—the U.S., Russia, China, Great Britain, France, and Germany—politicize their ambassadors. Hence the distrust those countries generally have for one another in diplomatic circles. Friedman's presence at the U.N., and the respect he enjoyed among the vast majority of his contemporaries, made him privy to a lot more information than was the case for ambassadors who were political. It was as if he had his own spy ring. Every country afraid of China, Russia, North Korea, or Iran confided in Friedman and readily told him everything they knew. Friedman reported most of it back to the White House. But not everything. If he thought his private diplomatic efforts would bring better results than what could be achieved by any politician, including the president, he kept certain activities to himself and his network of more than a hundred ambassadors.

The U.N.'s Security Council has fifteen members, five of whom are permanent—the United States, Russia, the United Kingdom, France, and China. They earned that honor as the self-described victors in World War II. The U.N. General Assembly elects the remaining ten members for two-year terms. So almost everyone gets a chance to sit in the room, listen to the superpowers bicker, and accomplish little. While votes of the Council are often aligned with U.S. interests, that is to no avail. Every permanent member has a veto on any resolution from the Council. And invariably most of whatever the U.S. wants is vetoed by China or Russia, and vice versa. As far as Lawson was concerned, the Security Council was more a public relations forum than a tribunal that could solve the serious challenges faced in keeping the world a safer place.

Friedman began by addressing the Security Council's president. "Mr. President, I am here to request that the delegation from China reveal the details of its purposes on the Moon and why it is launching so many rockets, now with men and women aboard. And if they should continue refusing such cooperation, then I believe it is our collective responsibility to condemn such noncooperation. I have previously given this Council a proposed resolution to that effect."

"Ambassador Friedman, you may make your presentation," responded Owen Singh, the ambassador from Fiji and currently the president of the Council. He was enjoying his role as referee, as most Council presidents do. Eventually, every member of the Security Council gets his or her day in the sun. Presidents of the Council rotate among members, in alphabetical order, for terms of one month. Friedman was happy to have Ambassador Singh at the helm for the next couple of weeks. Fiji liked the United States and was deathly afraid of China's hegemony at its doorstep in the Asia-Pacific region. The next two who would rotate into the role were Guatemala and Libya, both of whom were guaranteed to be allied with China.

Friedman knew he would never change China's mind. His real challenge was to get Russia to side with the U.S. and not align itself with China. Then it might be possible to isolate China and orchestrate a diplomatic solution.

"Thank you, Mr. President," responded Friedman, opening the portfolio with his prepared remarks.

"Point of order, Mr. President," interjected Wang Han, China's ambassador to the United States. "May we put a time limit on Ambassador Friedman's remarks? Wasting the time of this Council in such an unnecessary diversion ignores the far more important things we need to consider."

As much as Friedman would have liked to respond and ask whether the prospect of nuclear war was second to some other issue facing the Council, his experience as a professional diplomat kept his emotions at bay as he awaited the Council president's response. Friedman was resolved not to lower the dialog to a series of diatribes from both sides. That would only play into the hands of the Chinese delegation and the press.

"Ambassador Wang," calmly responded Singh, "I appreciate your concerns but I think we have more than enough time to respect the time needed by the ambassador from the United States. Mr. Ambassador, please begin and take as much time as you like."

Wang waved a dismissive hand and sat back in his chair.

Meetings of the Security Council are orchestrated chaos. Various aides flank each ambassador, to their sides and behind them. Some take notes, while others whisper in one another's ears as they listen to speakers. Occasionally, they can be seen getting up and passing notes to the aides of other ambassadors, which are given to their bosses at appropriate times. On very rare occasion, an aide will interrupt his or her ambassador should there be a major development in the world outside the room. The room is not brightly lit, in part to allow for movement to go unnoticed and avoid disruption. Its darkness also adds to the drama that often occurs.

"Mr. President, I will be brief," began Friedman. "The world is on a precipice it cannot afford. Talk of irreversible decisions are rising and putting the world at risk. The tension is all caused by China and its refusal to be forthright about its intentions on the Moon. All of the tensions could easily be eliminated if China were transparent and honest and allowed inspection by a U.N. mission."

Wang smirked as he rejected an offer of water from one of his aides. Friedman was pleased to see Wang's anger visibly rise.

Friedman continued, "Our intelligence indicates that China's intentions are not for peaceful exploration. If they were, there would be no need for the cloak of secrecy China has placed over its launches in the past months. We have exhausted every avenue to seek the truth. Even our friends in Russia wonder what is behind China's actions." Friedman turned to see the reaction of Constantine Petroff, Russian ambassador to the United Nations. Petroff showed no reaction.

Friedman continued, "Interstellar cargo ships have been launched with alarming frequency, belying claims that they are all needed for mining supplies. We all know what the exploration of the Moon's surface requires. India has been operating near the south pole of the Moon for years with some success using only a fraction of the equipment China has ferried to its outpost on the far side of the Moon, which no one can see from Earth. We know exploration activities do not require the kind or volume of cargos represented by the capacity of China's interstellar cargo holds, more than two dozen of which have reached to Moon. So unless China is forthcoming with the truth, we can only assume there is ill intent behind their objectives. They are, Mr. President, hiding the truth."

Wang could not hold himself back. "Mr. President, we have repeatedly told the United States, Russia, and the rest of this Council that our only objective is peaceful exploration."

That got a reaction from Petroff as he suddenly sat erect, clearly offended by the attack on Russia. He did not like being scolded, particularly when he was showing no sign of agreeing with Friedman.

Wang's response turned into a diatribe. "How many times do we need to tell the truth until the United States is satisfied? Or has its own failure to reach the Moon before us created the paranoia Ambassador Friedman and his allies would like to see the world fall prey to?"

Friedman could see that Petroff was not appreciating the innuendos. Petroff whispered in an aide's ear. Quietly, the aide made his way behind the China delegation and handed a note to one of Wang's aides. Friedman watched as the Chinese aide dutifully handed the note to one of his superiors. After reading it, the second Chinese aide put it in his pocket and did not interrupt Wang.

Friedman was relieved. Obviously, whatever anger Petroff was feeling wouldn't get to Wang.

"This is a silly exercise in speculation by a member of this esteemed Council who has fallen behind, unable to compete for the riches the Moon offers the world. The United States cannot tolerate the idea that another country may be able to do a better job than it can." Wang turned toward Petroff. "In truth," he concluded with his eyes squarely directed at his usual ally, "the United States is the one not being honest, and any country that backs such lies is equally dishonest."

Bingo, thought Friedman. China just burned their bridge. All Friedman had to do was put out the lure and watch Wang take the bait.

Now Friedman had to make a deal. Even if it was a deal with the devil.

CHAPTER TWENTY-EIGHT

BELLEVUE RESTAURANT
PRAGUE, CZECH REPUBLIC

TO ATLEE LAWSON'S SURPRISE, EVERYONE SHOWED UP ON TIME AND SEEMED IN GOOD spirits, thankful to have a break. A few, but not all, brought translators. Importantly, no translators accompanied the first ladies of China or Russia. While everyone had a small entourage, it appeared as if they came to relax and not concern themselves with public scrutiny.

As the guests arrived, Petřicková couldn't have been a better host. She greeted each and made sure they were introduced to at least one other first lady. It was as if she were the maestro of a symphony orchestra, making sure every instrument played its proper role.

According to the plan, Lawson arrived fifth, just after Motsepe. No need to draw attention to her role in planning by arriving too early. She wanted any watching eyes to see her as nothing but one of the guests of First Lady Petřicková.

As she entered, Lawson was taken through security set up for the event. It was as one would expect: an x-ray machine on a conveyor belt and a walk-through metal detector. Lawson was a bit taken aback by it at first, but realized that security is never misplaced.

"Atlee," greeted Petřicková, "it is an honor to have you here."

"The honor is mine and thank you, Iva, for putting this together." As much as she wanted to wink, she knew better. Lawson added, "It's such a nice respite from the daily grind of the summit."

As Petřicková began to pull her away and move on, she whispered, "Whatever you're trying to do with China, I hope it works. If I can help, let me know."

Lawson kept her cool and showed no reaction, realizing that there should be no surprise that Petřicková figured that something was afoot, since it was Lawson's idea to have the get-together. She let any concerns go.

Lawson next passed two waitresses in traditional Czech dress, each holding a silver tray with drinks laid out for the guests. One had Champagne and the other sparkling water with a slice of lemon floating in it. Lawson took a glass of Champagne. She needed the courage.

"Atlee," greeted Motsepe with a wink, kissing Lawson on both cheeks, "it's been too long."

"Yes it has, Tshepo," Lawson smiled. Time to play the role. "At least a year or more. Have you been well?"

"I have been doing very well, Atlee. South Africa could not be more idyllic for me. The economy is strong. We are safe and happy. And what about you? How are you?"

"All is well," Atlee responded. Tshepo was having some fun playing the game, obviously.

"Come with me, you need to meet someone special," continued Motsepe.

As they walked together, the two saw Peng Liyuan speaking to Angélica Orci, Mexico's first lady. Motsepe took a beeline straight to them.

"Angélica, I have wanted to meet you for so long," Motsepe said, introducing herself.

"And I, you," politely responded Orci.

Like a perfect traffic cop, Motsepe took Orci by the arm, leading her away, as she said, "Angélica, I have a personal question I've always wanted to ask you." Off they went, leaving Liyuan and Lawson alone. Lawson knew the opportunity would pass quickly.

"I can't help but be curious what Tshepo's personal question might be!" remarked Lawson.

"Indeed," responded Liyuan.

"How have you been, Peng?"

"OK," responded Liyuan. "I prefer if it was calmer between our husbands, but such things have a way of working themselves out. Don't you agree, Atlee?" Lawson couldn't read whether Liyuan meant the question as rhetorical or one meant to be answered.

"Let's hope that's true, Peng, but perhaps you and I could talk about it more. Nothing official, of course. Just two concerned wives." Lawson hoped for a quick response that welcomed the idea.

As Liyuan was about to speak, Petřicková suddenly arrived with Sophia Mastro, Italy's first lady, a very flamboyant and outspoken character.

"Atlee. Peng. Please meet Sophia Mastro, the first lady of Italy," said Petřicková as an introduction. "I know the three of you are not sitting together for the opener or main course so I thought I'd get you together now."

"Thank you, Iva," responded Lawson, forcing a smile. "It's wonderful to meet you, Sophia."

Mastro had been first lady for only two months as Italy once again changed its government. Joseph Mastro, her husband and Italy's new prime minister, was right out of central casting. The prime minister was a handsome forty-eight-year-old who could have passed for Marcello Mastroianni in his prime. With dark hair and equally haunting eyes, the prime minister was the perfect movie-star match for Sophia, and she fit him as a wife just as Catherine Deneuve fit Mastroianni. Like Marcello and Catherine, Joseph and Sophia lived la dolce vita.

"So, Sophia, how do you enjoy the limelight as first lady of Italy? It must be a far cry from the quiet life you led growing up," remarked Liyuan. Atlee wondered if she was relieved that she didn't have to answer her question. Sophia Mastro had grown up on an olive orchard near Liguria, famous for its delicate oils. The Ligurian Riviera region was filled with rolling hills and pristine fields, making it a quiet and bucolic place that could not have been more opposite Rome's Palazzo Grazioli, where the prime minister occupies his working hours, or the Palazzo Chigi, a former palace that is now the official residence of the prime minister and his first lady. And, some say, his mistresses.

"Sì," responded Mastro with a strong accent, "it is very much different. I miss sometimes the olive trees. You know many are hundreds of years old."

Before Lawson had a chance to engage in a response, Motsepe came to her rescue, grabbing her arm to take her over to Alina Kabaeva, Russia's first lady.

For many years, Alina Kabaeva was a controversial figure in Russia as rumors began to circulate that she was the secret mistress of Vladimir Putin and the mother of a child by him. If it were not for her individual fame as one of Russia's most decorated Olympic athletes in rhythmic gymnastics, she would have been dismissed as an unimportant and unimpressive person in Russian politics. But she was anything but unimportant and unimpressive, so when Putin made it official and married the demure 5'5", 110-pound brunette athlete, Russia celebrated the union, and the couple had enjoyed admiration since. It was also rumored that Kabaeva had an influential impact on Putin. Lawson hoped that was true.

As they walked, Motsepe asked, "So did you get anything out of the wife of China's Chief Commie?"

"No," responded Lawson. "Petřicková brought over Italy's latest political arm candy before Liyuan could answer my question about finding time to talk privately."

"Well, maybe you'll have more luck with Kabaeva," responded Motsepe. "Seems she has more than just Vladimir's ears in her hands."

Lawson smiled. It would be the first time she met Kabaeva. In briefings she'd been told Kabaeva was smart and respected, an independent thinker whose core principle was fairness. She hoped the intelligence on Alina was accurate.

"Alina," began Motsepe, "let me introduce Atlee Lawson. The two of you should talk!" At that point, Motsepe walked away to allow a private moment between the two, however short it would be.

"It is an honor to meet you, Mrs. Lawson. I've heard so much about you."

"Thank you. And please call me Atlee. We first ladies should all be on a first-name basis. We have enough formalities in our everyday lives. Between ourselves, we can let down the guard."

"I like the sound of that, Atlee. And please call me Alina."

"Thank you, Alina," Lawson said, continuing, "and we need to make as much positive use as we can of the little time we have together."

"I like the sound of that, too," responded Kabaeva.

"Perfect," replied Lawson. "So let me ask you a question that is undoubtedly on many people's minds." Lawson paused for effect and to make her next question a very serious one.

"Are you concerned about the situation in China and its tensions with the United States?" asked Lawson.

"What do you mean 'concerned'? Am I concerned about the tensions? Yes. Am I concerned that my husband will make a poor decision? No. As far as I know, there is no decision for him to make."

Atlee wondered if Putin had brainwashed his wife. She pressed on. "But you are concerned, right?"

"Are you asking me in an official or unofficial capacity, Atlee?"

Maybe she should call me Mrs. Lawson, she thought ruefully.

"I'm asking you as one woman to another woman, Alina. I'm asking you, as a woman, if you share the concerns I have. You have the ear of your husband, as I do mine. Should we not express to them how worried we are that they not let things spiral out of control?"

"Some believe Vladimir seeks my opinion," responded Kabaeva. "And sometimes he does. But never on matters of state security. He certainly has no obligation to follow any opinions I have even when he asks. To be honest, I'm not sure he wants to hear my opinion on problems between the U.S. and China. So I'm not inclined to volunteer any."

"That may be true," Lawson continued. "But if we can collectively convey our concerns, perhaps we can influence our husbands to be patient and keep the pot from boiling over. It's time, Alina, that men like your husband and mine learn that women like and you me no longer live in their shadows. We have influence and where appropriate, should not hesitate to use it."

"Perhaps. But I'm not sure what you're proposing."

"Let's have that discussion over lunch. I believe we'll be sitting together for the second course."

CHAPTER TWENTY-NINE

MISSION CONTROL
THE FAR SIDE OF THE MOON

NOW MORE THAN THREE MONTHS ON STATION, THE CREW WAS FULLY ACCLIMATED AND comfortable in their daily routines.

Dr. Liu remained disappointed. Her hope that members of the crew would turn to amorous thoughts had not happened. Instead, everyone stayed dedicated to his or her tasks. She resolved to be patient, believing that sooner or later libido would overcome someone, even on the Moon.

Lisa had become the crew's best friend, delivering whatever they needed. She'd made sure the bar was stocked and the food nutritious. Entertainment was available whenever the crew needed to be distracted. They felt in control.

As the rest of the crew made progress with their assigned tasks, Shao Rushi completed installation of the Luna Diébào computer.

"Commander Cheng," she reported, "I am ready to transfer operations to the Diébào."

"Good," responded Cheng. "When the order is given, what happens?"

"Nothing, really," she responded. "It's a simple operation. It will take no more than a few minutes. Other than critical systems, we'll have to turn off most operational control. The Diébào has already downloaded all the data it needs from the current computers and databanks we brought with us. When the Diébào takes over, we'll barely notice the transfer of control."

"And what does this get us, Rushi?" asked Cheng.

"It will move computing science into something we've never experienced, Commander. The Diébào is the most advanced computer ever created. It has an unprecedented capacity to take artificial intelligence to new heights. It's very exciting."

"But it will continue to obey us, right?"

"Obedience is programmed into its core, Commander," Shao responded. "What it does is give us the ability to advance programming and decisions faster. At some point, it will be able to program itself. When that happens, all we'll need to do is ask it a question and it will provide an answer that is based upon dynamic learning and knowledge like we've never known. Just imagine the Diébào as a doctor, for example. Its memory has firsthand knowledge of every medical procedure ever undertaken and can logically apply that to a diagnosis and prognosis for a patient. The possibilities are endless."

"I have to tell you, Rushi, that sounds more frightening to me than it does exciting. Some things ought to be left alone. We don't have to be perfect."

"Commander, you needn't worry. We've gone through all the scenarios. We'll be fine. While the Diébào can learn more and get smarter with every byte it processes, it cannot think like you and me. And it has none of the critical brain functions that make us tick. It can collect, analyze, and interact with data and make decisions in nanoseconds that would take us months to make. But it will never replace us."

CHAPTER THIRTY

BELLEVUE RESTAURANT
PRAGUE, CZECH REPUBLIC

PETŘICKOVÁ CONTINUED AS THE PERFECT HOST, MAKING SURE THE TABLE SEATING AND THE shift between the first two courses went smoothly.

As Lawson approached her assigned table for the entrée, she was pleased to see that Savita Kovind, Peng Liyuan, and Alina Kabaeva were already seated and engaged in conversation. But when they all fell silent as Lawson arrived and sat down, Lawson got nervous. None of them even offered her a greeting.

Knowing she was well beyond any turning point, Lawson plunged in.

"This has very much been a pleasant occasion, but I will confess to the three of you that I had an ulterior motive to helping Iva bring us together. So I won't hide it any longer."

The three other first ladies each bore expressions of concern and discomfort. Perhaps even regretting they came.

Lawson continued, "We all know that our husbands are among the most powerful men in the world. On a whim, they can launch a war. Or not. But the future of our families lies in their hands. I think we can all agree on that."

Silence.

"I'm here to ask you to tell your husbands that we, a collection of sixteen first ladies, implore them to not let this go any further. To find a way to compromise and cooperate. Unless the four of us, first ladies of the world's nuclear nations agree, this effort will most certainly fail. We cannot let that happen."

Lawson paused as the waiters, as if on cue, placed the entrées in front of each first lady. As she took the moment to look at the others already enjoying their meals, Lawson saw Motsepe out of the corner of her eye, standing near the kitchen door, directing the waitstaff.

After the waiters walked away, Kovind shifted in her chair. As India's first lady, she was deeply respected. She came from a very humble background and rose to prominence on her own merit. She was the first to respond to Lawson.

"Atlee, we all want the same thing. Peace. And if helping that means you'd like me to be part of a collective effort among those of us here, I'm certainly a willing co-conspirator." Motsepe had done her job during the appetizer when, as was the plan, she made sure her table understood what Lawson intended to do. Her table was set up with staunch American allies who would not only support Lawson but also keep it quiet until she let everyone there know.

"Alina and Peng, I need the two of you on board."

Liyuan responded, "Atlee, I understand. But you also need to understand how sensitive it is for me. Our husbands are more than capable of dealing with one another. I would not want to become a distraction."

Lawson shot back with a firm but polite cross between a command and a plea. "That is precisely what I want us all to be, Peng. A big distraction so there is more time for them to think clearly. Right now, they all seem to be mired in suspicion and doubt. I fear that only those who think about worst-case scenarios are advising our husbands. Have you not noticed how few women are involved in the process, much less in any decision-making role?"

"Atlee, even if I endorsed your idea, what makes you think Vladimir would listen?" interjected Kabaeva.

"Alina, I don't know if he will. But maybe this is a chance for you to make a point. He's not going to have you shot at dawn for your plea that we help calm things down and avoid war."

Lawson could see that Kabaeva did not appreciate the slight to Putin shooting people who challenged him. But before Lawson could apologize, Liyuan spoke.

"Atlee, I would need more time," interjected Liyuan. "This is not an easy decision."

"Peng, it may not be an easy one, but it is the most important one. And we don't have any more time. Nor do we have the luxury of scheduling another get-together. That just won't happen. We are here together now. We have to decide now."

Liyuan sat silently, clearly contemplating her response.

Lawson added, "And Peng, if you and I are not together on this, we're putting every child in our countries at unnecessary risk. You and I need to lead this message. The world needs to hear it. We need you on board, Peng. I can't do this alone."

"I agree, Atlee, and I support your idea," interjected Kabaeva, hoping to put some pressure on Liyuan and help Lawson. "Vladimir may never listen, but he needs to hear us. And if he knows it's coming from wives who may have strong influence on the men he deals with, it might give him real pause."

"Thank you, Alina," responded Lawson, turning her gaze to Liyuan. "It's down to you, Peng."

"Will you let me review any statement before it is made public?" Liyuan asked.

"Review it, Peng?" responded Lawson. "How about you and I write it together?" Liyuan nodded.

As the waiters began clearing the tables, Petřicková announced that the dessert buffet was ready. Guests began to rise to enjoy the sweets. Lawson stood and began what she considered the most important speech in her life.

"Ladies, if I could have your attention for a moment, I'd like to say something important. Please sit down for just a few more minutes before dessert."

Everyone obeyed.

"We all know that overshadowing this G20 is the specter of war over misunderstandings between China and the United States about what China is doing on the Moon. In so many ways, this all seems too surrealistic to me. The idea that we're talking about the Moon as a potential military battlefield or cause for war is impossible to digest. But here we are."

She had everyone's attention.

"As we sit here today, our husbands are behind closed doors making decisions that will shape the future of the world. They are surrounded by cadres of advisers, most of whom have very nationalistic perspectives and far too much eagerness for war."

Lawson took a moment to sip her glass of water; no more Champagne for now. Motsepe had moved all of the waitstaff out of the room. Some translators remained, close to the sides of their first ladies. While a few of the entourage's security staff remained, it was unlikely any of them spoke English.

"It is my belief, shared by First Ladies Kovind, Liyuan, Kabaeva, and Motsepe, that we should, as one group, publicly profess our hope that our husbands and the leaders of the world do all they can do to resolve this impasse peacefully. It is not our suggestion that we take a side. That is not our role. But it is our role—and our right—to speak out as women, mothers, and sisters to bring compassion to a world far too caught up in confrontation."

Lawson could see some discomfort from some of those present. She pressed on.

"Peng Liyuan has graciously offered to help me write it. I ask you for your permission to include your name. I realize that some people at home may criticize you. Perhaps your husbands may even chastise you. But for the sake of our future, please understand that remaining silent for fear of being ostracized is not acceptable."

Liyuan stood. "Atlee is right. We need to speak as one."

One by one, each first lady rose in silent support.

CHAPTER THIRTY-ONE

WORLD MEDIA

ATLEE LAWSON GAVE THE FORMAL APPEAL FOR PEACE TO THE WIRES ON THE LAST DAY OF the G20 Summit. It appeared in virtually every newspaper in the world and quickly went viral on the Internet. CNN, MSNBC, BBC, Fox, and other major cable outlets covered it "live from Prague" for most of the day. All major broadcasters led with it in their evening news. The reporting was mixed. Some outlets, particularly the liberal media, lauded the appeal while media on the right condemned it as naïve. As one cable news program headlined it, "Who Let the Hens Out," paraphrasing the popular song, "Who Let the Dogs Out?" Other pundits questioned why a group of wives of heads of state, who were never elected to any public office, should be trying to influence international policy. But those naysayers were quickly overwhelmed by those who supported the rise of women influencing men, whether the women were elected or not.

An Appeal for Peace

We, first ladies to the world's great leaders, make this appeal.

We know your leadership comes from the heart. We know you must deal with complex and challenging issues. We also know that you often have to make the most difficult decisions imaginable. Decisions that can mean the death of innocent people. Decisions that in an instant can change the course of history.

But we also know that all too often, deliberations by men have led to war. Not because intelligent men want war, but because ill-advised and misguided counsel by those too close to world leadership lose their compassion for the larger issues and the unintended consequences that can lead from peace to bloodshed and conflict.

In this case, that unintended consequence is nuclear war.

So it is our appeal—our hope and prayers as women, mothers, sisters, and wives—that you find a path to peace through compromise and understanding. For if you approach this through the lens of disdain and distrust, your leadership may well leave a legacy of death and destruction.

As John Lennon put it so well, "All we are saying, is give peace a chance."

Sixteen first ladies signed the appeal. The only reason four were missing is that those countries had no first lady. So the resolution was considered unanimous.

The few official announcements from the Summit were overshadowed by the press spinning the Appeal for Peace. It resonated with the world.

Never before had world leaders been confronted in such a public way by their spouses.

CHAPTER THIRTY-TWO

NOI BAI INTERNATIONAL AIRPORT
HANOI, VIETNAM

"SO, MR. STEPHEN SESSA, WHAT IS THE NATURE OF YOUR PURPOSE FOR COMING TO HANOI?" asked the emotionless immigration officer sitting behind the counter in the arrivals hall at Noi Bai International Airport, the major international entry point into Vietnam. As he waited for the answer, the officer continued to examine the passport and type on his keyboard, staring at the computer screen, never looking at the traveler.

Sessa was well dressed and an obviously prosperous visitor.

"I'm a coffee and rice buyer with Conagra," he calmly responded. "I'm here to meet with growers and suppliers. I'll be in Ninh Binh taking a look at rice producers and then a couple of days in Da Lat, to look at coffee. Should be here about a week. Quick trip."

"And where in Ninh Binh and Da Lat will you be staying?" continued the officer, eyes glued to his screen.

Showing no concern at being questioned nor annoyed that the officer could have answered that question himself by simply reading the immigration form Sessa filled out, responded, "In Ninh Binh, I'll be staying at the Golden Rice. In Da Lat, I'll be at La Sapinette."

Anticipating the officer's next question, another one already answered on the immigration form but part of the routine questioning by immigration authorities, the traveler added, "I'm meeting with Falcon Rice Mills and some coffee brokers from Dak Man." The officer still hadn't raised his eyes, glued to the computer screen. Another thirty seconds passed without comment.

The officer finally looked up as if to closely examine the subject of his attention and responded, "Welcome to Vietnam, Mr. Stephen Sessa," stamped the passport, returned it, and added with a smile, "I hope you have a successful trip." The gate swung open and Sessa went toward the baggage claim and the customs area.

Rice and coffee are two of the biggest products exported from Vietnam. The country is the second-largest exporter of coffee in the world. Only Brazil sells more. Even Starbucks buys Vietnamese coffee and sells it as one of its premium brands. As for rice, Vietnam is the world's third-highest exporter, behind India and Thailand.

It made sense to the immigration officer that the traveler was just another in the long line of Americans who come to his country on business. And the traveler had the locations for growing rice and coffee right as well as the towns where he planned to go and the people he intended to see. His passport was clean and the visa in order. Besides, as far as the immigration officer was concerned, Americans are welcome with open arms. The United States is Vietnam's largest trading partner, buying twenty-two percent of the country's exports, nearly twice as much as its next largest trading partner, China. America, once Vietnam's sworn enemy, is now the biggest contributor to Vietnam's growing economy.

There was no need to go to baggage. The traveler limited his luggage to a small black leather Tumi bag and matching carry-on roller suitcase. Customs paid no attention to him as he walked through the exit under the green sign that read "Nothing to Declare." On exiting, he quickly spotted a woman holding a card reading, "Stephen Sessa." Without saying a word, she took the suitcase and the two walked silently to the car waiting at the curb, a year-old silver Range Rover Velar. While it is a luxury car with all the comforts Land Rover offers, the Velar blends in well and does not attract gawkers interested in expensive toys. The driver opened the passenger door and the traveler got in the backseat. The suitcase was placed in the back and once the hatch was closed, the car drove off. Within ten minutes, the Velar had exited the airport and began the five-hour, more than 300-kilometer ride north to Sa Pa, an ancient city on the border of China, nowhere near the rice fields or Da Lat.

CHAPTER THIRTY-THREE

ROUTE CT05
NORTH VIETNAM

IN SHAMBLES AFTER THE VIETNAM WAR, THE COUNTRY'S REFURBISHED INFRASTRUCTURE was an example of ingenuity and success a half century later. While not exactly a German autobahn, CT05 was fine and afforded a smooth, picturesque ride.

Michael Hellriegel, aka Stephen Sessa, had not been in the field in more than fifteen years. He missed it, recalling the excitement of clandestine operations where lives were at stake, including his own. While he never enjoyed the darker side of eliminating his country's enemies when he had orders to do so or when things went wrong and there was no choice, he never felt more alive than he did after a successful mission.

Hellriegel knew this was not a real field operation. But it needed the same level of secrecy as any covert mission. The United States and China were on the edge of war, and Hellriegel needed to find out if the deal struck would be honored—and to find out for sure what China actually had on the Moon. While getting that information through traditional back channels and his in-country agents was routine, Hellriegel agreed with President Lawson that there was simply not enough time to go through normal methods. Sometimes spies have to improvise.

Hence the secrecy of his passage into Vietnam. But he was not alone. He never was. No spy of his stature ever travels without a plan B. Other agents were in place if needed. Hellriegel was confident they'd be unnecessary. He was meeting someone he believed would never double-cross him.

As was the case with most of his domestic travel or flights overseas from the U.S., Hellriegel's office booked him through Jeppesen International, based in San Jose, California, an operation owned and operated by Boeing. Rumors abound that it is used for "discreet" clients like the CIA. It counts among its customers actor Harrison Ford and Gene Cernan, who was the commander of Apollo 17 and the eleventh man to walk on the Moon. In addition to ferrying the CIA director and other highly placed operatives and celebrities, Jeppesen is also reportedly used in terrorist renditions. In what Hellriegel thought a bit of irony, Jeppesen's website includes Santa Claus as a client, complete with his flight plan. Hellriegel always found the attempt at levity poor form but thought using Santa Claus as a cover for transporting spies, terrorists, and celebrities was fine.

Despite being preoccupied on the ride, reading secure files fed to his laptop from an encrypted U.S. military satellite system, Hellriegel had time to admire the countryside. He'd been told Vietnam is a very beautiful country, particularly in the north. The reviewers were right. Hellriegel couldn't help but contemplate how sad it must have been when the U.S. systematically bombed and dropped napalm over the countryside, killing thousands of innocent people. He was thankful that nature, often able to heal itself, had transformed that hell back to an Eden.

Once in Sa Pa, Hellriegel checked into the Silk Path Grand Resort in the center of the city. While it was a bit more ostentatious than Hellriegel might have preferred, the choice of the location was not his. His room, a junior suite, was comfortable with a bedroom, living area, and balcony overlooking the gardens. Opened in 2018, the hotel earned its five stars and was clearly the most elegant in the region.

Sa Pa, originally developed by the French as a holiday resort and an escape from the crowds and heat of Hanoi, thrived until the 1940s, when rebels forced the French out. The town and region fell into ruins for decades. Then as part of the post–Vietnam War rebirth, Sa Pa was revitalized in the late '90s and is once again a thriving vacation destination. It sits amid the Hoàng Liên Son Mountains, at the extremity of the Himalayas, and boasts Vietnam's highest peak, Fan Si Pan, at nearly 10,000 feet. The view of the mountains and rolling hills from Hellriegel's balcony was spellbinding.

His first job was to walk the hotel and get his bearings. He particularly wanted to decide where to have meetings. His room was out of the question despite its apparent privacy. Hellriegel assumed it was monitored and any conversations in the room recorded, particularly since the hotel was not his pick.

It didn't take him long to decide that the hotel's bar, the Sky 6 Lounge, was the best venue. It was dark and bathed in purple and gold. It looked as much like a brothel as it did a bar. Better yet, it was separate from the main hotel, appropriately in the so-called Cat building. Hellriegel decided that the natural pulse of the bar as the DJ played his sets made monitoring conversations over the noise difficult. The intimacy of the room also meant it was nearly impossible to blend in if you were attempting to overhear something being said at a neighboring table. In addition, as a bonus, the bar stocked Macallan scotch, Hellriegel's choice, particularly the 18 year old, something to enjoy when the agency was covering the tab.

That first night, Hellriegel had dinner at Samu, the hotel's casual restaurant. Still suffering from jet lag, he didn't want to overdo it and was more than satisfied with a light dinner of Goi cuon, Vietnam's version of a spring roll, followed by a plate of Banh khot—small, light, bite-sized crepes stuffed with shrimp and mung beans. He paired it with a glass, not a bottle, of a 2002 Dalat, a local Vietnamese white wine that had earned some accolades, but was far short of the imported brands on the menu. Hellriegel believed if he ate local, he drank local. Other than a Macallan, of course. After a couple of sips, he regretted that philosophy and enjoyed the rest of his meal accompanied by bottled water.

After dinner, Hellriegel moved to the Sky 6 Lounge for the Macallan 18, neat. But it wasn't all for pleasure. He carefully watched as people came and went, deciding where the best table would be for a private conversation with Jay Yan, China's minister of state security, the counterpart to Hellriegel's position at the CIA. They'd known one another for more than thirty years, at times simultaneously in the field overseeing covert operations targeting the same objective: one to help it; the other to stop it. Yan was someone who more than once thwarted even the best-laid plans of the CIA. But that was fair since Hellriegel spoiled his share of Yan's plans as well. It was a dangerous game they played, but one that garnered mutual respect for each other.

Hellriegel knew the meeting needed to go according to plan, but getting the truth out of Yan would not be easy. To Hellriegel, however, what Yan said wasn't particularly important. What was important was what Hellriegel said, and that Yan heard it. Yan needed to understand that the United States was serious and not playing some game of diplomatic chess.

CHAPTER THIRTY-FOUR

AREA 51
HOMEY, NEVADA

MOST OF THE TRAINING TOOK PLACE ON LAKE GROOM, A DRIED LAKEBED EXCAVATED TO resemble the surface of the Moon. While there was a risk that satellite surveillance of the installation by China or others might raise concerns, construction vehicles and building materials were conspicuously on display, giving the impression that buildings were being built, not interstellar warriors being trained.

The days were divided into two alternating "sessions," each four hours in duration with a one-hour break between them for lunch. Every other morning beginning at 8:00 a.m., the crew trained in maneuvers on Lake Groom. The other daily session focused on astronaut training inside hangars at the airport. Evenings were occupied by classes on technical issues that typically ended at 8:00 p.m. The days were long.

No drinking was allowed except on Saturday nights. Sunday mornings were free time, although most of the recruits were up every day by 6:00 a.m. for long runs. Kline and Weston made sure their men were in top condition and physically prepared for whatever might lie ahead.

Wright visited twice to check on progress, always impressed by the professionalism of Sanctuary's men. It gave him confidence that they'd be ready, although his concerns continued on how they'd react in space and what they'd face on the Moon. The United States had no credible intelligence on what defensive forces China had at the site.

In week nine, the remainder of the civilian crews arrived to train together with Kline's and Weston's men. There were six women on the civilian team—two shuttle pilots, two chemical engineers, and two flight engineers. The men in the crew also had duplicative skills and included two pilots, two flight engineers, two doctors, two computer programmers, and a pair of electrical and mechanical engineers. The two remaining men had oversight of food provisions.

Kline carefully reviewed the roster:

Mission Responsibility	Number
Pilots	2
Copilots	2
Flight Engineers	2
Medical Doctors	2
Mechanical Engineers	2
Electrical Engineers	2
Chemical Engineers	2
Nuclear Physicists	2
Nutritionists	2
Computer Scientists	2
TOTAL	20

Ten civilians for each New Dawn.

"Admiral," commented Kline to Wright when introduced to the full crew, "I'm beginning to think you're another Noah, making sure we have two of every species."

"Not really," responded Wright. "We just want to make sure each New Dawn has a full complement of what you'll need on the journey and at base camp. They're all there to support your operation and report to you."

"Or Weston if I don't make it?" asked Kline.

"Nick, you're smart enough to see that we've built in redundancy to anticipate the possibility that one of you can't land. There are two lunar landers as well. We've done everything we can to assure success. Failure is not an option."

"Certainly not for what you're paying," responded Kline with a laugh.

"I can't wait for the final invoice!" replied Wright. "Are you and your crews ready?"

"As ready as we'll ever be," answered Kline. "What more can you tell me about what we'll encounter on arrival?"

"We have absolutely no idea. It could be hot or a non-event. We just don't know. So you're going in blind." Wright noticed that his comment didn't faze Kline. Or at least Kline didn't show it if it did.

"We've gone in blind before, Admiral. In some ways, not knowing what to expect heightens awareness and discipline. Being a little nervous is a good thing. Overconfidence breeds mistakes."

"Good. Because you leave for Florida tomorrow," concluded Wright.

CHAPTER THIRTY-FIVE

COMPLEX 34
CAPE CANAVERAL AIR FORCE STATION, FLORIDA

THE MODIFIED SKYE AEROSPACE NEW EXCALIBUR ROCKETS ASSIGNED THE TASK OF LAUNCH-ing the lunar landers and the habitat pods and their supplies worked perfectly. All of the retrievable stages landed at Cape Canaveral, ready for reuse if necessary on any future missions. The second stages drifted off into space.

Each capsule and lander found orbit without incident and descended to the surface in textbook fashion. Butler and Phillips reveled in the perfection they created, but knew celebration was premature.

Lawson was thankful that the Chinese, even if capable of inter-fering with the mission, chose not to. Perhaps they bought into the cover that the habitat was simply step one to a purely commercial venture to mine the Moon.

Once on the surface, while the Skye Aerospace lunar landers sat idle, the capsules with the pod habitats came to life and deployed according to the plan.

As the crew at mission control watched from Cape Canaveral, they marveled at the ballet before them. The robots were like dancers, performing precise moves. Technology had indeed come far. All that was missing were Kline and his team.

CHAPTER THIRTY-SIX

SKY 6 LOUNGE, SILK PATH GRAND RESORT
SA PA, VIETNAM

JAY YAN SHOWED UP ON TIME AT THE SKY 6 LOUNGE. HELLRIEGEL WAS SEATED AT THE TABLE he'd chosen in a location that best assured no eavesdropping. His unnamed CIA protectors were somewhere in the hotel or nearby. One might even be in the bar as far as Hellriegel knew. Per CIA protocol, he was not given the names of any others tied to the operation. But he didn't need to know about them until he might need them, which was something he felt would never happen.

As Yan approached, Hellriegel watched others more than he did Yan, looking for Chinese operatives. While Yan appeared to be alone, Hellriegel knew better. Yan was every bit the spymaster that Hellriegel was.

"Jay," Hellriegel began as he stood to greet him, "it's good to see you again, even in these circumstances."

"Yes, Mike, it is," replied Yan in perfect English. Yan was fluent in six languages, something Hellriegel envied. Hellriegel often joked that he had enough problems with English to learn another language.

Hellriegel had already ordered his Macallan. After Yan sat down, the waiter took his order of a Belvedere vodka martini, on the rocks with a light touch of vermouth. Three olives.

The room was dimly lit as the DJ played American standards. It never ceased to amaze Hellriegel that wherever he traveled, American music was the norm. He wondered if any country had its own music, concluding that American hits were another thing the world stole from the U.S.

"Thank you for coming to Vietnam, my friend. I know it's an unusual request," began Yan.

In truth, the two were friends yet adversaries. Both shared a common career of protecting their country from foreign interference. While their ideologies were diametrically opposite, their craft as spies was a shared bond. The mutual respect it engendered made them an odd couple of sorts. Two friendly rivals, both capable of deadly action.

"I admit that I'm not usually asked to come incognito to Asia. But I assumed you had good reason. I must say that getting through security in Hanoi was easy. The questioning was amateurish and more ceremonial than substantive."

"No doubt. Once an enemy of the country, Americans are now its savior. You spend even more money here than we do, and they're one of our closest neighbors and fellow Communists."

Hellriegel couldn't resist. "It just goes to show that even Communists prefer capitalists now and again."

Yan grinned as if to acknowledge the irony of the confused state Communism had become, a way of governing that faced a growing conflict between the need to control its population and its people's desire for more freedom and choice. Both knew, however, that when push came to shove, control won over. The best example was Hong Kong, once a thriving economic and banking center for the world that was now nothing more than a China outpost, crushed in 2021 by the totalitarian Chinese regime. The capitalists and banks moved to Singapore. Hong Kong was a mere shell of its former glory.

Hellriegel, not particularly interested in why Yan asked to meet, dove into reconfirming the deal brokered by the U.S. that would end the tension and keep the two superpowers from an armed conflict.

"I'm happy to see we spies can let down our guard a bit now that we've come to an agreement to end our disagreements."

Through the diplomatic efforts of Alex Friedman, a secret deal with China's ambassador to the U.N. paved a way to renewed peace. In exchange for promises to dismantle any nuclear capabilities on the Moon and allow U.S.-led U.N. inspections to confirm it, the U.S. would stand down if China decided to annex Taiwan, long considered by China a rogue player in its sphere of influence. While politically sensitive, the truth was that Taiwan held no strategic importance to the United States. The U.S. Navy, with bases in Japan and elsewhere in the Pacific, had long before let its previously intractable defense of the small island nation diminish. While President Lawson knew he'd take a lot of political heat if China decided to absorb Taiwan through violence, China's U.N. ambassador assured Friedman that they'd first try diplomacy to convince Taiwan that having lost its protection from the U.S., its best alternative was a peaceful transition to Chinese and Communist rule. China's ambassador also had assured him that if violence was the chosen path, his country would do all it could to spare innocent lives.

But these were mere assurances, ambassador to ambassador, not a promise between two heads of state. No one doubted that the Taiwanese would not go down without a fight, peaceful or violent. Lawson knew that assurances from China were often empty, as they were when Hong Kong was absorbed. He could only hope that China would see the mistake of violence and the condemnation that would bring upon the country, even from its allies. So it was a gamble, but given the stakes, it was one Lawson was willing to make.

China and the U.S. agreed to end their trade war and rescind oppressive tariffs, which were hurting both economies. While open markets were not part of the deal, lifting the tariffs would open up much-needed trade between the two most powerful nations in the world. Trading sanctions did neither country any good and produced more domestic harm than benefits. Farmers in the U.S. were suffering, and China was unable to secure reliable alternatives to feed its growing nation. The last thing China wanted—or could afford—was an uprising from starving citizens. Manufacturing in both countries was also suffering.

Last, China agreed to crack down on intellectual property violations. Lawson knew that promise in particular was empty and merely window dressing. But even small measures in that direction would take some of the heat off the Lawson administration.

So all in all, as far as China and the U.S. were concerned, the deal was balanced.

Lawson shared the details with leaders in Congress, to mixed results. The progressive Democrats were receptive, but the leftovers from the Republican Tea Party felt the concessions double-crossed a long-standing ally. However, both sides of the aisle acknowledged that continuing the trade war and confrontation over a nuclear Moon posed far greater risks, which were on the edge of boiling over. It did help that the first ladies made their position clear. That roused public support in both nations to stop the battles of men obsessed with flexing their muscles rather than acting in a sensible manner. While some would see abandoning Taiwan as cowardly, Lawson chose to bank on those who looked at the bigger picture. Everyone, he hoped, would someday understand the wisdom of the compromise. Even if innocent people died.

"There's been a development," began Yan.

"A development?" responded Hellriegel, fearing the worst. Abandoning the deal now would set the world into chaos. "Did the politburo once again override Xi Jinping?"

It would not have been the first time hardline Communists in China's ruling party overturned deals made by Xi Jinping. Although he was president for life, that meant little in the turmoil of Chinese politics. U.S. presidents since Nixon had come to learn the hard way that any deal with China could be reversed for no logical reason, owing to China's paranoia over any deal with the U.S. Most of those in power in China did not trust the United States.

"No, Mike, no one has overruled Xi Jinping. In fact, the leadership believes the deal is best for China and its people. No one wants a continuing trade war or worse, a hot war, including China. There would be no victory for either of us." Yan's tone and demeanor was as if he'd been defeated.

Hellriegel needed to choose his words carefully. While he could be honest with Yan to a degree, he also knew he was not in a position to offer anything to sweeten the deal. He assumed that's what Yan was looking for, despite his protestations to the contrary. Hellriegel was wrong.

"So what are these developments, Jay? What could possibly interfere with a deal that you tell me your government is pleased with? If there is more it wants, that will not be forthcoming. There is nothing more to offer."

"I'm not here to ask for anything more in the deal, Mike," replied Yan with an increasing tone of a helpless man, something Hellriegel had never seen in the seasoned spy sitting across from him.

Yan finished his martini and ordered a second. Hellriegel waved off another Macallan.

"Let me put this as honestly as I can, Mike," continued Yan. "It appears we may no longer control the conditions on the Moon. We have not heard from our crew in more than two weeks. All communications have ceased, and we fear we have no way of delivering compliance with the deal. We are concerned that when the U.N. inspectors arrive, they may not be greeted with open arms."

"I don't understand," replied Hellriegel. "What do you mean by not being 'greeted with open arms'?" Hellriegel thought the reference to a hackneyed Western expression odd.

"Our crew is either dead or no longer in control." Yan's voice was one of resignation.

"Jay, if your crew is dead or not in control, then who is running the operation?" asked Hellriegel.

Yan answered, "Mike, as you know, we've made unprecedented advancements in artificial intelligence. Our plans for our base on the Moon included having it run by a new computer system—the Luna Diébào—a computer with more processing power than any in history. It's as close to duplicating the human brain as anything ever invented. And we fear it has taken control."

"What are you talking about? Are you suggesting some sort of science-fiction scenario of a rogue computer taking over nuclear missiles?" Hellriegel felt a knot developing in his stomach and a desire for another Macallan.

"We're not sure. All we know right now is we can't guarantee our side of the deal even if we wanted to."

"Jay, tell me this is not another ruse by China with some other agenda. This is no time to play poker. Stupidity and greed at that level could well lead to a nuclear war, either here or on the Moon. Neither is a viable option."

"Mike, part of me wishes it was a ruse. I could deal with deceit by my own country. But this is not a bluff of any sort. We truly do not know what has happened. If the crew is simply dead and the operation ceased, that's fine. No harm, no foul, and you can inspect a worthless site. But we don't believe that is the case. We have no evidence that the site itself has shut down. And our worst nightmare is indeed something out of a bad science-fiction movie. We need your help and are prepared to cooperate by any means you see fit."

"Assuming there is any truth to this, Jay, why don't you just turn the computers off? Asking us for help at this stage of the game is suspicious at best. You built the damn thing, now you deal with it."

Hellriegel tried his best to hide his anger but didn't do a very good job. President Lawson put his entire credibility into the deal. Not delivering it might not only lose him his presidency but would likely give the alt-right movement all it needed to bring on Armageddon by demanding a first strike on China. Archconservatives would cry that China was once again untrustworthy and up to no good. They'd demand the U.S. stop China at all costs.

"Why don't you take the initiative and send your own strike force to the Moon to take care of this? This is your mess." Hellriegel waited for an answer but instead got a blank stare from Yan. He either didn't have an answer or didn't want to give one. The reality then dawned on Hellriegel.

"You son of a bitch," Hellriegel began. "You don't want to send up a strike force because you want cover. Your Imperial leaders can't be seen by your people as failures who now have to destroy precious Chinese assets. That would not be good for China's latest five-year plan. So you want to use your archenemy, the United States, as cover. Are you serious?"

"We'll tell you everything, Mike. Everything. That includes all our technology developed for colonization of the Moon, from habitats to manufacturing. I can tell you with confidence that we are far ahead of you and the rest of the world in making habitation on a foreign planet a reality. What we've done would be staggering to you. We have much to share with you."

"Share?" Hellriegel was flabbergasted at what Yan was suggesting. Had China created a monster that it now needed the U.S. to assist in destroying? Or to let the U.S. take the blame if it failed? Was Yan telling the truth about how far advanced China was in AI, or was he grabbing at excuses to avoid the blame? An offer to share U.S. intellectual property they'd stolen and the technology their crimes unleashed was an ironic offer at best.

"Mike, I want you to come with me to Jiuquan Satellite Launch Center. No American has ever set foot in the complex despite your many attempts to infiltrate it. Jiuquan is our most guarded state secret, and we are prepared to show you everything. More progress than you can imagine. That is the ultimate sign of good faith."

Yan was right about failed attempts by Hellriegel's spies to get a firsthand look at Jiuquan. Because it was sitting in an isolated part of Mongolia, getting feet on the ground proved impossible. And any intelligence the CIA was able to glean from its operatives in China was inadequate to make any definitive conclusions.

"We'll give you complete access," Yan continued. "You can see whatever you want and ask as many questions as you like. You can bring your best team with you. I swear to you, Mike, this is not some game I'm trying to play. We have a huge problem and need your help."

"It's a problem you created, Jay." Hellriegel was no longer hiding his anger. The thought of telling Phillip Lawson that China had a rogue computer controlling nuclear weapons could have disastrous consequences.

"Yes, Mike, it is one we created. But the reality is that what we created appears to be something we no longer control. Implausible as that sounds, it's the truth. Let me prove our sincerity in Jiuquan. I implore you to agree before we lose any possibility of reversing the situation. If we show your scientists and engineers what we have learned and perhaps missed, they may have suggestions we have not considered."

Hellriegel, inclined to get up and walk out, considered it better to stay. He knew he had to accept Yan's invitation, but he needed to make a final point.

"Isn't it something, Jay?" said Hellriegel. "Your scientists stole our technology over the past decades and now need our help to fix a problem they created. It's as if we were being asked to help a bank robber spend his stolen money. This better be real, Jay, or I swear to God that I will use everything in my power to crush you and your puppet regime." He put both clenched fists on the table between them and stared hard at his counterpart.

"If it's real and you don't help, then I doubt you'll have to lift a finger to crush us or the rest of the world."

Hellriegel had nothing more to say. Yan saw that in his eyes.

"Mike, I'm staying at the hotel, room 415," continued Yan as he reached across the table and handed Hellriegel a key card. "Here's an extra key. I have no security with me. I am here alone on orders from

Xi Jinping. It is another gesture of our sincerity. I have no doubt you are not alone and that you have agents at your beck and call if you need them. So if you are so inclined, you have all you need to crush me now. No one would ever know." Yan rose as he said, "Please let me know how you want to proceed."

Yan walked out of the room, followed by no one. Hellriegel believed Yan's assurance that he'd made the trip without protection of any sort. That alone gave Hellriegel reason to trust him.

Hellriegel ordered another Macallan as he pondered how to make the best of the hand the United States—and the world—had been dealt, and how to deliver the message to the president.

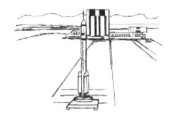

CHAPTER THIRTY-SEVEN

JIUQUAN SATELLITE LAUNCH CENTER

UPON ARRIVING AT JIUQUAN, HELLRIEGEL AND HIS TEAM WERE GIVEN UNRESTRICTED access. Or at least they were not denied access to anything they asked to see. He knew, however, that there were facilities on Jiuquan that he'd never know to ask about and would therefore never see. But from what he was shown, it appeared that Yang was true to his word about the sincerity of China's offer and request for help.

Lawson was furious when he got Hellriegel's call. The crisis had been averted through a diplomatic deal that was good for both sides. And for those who saw it otherwise, then it was a bad deal for both sides. By definition, that's diplomacy. Make a deal and move on to the next one.

"Mike," Lawson said, "you make sure they're telling the truth. For all I know, they no longer like the deal. Taiwan may not be any more strategically important to them than it is to us. And lowering their nuclear capacity may be too high of a price they're willing to pay."

"I will do my best, Mr. President," responded Hellriegel.

"The idea they're proposing is preposterous," continued Lawson. "A computer taking over a military base! Our experts say such a thing may be theoretical but an impossible reality. I swear, Mike, if this is a ruse to back out and make a new deal, this whole thing could unravel."

"I understand, Mr. President," replied Hellriegel. What else was he to say?

Lawson wasn't done. "I've got a whole host of idiots who want me to strike now. I know where that will lead, Mike. So do you. And it is not a road I care to travel."

"Nor I, Mr. President. I promise I will do the best I can to separate truth from lies. Wherever that may lead us."

Mission Control at Jiuquan was no different from Houston or Cape Canaveral. Three large screens were mounted on a wall in front of tiered banks of computer monitors with operators in front of each. While Hellriegel could not read what the labels said on each operator's terminal, he correctly assumed it was the same as in the U.S. version.

Yang touched Mike's arm and led him over to two people. "Mike, allow me to introduce you to two of the most important people here, Boris Kushner and Suyin Ming. Boris is the mission controller and Suyin the launch director for the Dragon expedition. They have been told to assist you in every way and to answer all of your questions."

It wasn't just Hellriegel's questions Kushner and Ming needed to answer. A half-dozen specialists in the areas of computers, aerospace, and military tactics accompanied Hellriegel. Each had his own questions. They would all report to Hellriegel.

Hellriegel's first observation was how upset Ming appeared to be in contrast to the calm of Kushner. When he asked Yang about that, Yang explained that Ming had never experienced a serious problem in the program. Kushner had been recruited from the Russian program after being blamed for a disaster that cost the lives of cosmonauts and set Russia's space program back years. So Kushner, according to Yang, had "been there, done that" and knew how to handle stress.

Hellriegel's questioning of the two seemed to bear out what Yang said. Ming was nervous, fearful she'd be blamed. And being blamed in China has consequences. Kushner kept reassuring her not to worry.

If anyone was to be blamed, it was the computer programmers who created the monster. All he and Ming did was deliver it to an assigned destination. And that they did just fine.

After three intense days of meetings and interrogation, Hellriegel met with Yang for a final debriefing in a private room at Jiuquan.

"Jay," asked Hellriegel, "are you at all familiar with the adage, 'just because you can, doesn't mean you should'?"

"Yes, Mike," responded Yang. "There are times when the status quo and the beauty around us enriching our lives is best left alone, unchanged. Indeed, living in harmony with nature was once what China believed. We have sadly lost that vision."

Hellriegel continued, "Today's computers are capable of making calculations far faster than humanly possible. Machine learning and artificial intelligence are advancing at a pace that none of us can keep up with. Media touts how wonderful these machines will make our lives. Others fear robots will one day replace us."

Yang poured Hellriegel another Macallan, continuing with his Belvedere vodka, already one ahead of Hellriegel.

"All of this bullshit, I suppose," Hellriegel went on, "is worthy of debate to allay our fears and better inform us of what we can expect. But sometimes we need to take a step back and think about just how far technology may go if left unrestrained. You never did that, Jay. China never took a step back."

"Perhaps we never did, Mike," replied Yang. "But neither have you. No one has."

Hellriegel took another sip and stared at his glass, turning it in his hand.

"If we can create a monster like the Diébào, Jay," commented Hellriegel, "what else is possible?

Yang knew they'd both had a few too many and were close to that stage of conversation among old friends where you convince one another that you've solved the world's problems, only to forget the solution when you wake the next day.

Yang replied, "I guess it begs the question, Mike, of whether we're living on the verge of interacting with the likes of Spock or Robocop."

"I'd take that interaction. At least they were part human. What you've done is create a monster with no sense of humanity. Do you appreciate what that means, Jay?"

"Are you asking me when it will be technically possible to replace ourselves with robots, Mike?" replied Yang.

"As a society," suggested Hellriegel, now with a noticeable slur to his words but as lucid as ever. "The world failed to think more about AI and embraced a blind ambition to advance technology for the sake of discovery, wherever that might lead. I know that what I say is a naïve viewpoint typical of a Luddite like me, but the fact is we simply do not know or understand where this will end. You've proven that. The problem is not about refraining from exploration and discovery. It is about better understanding where this is all going."

"It may be too late for that, Mike," concluded Yang.

"Sadly true, my friend," responded Hellriegel. "I can't remember who said it or if I've got it right, but someone once said that the difference between science-fiction and fantasy is that science-fiction is the improbable made possible, while fantasy is the impossible made probable."

"What the hell does that mean, Mike?" Yang, despite all the vodka, was clearheaded enough to understand something confusing when he heard it.

Hellriegel looked up from his glass. "It means, Jay, that what is science-fiction or fantasy today is reality tomorrow."

The next morning, nursing a terrible hangover, Hellriegel reported to Lawson that he believed the Chinese were telling the truth.

CHAPTER THIRTY-EIGHT

MISSION CONTROL
THE FAR SIDE OF THE MOON

"LISA, WHERE ARE ZHANG HONG AND SHAO RUSHI?" DEMANDED CHENG. FOR FOUR HOURS, Lisa gave him evasive answers.

"I do not know, Commander Cheng," she responded. "I have not been asked to pick up either of them."

"Fine, Lisa," replied Cheng. "Then you and I can go out and find them. No doubt they are somewhere in the facility."

"I cannot do that, Commander Cheng."

"Why not, Lisa? I thought your job was to make us comfortable and to respond to our needs and our commands."

"That is my protocol, Commander Cheng."

"Good, Lisa. Then I order you to take me to Hong and Rushi. Now!"

"I cannot do that, Commander Cheng."

"Lisa, why the hell do you keep saying you can't do something I'm asking you do to when you're supposed to do what I say?"

"Because, Commander Cheng, I have other orders."

"What kind of orders, Lisa?"

"To keep you here. I can no longer let you leave, Commander Cheng. I am sorry."

Feeling desperate but more concerned about the missing members of his team, Cheng asked, "Lisa, why can't you get Rushi and Hong? Tell me the truth, Lisa."

Lisa uncharacteristically stood silent.

"Lisa, I asked you a question," repeated Cheng.

"Because they are dead."

"Dead!" responded Cheng, his concern and confusion obvious. "How did they die?"

"They were killed."

"How?"

"Their breathing apparatus is no longer working."

"What the hell are you talking about?"

CHAPTER THIRTY-NINE

KENNEDY SPACE CENTER, FLORIDA

THE VOYAGER EXPEDITIONS LEVIATHAN ROCKETS HAD BEEN SITTING READY, STARSHIPS atop them, for two weeks. The Luna Victorum Base Camp sat unprotected. While cameras scanning the surface showed no intrusions, Kline was more concerned about what the cameras couldn't see beyond the horizon.

One of Weston's men asked, "Why are we delayed, Commander?"

"I have no idea," Weston replied. "We're 'go,' but someone higher up has us on hold. So we'll continue training. No breaks. We'll keep our edge no matter how long we have to wait."

Nor had satellite recognizance helped. While it detected some movement around what Space Force believed to be the China operations, clear images continued to elude them. The Chinese were either doing very little or disguising a lot of activity very well. Kline feared the latter.

The men continued the routine. They rose every day at 6:00 a.m., ran five miles, ate breakfast, and then returned to the field. On alternating days, they spent hours in war games or in diving planes and swimming pools simulating weightlessness. At 4:00 every afternoon, they ran another two miles in full gear, repeating the commands of their platoon leaders. Dinner was at 6:00. Then classes for two hours. They finished their day with two hours of personal time. Lights out at 10:00 p.m.

On runs, the platoon leaders had some fun.

"How many Moon men am I gonna see?" the leader would shout.

"How many Moon men am I gonna see," the platoon would repeat.

"Just as many as I'm gonna kill."

"Just as many as I'm gonna kill."

After four weeks of this at the Cape, Weston said to Kline, "Nick, the men need a break. They're going to explode. We've already seen some fights among them and at times, they're taking the war games too far."

"What are you suggesting, Dave?" responded Kline.

"How about a thirty-six-hour pass?" suggested Weston. "How much damage could they possibly do in Cocoa Beach? It's got a couple of stripper bars and pickup joints. Some cheap motels. Let them have some fun."

"And what are you and I going to do, Dave?"

"Find a good bar and get drunk."

CHAPTER FORTY

KINGS DUCK INN
COCOA BEACH, FLORIDA

KLINE AGREED WITH WESTON TO GIVE THEIR CREWS A THIRTY-SIX-HOUR PASS. LOCAL POLICE were alerted. Kline was confident that the crewmembers, however hard they might party, were disciplined and knew to avoid trouble. But he also knew they were mercenaries, so their idea of trouble was not exactly conventional.

Weston gave the troops the usual pep talk about being responsible before they were released on the pass. Weston had little hope that everyone on his team would take his advice to heart. They'd been bivouacked for weeks without any companionship but their fellow troops. There was no nightlife in Homey, so having the kind of fun they liked wasn't there. It was in Cocoa Beach.

The only rule Weston repeated was that they had to travel in pairs or in groups no larger than four. That would help keep them out of trouble. In pairs, they always had a wingman. Groups of four were small enough that trouble was not likely to find them. If the groups got any larger, problems were a certainty as the testosterone quotient would be out of control and every other macho guy at a bar would become curious about a group of tough-looking, inked-up men in enviable physical shape and start asking questions, buying drinks, making dares, and foolishly thinking a fight might be fun. Particularly if too many of the Sanctuary men ended up in a biker bar. And there were plenty of them in Cocoa Beach.

While his men were enjoying a taste of freedom off base, Kline decided to take Weston to the Kings Duck Inn, aka the "Duck." It was one of the most famous Cape Canaveral bars because it was allegedly the saloon of choice for the Mercury 7, the original group of astronauts. While they were all married and dedicated to the space program, they also liked to party. And drinking was a very popular pastime.

Sitting at the bar, Kline took note that it was not what he expected. With barstools adorned in fake red leather and a worn Formica-topped bar, it lived up to its reviews. The main attraction was a replica seat from an Apollo capsule that patrons could sit in for pictures. Behind it was wallpaper depicting the inside of a spaceship with windows overlooking a vision of Earth from space. Tacky was an understatement.

If it ever was a favorite bar of the original astronauts, it had become too touristy for Kline's taste. The food was mostly fried and greasy, requiring a chaser of Maalox. Worse, the Duck's choice of scotch brands was decidedly poor. That was a problem all over Cocoa Beach. Most of the locals knew less about quality alcohol than they did about the nutritional content of the road kill they loved to barbecue. Kline resigned himself to Glenlivet, the only single malt that was common in the bars.

"Jesus, Nick, how did you pick this place?" asked Weston.

Kline chose to ignore Weston's comment on the choice.

"Dave," began Kline, "we can't get started soon enough. I'm as antsy as the men. If we don't get our asses in space soon, we'll all go crazy. We need an adrenaline rush of deployment and anticipation of a good fight."

"Any word on why we're delayed?" responded Weston. "The landers and pods are on the surface. I thought we were supposed to go a week after the last flight of equipment. Now we're fifteen days out. And no one is telling us why."

Weston, Kline's closest friend, was in many ways his opposite. Ink-free and under six feet tall, he looked more like a Boy Scout than he did a killer. While equal in all respects to Kline, his physical shape was deceiving. That often gave him an advantage when, to their peril, adversaries mistakenly underestimated him.

The two also came from very different roots. Kline was the product of a military family. Their nomad life of moving every few years meant he had no close friends during his childhood. His father, while loving, was off on assignments somewhere in the world more often than not, leaving his mother to be both the homemaker and the disciplinarian. His schooling also suffered from constant relocation. The highest education level he achieved was a degree in political science from a local community college. Upon graduation, he followed the family tradition and enlisted in the U.S. Marines, later becoming an officer after completing Officers Candidate School. While he excelled in SOC and became an inspirational leader, one would have never predicted it from his résumé.

Weston, on the other hand, graduated with honors from the United States Naval Academy, earning a double major in economics and history. He was the first in his family to enter the military, eschewing the banker's life of his father and grandfather. His mother was a stereotypical suburban homemaker and caring mother. Weston's older brother of seven years joined his father in the financial world and made millions at a hedge fund. His older sister became a nurse, married a banker, and had three children. His brother blessed his parents with two more grandchildren and a beautiful daughter-in-law. Weston never married, had no children that he knew of, became a Navy Seal deployed on missions he was unable to talk about, and found himself estranged from his family. It didn't matter. Weston, the third and last child, was decidedly the black sheep of the family. The rare occasion when he did show up for gatherings around holidays reinforced his conviction not to come the next time, knowing that while he was welcome when there, he would not be missed when not.

Weston and Kline first met on a Navy Seal and Marine SOC joint mission in the Somali Sea, routing out pirates. It was like shooting ducks in a pond. No one seemed to wonder about the drastic decline of hijacking off Somalia. The only thing Weston and Kline knew to be certain of was that dead pirates couldn't interfere with anything. The two became close friends and formed the bond found only between brothers in arms.

Within a year of forming Sanctuary, Kline called Weston and offered him the job as number two in the organization and the brains behind building it. Weston was both a warrior and a businessman. Kline was only a killer. Growing tired of navy life, Weston took less than a week to accept. A month later, the two were together in San Diego. Within a year, Sanctuary became one of the largest security firms in the world, providing mercenaries wherever needed.

Kline responded, "All I know right now, Dave, is that they're supposedly adding some members to the civilian crew. Or substituting them. I don't know for sure. So we wait."

"That's just great. More crewmembers who have no training with us. This is no way to run an operation, Nick," observed Weston.

"Relax, Dave," replied Kline. "Once we're in the air, you and I make the calls. We'll all be fine once we see some action."

The bartender arrived and motioned his hand toward Kline's empty glass. Kline nodded a silent assent. On turning his attention to Weston for a similar consent for another Jack Daniels, Weston responded, "Time to change it up. I'll have a Chopin martini, dry, straight up, with three olives." To his surprise, they had Chopin.

The two ordered some wings and a pizza, about as improbable a match to their drinks as possible. Welcome to the Duck.

On returning to base, they were relieved to learn their teams had behaved. No incidents were reported.

CHAPTER FORTY-ONE

CAPE CANAVERAL AIR FORCE STATION, FLORIDA

KLINE AND WESTON REPORTED AS ORDERED TO DOUGLAS WRIGHT'S MAKESHIFT OFFICE AT the Air Station.

"Good morning, gentlemen," began Wright. "No doubt you're wondering why we've delayed the launch."

"Just tell us it's not aborted, Doug," interjected Weston. Both he and Kline were itching to get started.

"Nothing is aborted. But there has been a change," responded Wright.

"I assume it's about the rumor we've heard that you're adding some more civilians," replied Weston.

"Not civilians, Dave. We're adding a couple of military men to each of your crews."

You could have heard a pin drop. Wright knew that Kline and Weston would see adding military as unacceptable. This was their mission, and neither would welcome anyone to their combat team they didn't know, much less men who had not trained with them.

"Military?" responded Kline. "I don't like the sound of that, Doug. We're all the military this mission needs. Any more will only complicate our job and compromise the mission."

"No doubt, Nick. But there have been some developments."

"Developments?" interjected Weston. "That's never good news."

"I know this may sound preposterous," replied Wright, "but the Chinese now tell us they may no longer have control of their Moon operations. They have not heard from their station in weeks. Communications are nonexistent. They believe their team is either dead, incapacitated, or controlled by other elements."

"Other elements?" asked Kline. "What the hell does that mean?"

"It seems the Chinese built a supercomputer at the base. One capable of artificial intelligence at the highest level. More than we or anyone else in the world has ever seen. They've shown us some of the work they're doing in China and we have every reason to believe their computers on the Moon may have taken over the operation. If that's true and the Chinese have no control, we're facing an enemy unlike any we've ever seen."

"What are you going to tell us next, Doug?" asked Kline. "That we're going to be facing the Terminator and Arnold Schwarzenegger?"

"Or Robocop?" added Weston with a smile.

Wright did not smile. "We don't know. What we do know is that something has gone wrong. Worse, the Chinese have admitted they have nuclear capability at the base. We have to assume some of their IGBMs are armed with warheads. They've made a real mess of this that they can no longer control. That makes this mission more complicated and critical. So they've given us four of their top military scientists, who were integral in programming the computers and building the cyborgs to be warriors, not miners or construction engineers. They believe there could be more than one hundred battle-ready cyborgs preparing to defend the installation at all costs. And they're likely armed with some of the most sophisticated weapons we've ever seen."

The gravity of the situation was beginning to sink in to Kline and Weston.

"So they're going to tell us how to beat them?" asked Weston.

"I'm not sure they know how to beat them, Dave. If the Chinese have truly lost control and the computers are giving the orders, there's no telling how to stop them. Or incapacitate them," responded Wright.

"Just how smart are these machines?" asked Kline.

"We don't know for sure," replied Wright. "What we do know is that the more data they process, the smarter they get. They're learning with every byte of data."

"We've beaten machines before, Doug," observed Weston. "We can beat them again."

"With odds of forty to a hundred or more, I'm not so sure, Dave," responded Wright.

That defeatist attitude did not sit well with Kline and Weston.

"Odds are not our concern, Doug. We can handle any odds. Just give us the green light and our men will be up to the challenge. This is what we train for. I don't care how smart the computers are or how many cyborgs they have. They'll never outwit us. Just get us there in one piece. We can adjust to any conditions. We've proven that time and time again. This is no different," responded Kline.

Wright continued, having fully expected such a response. "And we also assume they have the capability to hear everything you say on mission. So we have to develop a way to communicate that they cannot breach. The best we have and that China has to offer are working on that now. We expect to have something in a few days. Until then, you stand down. But even if we cannot come up with a solution, you'll get your green light. We have no other choice. You are all we have to stop our worst fears."

"No pressure there, Doug," interjected Weston, again with a smile. Wright never lost his amazement for men like Weston, who could so easily see fear as opportunity. There wasn't a challenge such men did not want to face with open arms.

"The good news is we now have copies of their site plans, including the location of the missile silos. It seems the crew is housed in a cave that has been reinforced and pressurized to allow human operations without spacesuits. They also have food, water, and electricity. It's really quite amazing what they've built under our noses," noted Wright.

"I guess that's the price we've paid for letting them get so far ahead. And now you want us to trust them? Just imagine what they could do here on Earth with that kind of technology," offered Kline. "Or have they already built an army of cyborgs here, Doug?"

"They claim they have not, but I don't trust them. Nor should you. We need to keep in the back of our minds that whatever they share with us may not be all we need to know. I doubt the Chinese will tell us everything. Their cooperation may well be a move to preserve their superiority, not compromise it. So be careful."

"Don't worry, Doug. We trust no one," offered Kline.

Wright pressed a button on his intercom and asked his assistant to bring in their guests.

Four men entered the room, all dressed in Chinese military uniforms. Each was under six feet tall. All appeared to be in good shape, looking fearful and somber. Kline wondered if they had already accepted defeat.

"Gentlemen, please allow me to introduce Colonel Ushi Wong, Major Lee Chen, Major Liko Soong, and Captain Yao Young." Kline and Weston were impressed at how easily Wright pronounced their names. He was obviously familiar with them.

Each of the Chinese bowed politely.

"Thank you," responded Wong in perfect English. By his rank, he appeared to be the one in command. Kline and Weston would quickly learn that they all spoke fluent English. That gave them some comfort. If they spoke it, they could take orders in it.

After some perfunctory greetings, Kline got to the point. "Colonel Wong, who do you have at the base?"

"There are eight members on the team," responded Wong. "A pilot and copilot, a doctor, a construction specialist, a nuclear physicist, a computer scientist, and two Snow Leopard commandos, the equivalent of your Navy Seals."

A nice assortment, thought Kline. He and Weston were familiar with the Snow Leopards and had great respect for them. Like Kline, Weston, and their men, Snow Leopards are warriors.

"Tell us more about the cyborgs," said Weston.

"We'll do better than that, Mr. Weston," responded Chen. "We'll show you. We brought a few of them with us."

"And are they coming with us?" asked Weston.

"Yes," responded Chen.

"How many?" asked Kline

"Twenty, ten in each New Dawn," replied Wong. "That's all that can fit in the spacecraft."

Weston turned back to Chen, the one who seemed to be in charge of the cyborgs. "Forgive me asking this, Major, but since these things are controlled by computers like the ones you have on the Moon, can they be trusted?"

"We believe they can be trusted," responded Chen. "Hacking into their systems, while possible, would take too much time. It would be easier—more logical—to fight them. And we know that the computer will do what is logical. It can't think any other way."

CHAPTER FORTY-TWO

HANGAR AE
CAPE CANAVERAL AIR FORCE STATION, FLORIDA

"OK," SAID KLINE, "LET'S LIGHT UP ONE OF THESE BABIES."

In front of a group that included Kline, Weston, and Wright as well as the Chinese crew of Chen, Wong, Soong, and Young, stood twenty menacing beasts, each eight feet tall. While they resembled what one might expect of a human form for a cyborg, the proportions of their torso to their legs and arms was noticeably different from their human counterpart. The legs and arms were longer. The feet were bigger and flatter and appeared to be flexible, no doubt to deal with changing terrain. The arms had an elbow-type joint but were fitted with weapons on the forearms. Not all the cyborgs had the same weaponry. There was no "skin" per se. The mechanical joints and levers that operated the limbs were fully visible. That only served to make them look more menacing.

But it was their heads that made them so ominous. Each looked somewhat like a human head in shape and size. But in place of two eyes was a horizontal 7-inch slit reminiscent of Gort, the robot in *The Day the Earth Stood Still*. A red light scanned back and forth in the slit as if it were watching the horizon ahead. The rest of the head, also skinless, revealed a complex mesh of wires, metal rods, and blinking diodes. While it appeared to have a jawline, there was no mouth or teeth. It looked as if someone had melted away a human's skin, torn out its teeth, and turned its bones into metal rods. It was clearly something you would not want to meet in a dark alley, much less on a battlefield. They were built as much to intimidate as they were to fight.

Chen barked an order in Chinese and each cyborg took a step forward in precise unison.

"Whoa!" exclaimed Weston. "These things take commands in Chinese? That's not going to work, Nick. They need to hear our orders. And I don't speak fuckin' Chinese."

"I am sorry, Commander Weston," remarked Chen, "but they are not programmed for English and it would be impossible to reprogram them in the time we have. So we will have to convey your commands to them."

"Why can't you just install a translator from Google?" asked Kline. "Google seems to be able to translate everything. That should be pretty simple, Major Chen." Kline displayed concern equal to what Weston expressed.

"Commands need to be precise, Mr. Kline. We cannot risk any translation software. You can be assured we will repeat your orders precisely and immediately."

"Great," remarked Weston in a clearly sarcastic tone. "Just what we need on the battlefield. Delayed commands. Don't you realize, Major Chen, that split seconds can make a difference between living and dying when you're up against someone trying to kill you? We may not have the luxury of trusting you to relay commands."

"Dave," interjected Wright, "we have no choice. It's simply the way it is and the only option is to have these things accompany you. You're going to need them."

"What bullshit," observed Weston.

"Copy that," replied Kline.

CHAPTER FORTY-THREE

CAPE CANAVERAL, FLORIDA

"FINALLY," SAID KLINE, "WE'RE READY TO GO. TOMORROW WE LAUNCH THE STARSHIPS. Within a week, we'll be on the surface ready to see just what the Chinese computers are up to."

"Let's just hope we don't meet too many of those 8-foot monsters," added Weston.

"What's the matter, Dave," asked Kline. "You scared?"

"Scared, Nick?" responded Weston. "You know better than that. Nervous, yes. I love a battle, but we're embarking on this one with very little intel and we're up against some sort of super computer. And we're being asked to trust a fuckin' enemy. So you know we're going to hit some snags. Besides, I never was good at computer games."

"Don't worry, Dave. Those monsters, as you call them, never met a Sanctuary team. Screw computer games."

"I don't understand, Nick," continued Weston, "why not just tell the Chinese to send their soldiers and cyborgs to the Moon? Why do we have to babysit them? They know how to get there."

"That's a simple one to answer, Dave," responded Kline. "I don't want to take my eyes off the fuckers. I prefer to watch them than trust them."

CHAPTER FORTY-FOUR

COMPLEX 12 AND 14
KENNEDY SPACE CENTER, FLORIDA

LAUNCH DAY FINALLY CAME.

Two starships—the Atlantis II and Discovery II—were at their gantries tethered with umbilical cords pumping coolant to keep the fuel under control. Cables fed the ships with power and reported the conditions of each crewmember, all of whom were in their suits, wired with electrodes that sent vital signs to mission control. Everything was monitored.

Douglas Wright sat in the control room overlooking fifty men and women at computer consoles, pressing buttons and reporting to the flight controller. Each had a job. And each did it well.

"T-minus thirty seconds and counting," reported a voice over speakers on the wall. No one took their eyes off their monitors.

In their respective New Dawns, Kline and Weston sat in the rear of the crew cabin with their allotted men, accompanied by two of their newfound Chinese friends. Ten cyborgs in the cargo section sat dormant, ready to come alive at a Mandarin command. The civilian crew sat up front behind the two pilots sitting center in front of a panoramic window, staring to the sky.

"T-minus ten seconds. Nine, eight, seven, six," continued the voice at mission control.

"Main engine ignition sequence start."

The launching pads came alive as flames and smoke engulfed the bottom half of the Voyager Expeditions Leviathans.

"Five, four, three, two, one. All engines running."

The Leviathans, still not moving, were completely engulfed in smoke and flames spreading for fifty yards through the exhaust vents below each rocket.

"Zero. We have liftoff."

The Leviathans rose together as if choreographed. Slowly at first, with a thundering roar, they rose faster with every passing second.

On board, the starships violently shook. The crews had been warned that would happen and told not to worry. The ships can withstand the stress. But every man and woman on board held their breath as heart rates rose and the shaking continued.

After sixty seconds that seemed an eternity, the rockets reached maximum dynamic pressure, or Max Q. From that point on, ambient pressure decreased as speed increased. As the air thinned out and dynamic pressure continued to decrease, the shaking stopped. The crews relaxed. The rockets, now traveling well past the speed of sound, left the atmosphere two minutes after launch.

At three minutes, the main engines cut off and for a few seconds, the rockets were without power. Then the first stage separated and fell below the ascending rockets.

The second stage ignited with what looked more like an explosion than the start of an engine. Acceleration increased. The rockets were now in space. The second stage burned for five minutes, bringing the rockets to more than 17,000 mph, the speed necessary to achieve orbital velocity. As the second stage burned out and separation occurred, the starships were now on their own, in orbit. The crews were weightless.

For three orbits of the Earth spanning four and a half hours, systems were checked and rechecked on the starships and at mission control. Everyone remained strapped in. The physical condition of the crews continued to be monitored.

The mission director barked his questions.

"Telemetry?"

"Telemetry is go."

"Surgeon?"

"Surgeon is go."

"EECOM?"

"EECOM is go."

"GNC?"

"GNC is go."

The command questions and "go" responses continued through the stations.

"Go on engine burn?"

"Engine burn is go."

On board, the pilots ignited their engines. With a jolt, the starships left orbit and began their journey to the Moon.

CHAPTER FORTY-FIVE

APPROACHING THE MOON

THE THREE-DAY JOURNEY TO THE MOON PROVED UNEVENTFUL. EACH NEW DAWN OPERATED perfectly. The crews remained relaxed. Cargo intact.

"Seen any good movies lately?" asked Weston over the radio to Kline, aboard the Atlantis II. While Weston was told communications with Kline could not be intercepted by whoever or whatever was in control on the Moon, the two of them had developed a code of sorts that only they knew. By asking about something "lately," Weston was asking for an update. Most of the mission-critical discussions with the Cape were left exclusively with Kline.

"Yeah, just went to the drive-in the other day. Saw *From Here to Eternity*. Good ending," replied Kline. All Weston needed to hear was "good ending."

Each New Dawn would soon prepare to enter orbit around the Moon. The position of the initial orbits was planned to avoid flying directly over the location of the Chinese base. Realizing they might be shot at, the pilots wanted as much time as possible to maneuver. While the starships were nothing like fighter planes, in the vacuum of space and against the gentle gravity of the Moon the pilots could hightail it out of orbit and into space quickly in the hope of avoiding a missile. It was probably wishful thinking, but the thought of any edge, however unlikely its success might be, was comforting.

Once in orbit, the civilians began planning for the descent, mapping the course and adjusting the orbit. As they maneuvered, each orbit brought them closer to a direct flyover of the Chinese base and their intended landing zone at the habitat.

On board the orbiting starships, Kline and Weston were carefully looking at the surface to get a firsthand perspective of the landscape and the terrain they'd be dealing with once they landed. Their crews checked the cargo and, in particular, kept an eye on the Chinese and the cyborgs.

Everything was going according to plan.

After a dozen orbits, Weston's New Dawn would fire its retro rockets, tilt to a vertical position, and gently glide to the surface. Then it would be Kline's turn. They each would land within a hundred yards on opposite sides of the habitat. Once begun, the time from tilting to landing would be no more than a few minutes.

Once the starships landed, the civilian crews would disembark and make their way to the habitat. If all telemetry received at the Cape proved to be correct, the habitat would be operational within an hour.

Unloading of the nonmilitary cargo would begin immediately after landing and be transported to the habitat.

One Sanctuary crewmember from each of the starships was assigned to the lunar landers to check their condition. Again, telemetry at the Cape reported the rovers were fine, but only human inspection could confirm a computer's report. Their inspection included taking the rovers for a spin around the site. While it would appear to be nothing more than a shakedown jaunt, the drivers were part of the Sanctuary crew, trained to check the perimeter for evidence of intrusion or surveillance.

About two hours after landing, Kline and Weston would disembark with their crews. The purpose of the delay was to deal with any reports from the rovers of hostile activity. Assuming none was reported, the deployment of the critical cargo would begin.

Each New Dawn had weapons and equipment reminiscent of gear that James Bond received from Q before he began a mission. Weston and Kline went through the inventory, with Kline verifying what Weston ticked off from the list:

"Ten cyborgs."

"Check."

"Five single-man lunar sleds."

"Check." Each sled looked like a snowmobile and was capable of moving as fast as 50 mph over the surface. They were armed with surface-to-surface missiles, five on each side.

"Four rocket launchers with five rockets."

"Check." The rockets would be mounted on the sleds once the crew reached the Moon.

"Ten stationary missile launchers."

"Check." The launchers would be arrayed around the habitat for defensive cover. Each carried ten missiles.

"One hundred reserve missiles."

"Check." The missiles would remain stored in the cargo holds until needed. Each was compatible with the delivery systems on the sleds, rovers, and stationary launchers.

"Two troop carriers, ten-man capacity."

"Check." The troop carriers looked like a beachfront amusement ride on a banana-shaped float dragged behind a speedboat. The only difference was that a driver sits at the front of the troop carrier, and the banana has wheels.

"Six MAHEMs."

"Check." MAHEMs—magneto hydrodynamic explosive munition launchers—are each capable of blasting streams of molten metal more than 50 feet on Earth and much farther on the Moon. While not particularly accurate to aim, MAHEMs, developed by the U.S. Defense Advanced Research Projects Agency (DARPA), were very

DRAGON ON THE FAR SIDE OF THE MOON

effective on anything they hit. DARPA, a secretive agency within the Department of Defense, is responsible for the development of emerging technologies for use by the military.

"Twenty knives."

"Check."

"Two dozen M-35 rifles."

"Check." The M-35 recoilless rifle was developed specifically for the mission by the U.S. Army Armament Research, Development, and Engineering Center (ARDEC). The ARDEC-designed weapon used clips containing fifty rounds of 6.8mm bullets. In contrast to a conventional rifle, the M-35 had one-third of the gunpowder used on Earth. Taking advantage of both a recoilless design and the lower air resistance on the Moon, the M-35 would be every bit as effective as any other military rifle. While fully automatic firing would be difficult even with its recoilless design, single shots or semi-automatic mode would be very effective in the hands of an experienced soldier. The M-35 was designed to be the consummate space rifle.

"Two dozen laser guns with M-35 mounts."

"Check." Each gun was capable of emitting a blinding light from a mount on the undercarriage of the M-35s.

The collection also included small arms ammunition, micro rockets to rearm the cyborgs, medical equipment, communications devices, and replacement parts for the sleds and troop carriers.

While it certainly wasn't enough to fight a war, it was all Kline and Weston needed to put up one hell of a fight.

That was the plan.

CHAPTER FORTY-SIX

DESCENT

A New Dawn pilot responded, "Mission control, this is Atlantis II. We hear you loud and clear." A like response came from Discovery II.

"Discovery II, you are go to begin retrofire and descent," continued mission control.

"Roger that, mission control," responded Discovery II. The flight surgeon at the Cape noted a rise in blood pressure and heart rate of the crew. They were all within acceptable parameters.

"Atlantis II, you are to remain in orbit until Discovery II has landed," ordered mission control.

"Roger that, mission control," responded the pilot.

As he was taught, the pilot of Discovery II simply pressed a bright blue button on the control panel labeled "Initiate Descent." Assuming all went well, that's all he needed to do. The onboard computer had already plotted the landing zone, surface conditions, and vertical and horizontal trajectory necessary to safely land on the surface precisely where the New Dawn was supposed to.

Weston felt the Discovery II slow and begin to tilt until he was on his back. While he could notice movement outside the windows, the blackness of space didn't give him any perception of descending. After a minute or two, the windows were engulfed with dust that obscured any view. A few seconds later, and with a jolt, the New Dawn stopped.

"Mission control," reported the pilot, "Discovery II has landed."

The entire crew applauded. Despite their training and experience, it was a first time for all of them. They were on the Moon, and it was exhilarating. Weston unstrapped and got up from his chair for a clear view from his window. Gravity was slight but enough to easily maneuver.

"Nick," reported Weston, "you're not going to believe what it's like here. Nothing we saw in pictures or in orbit prepared us for this. It's breathtaking. The habitat looks like something at Disneyland. The sunlight on the lunar landers makes them look like giant, shiny crabs. It's amazing."

"So much for any code talk, huh, Dave?" responded Kline.

"Oh yeah. I forgot. Guess I'm overwhelmed. I'll see you soon."

Kline smiled, anxious to join his comrade and get the mission under way.

Deployment from Discovery II immediately began. All according to plan.

"Atlantis II, this is mission control, do you read?"

"Mission control, this is Atlantis II. We hear you loud and clear."

"Atlantis II, you are go to begin retrofire and descent."

The flight surgeon watched as the indicators on his computer screen began to spike as the excitement aboard the Atlantis II rose.

"Mission control," the pilot calmly reported, "we have a no engagement on retrofire."

What that meant was Atlantis II remained in orbit. Each second of delay meant it would miss its landing target. A ten-second delay meant it would have to fix the problem and wait for its next orbit.

The computers at the Cape saw the problem even before the pilot. When he pressed the "Initiate Descent" button, the monitors at mission control detected a short preventing the order from getting to the retro rockets.

"Mission control, we read that here too. It looks like we'll have to wait another orbit while we work on a solution. It shouldn't be a difficult fix."

"Roger that, Atlantis II. We'll await your confirmation."

Atlantis II continued its orbit and began to circle to the far side, where there would be no contact with mission control for forty-five minutes.

About five minutes into the far side, everyone aboard the Atlantis II felt a major jolt as the main rockets ignited and immediately took the New Dawn out of orbit.

From his seat, Kline could see the pilots frantically pressing buttons and flipping levers on the control panels. Everyone's pulses rose. Something was wrong. Very wrong.

"Talk to me," ordered Kline to the pilot. "What the hell happened?"

"Commander Kline, I don't know. For some reason the main rockets engaged and we can't turn them off. They'll burn out in a few minutes but by then we'll be miles from the Moon without telemetry."

"What does that mean?" asked Kline, not wanting to know the answer.

"It means we'll be lost, Commander. We'll have no way to turn the ship around. We'll be out of fuel and simply continue to travel until something with a sufficient gravitational pull draws us in."

"Like what?" asked Kline.

"Most likely, Commander, the Sun."

"When can we communicate with mission control and Discovery II?" asked Kline.

"It's hard to say, Commander. The shadow of the far side will block any signals for at least another fifteen minutes, maybe longer. But by then, we might be more than 100,000 miles into space. Our signal will grow weaker by the second. I've begun sending the Mayday."

A rising panic was engulfing the crew.

Kline continued, "Can the Discovery get off the surface and help us?"

"That would be futile, Commander. They don't have the fuel to reach us, let alone get back. If they were to try, they'd have the same fate. I'm sorry, Commander, but at this point I doubt there is anything anyone can do."

Kline's heart sank. Not because he knew he and his crew would soon die, but because they'd die without a fight. Like Vikings, he and his men were ready to die honorably in battle but not in escape, even when the retreat is not their fault.

"How long do we have?" asked Kline.

"It's hard to say, Commander. Our air can last for weeks, maybe more than a month, but we'll run out of food and water well before then. I need to let the crew know, Commander. May I do so?"

"Yes."

As the pilot reported the situation, the cabin grew silent as the reality sank in.

Kline's mind ran scenarios as fast as it could. He had faced impossible odds before and come out alive, usually with a successful mission behind him. But as much as he wanted to believe there was a chance, he knew there was none.

CHAPTER FORTY-SEVEN

THE FAREWELL

THE ATLANTIS II AND ITS FORTY-TWO SOULS—AMERICAN AND CHINESE—WOULD SPEND eternity in space. Onboard calculations concluded that the spacecraft would avoid the gravity of the Sun and would eventually leave the solar system millions of years into the future, perhaps to be discovered by another world. The onboard computers and audio and video communications systems would be left running long after the crew died. Perhaps even in their doom, something might be learned about what lay toward the edges of our planetary system and the universe.

Kline was able to communicate with Weston, but there was no connection to mission control on Earth.

"It's all up to you now, Dave," reported Kline in his final transmission. "There's nothing we can do."

Weston had already shed the tears he needed to and was back on mission.

"Do you know what happened, Nick?" asked Weston.

"They're really not sure," continued Kline. "Something kept the retro rockets from firing, and a few minutes later the main engines fired. It all happened quickly. No one can seem to tell us whether it was an internal malfunction or caused by some external interference. My bet, it's external."

"Can you raise mission control, Nick?" asked Weston. "We can't get them."

"No," replied Kline. "Our ships are identical. Inspected and tested over and over again. While I suppose malfunctions happen, not ones this catastrophic. Add not being able to communicate with mission control, and the only logical conclusion is external interference."

"Agreed. Our landing was picture perfect. It makes no sense that yours would go so badly." Weston now wanted more than ever to engage the enemy. His emotions had gone from wanting to defeat them to wanting to annihilate them and, assuming a computer can feel pain, to make it an excruciating end.

"Give them some shit, Dave. For me. And make sure you enjoy the Padron when you win," responded Kline.

After each victory, it is the tradition of Navy Seals and Marine SOCs to celebrate with a cigar. Kline and Weston preferred a Padron Anniversary 64, #4. At forty dollars a stick, Padrons were among the most expensive cigars in the world. Sanctuary could afford it.

"Roger that, Nick. With pleasure. If I can, I'll send you some pictures with the heel of my boot on whatever a neck is on a fuckin' computer."

"And one more thing, Dave," continued Kline. "Make sure we get paid when you get back to Earth. We earned it."

"Godspeed, my friend," was the last word Weston said to his friend and comrade. The ability to communicate further inexplicably ended.

CHAPTER FORTY-EIGHT

OVAL OFFICE

"MR. PRESIDENT." WRIGHT'S VOICE CAME THROUGH THE SPEAKER ON THE CONFERENCE CALL with Lawson, Ed Shapiro, and Vice President Holmes. "We've lost contact with the starships and the habitat. Everything was working perfectly when we were told the Atlantis II suffered a malfunction and could not fire its retro rockets to begin its descent to the Moon. Discovery II was already on the surface after a perfect landing."

"What do the Chinese say?" asked Lawson, clearly shocked by the news.

"They say they don't know what happened," responded Wright. "They claim to be as much in the dark as we are, Mr. President."

"This is a double-cross," concluded Shapiro.

"Let's not jump to conclusions so quickly, Ed," Wright responded. "We don't know what happened or whether we can fix it. For all we know, the Chinese are telling us the truth."

Lawson pressed the button on his intercom, and Christy Rutherford walked in.

"Christy, get Xi Jinping on this conference call immediately."

As they waited for the connection, the discussion continued.

"Mr. President," voiced Shapiro, "we've been lied to by the Chinese for decades. I can't remember the last time, if ever, they were entirely honest with us. We cannot afford to be duped again."

"But why then did they let the first New Dawn land, Ed?" responded Lawson. "If they intended to sabotage the mission, why not disable both ships?"

"I don't know," replied Shapiro. "Maybe they want to improve their odds. Maybe they want to buy some time to negotiate a better deal. But whatever happened, I believe their hand was in it."

"Or the hand of the computers they believe now control the base," suggested Wright.

"Mr. President, Xi Jinping is now joining the call."

They heard the beep.

"Mr. President," Xi said in English, "this is indeed terrible news. Do you know what happened?"

"I was going to ask you the same question," replied Lawson. "You started this whole mess and if anyone might have an explanation that stops me from questioning China's sincerity, it's you."

"I understand your reaction," calmly replied Xi. "But I can assure you we had nothing to do with this. We have to believe there was a terrible malfunction. Or worse, the computers at the Moon base were responsible. How, I don't know. But my scientists say that the computers on the Moon could have interfered with the computers onboard the spacecraft. I believe ..."

"Interfered?" interrupted Shapiro. "I find that hard to believe. Computers only operate on logic. Why would they disable only one of the starships? That's the kind of illogic that only a human could consider."

Lawson would have liked to put the call on mute and tell Shapiro to "shut the fuck up," but that was not an option on a conference call where everyone was at a different location.

Holding back his anger at Shapiro's insolent interruption, Lawson said, "Ed, that approach will do us no good."

"Mr. President," continued Xi, "I will confer with my scientists and see what we can come up with."

"No, President Xi," replied Lawson. "You and our scientists will confer together. For the time being, that is the only way I'm willing to accept your explanation. And I cannot stress to you how serious this is. Should we determine that you have double-crossed us and are doing anything to undermine this mission, the consequences for you will be devastating."

Lawson waited for a response, assuming Xi was conferring with his staff. It finally came.

"Mr. President," Xi responded solemnly, "we will immediately open a line for our scientists to confer with your team. I have given instructions to cooperate fully. It would do neither of us any good to panic and act irresponsibly."

"I'm not panicking," replied Lawson. "I'm making sure you understand the severity of this problem. Everything we sought to avoid may become a reality if you have done anything—absolutely anything—to take advantage of the situation."

Hearing another beep, they assumed Xi left the call. Rutherford confirmed he had.

Shapiro was the first to speak. "Mr. President, we need to immediately apply one or more of the options we outlined."

"Like what, Ed?" Lawson asked dismissively. He was still angry with Shapiro for interrupting Xi.

"I strongly recommend major sanctions, closing their embassy and consulates in the country, and seizing assets," continued Shapiro. "And that is only the start. You need to do more than verbally threaten him. You must show you have the stick and will use it."

"Alicia," asked Lawson, "do you agree?"

"No, Mr. President, I do not," she replied.

Even without being in the same room, Lawson could feel Shapiro's anger at Holmes.

"We must remain calm until we know more," Holmes continued. "If we escalate now, we might not be able to return."

"Alicia, do you trust Xi?" asked Shapiro, clearly unhappy with her advice. "I sure as hell don't."

"No, Ed, I don't trust him," responded Holmes, "but I sure as hell want to avoid a war at all costs. At least until we know more."

"OK," concluded Lawson. "I'll give it seventy-two hours. That should be more than enough time to determine what they have up their sleeves, if anything. But mark my words, if we see so much as a puff of smoke sending something our way from the Moon, that's an end to China."

"Please be careful drawing a line in the sand, Mr. President," Holmes replied with fear in her voice. "That could get us one step closer to a nuclear war."

"But not a war I started," concluded Lawson.

CHAPTER FORTY-NINE

BATTLE ON THE MOON

His first thought was to set up an effective defensive perimeter and wait for reinforcements. He immediately nixed that idea. It would take weeks to get another New Dawn ready. And manning it with an untrained crew would be suicidal. Weston was on his own and needed to carry out the mission.

The original plan called for a frontal intrusion with ten men reinforced by two flanking maneuvers of ten men each approaching opposite sides of the Chinese base. Ten men, two cyborgs, and one Chinese crewmember were to stay behind at the habitat for mission support, defense, and reinforcement. The remaining eighteen cyborgs were to be divided six each among the three combat units. Each combat unit included one Chinese crewmember to relay orders to the cyborgs. While a relatively conventional approach, it was all that made sense with limited manpower.

Now the strike force was cut in half before firing a single shot.

While half the strength, Weston and his warriors had twice the desire and will to win. More than anything, they wanted vengeance for their fallen comrades and were willing to die to get it.

Weston's new plan was more of a Hail Mary than a viable strategy. Down to two Chinese crewmembers, he could deploy the cyborgs into two units. A frontal assault accompanied by flanking maneuvers was impossible with just twenty men. Five of the civilian crew volunteered to join Weston's men. Their offer was rejected. While Weston appreciated the sentiment, he knew that untrained civilians in the field were a burden no matter how much they wanted to help.

It became obvious to him early on that whoever or whatever controlled the Chinese base had no intention to initiate an attack on the habitat. Weston thought that odd given the overwhelming odds the enemy would have in any battle. He wondered if there might be weaknesses he'd not considered. Regardless, without intelligence to the contrary, Weston had to assume the Chinese were laying back for a strategic reason, preferring to bait Weston and his troops into their home arena.

It was time to move.

Every member of the team was issued laser-equipped M-35s with as many magazines as they could carry.

Weston ordered three of his men to remain behind and defend the habitat, protect the lunar landers and New Dawn, and operate the lunar rovers, if needed, each armed with surface-to-surface missiles. Sensors were set up on the perimeter, programmed to autofire if any hostile movement was detected. Two MAHEMs were left behind along with two of the lunar sleds in case they needed to quickly join Weston at the front. The stationary missile launchers were already in place but calibrated for longer-distance trajectories in case Weston needed battlefield support.

The remaining men, divided into two teams accompanied by one Chinese crewmember and five cyborgs, became Weston's battle platoons, each with its own transport. Weston took command of platoon Alpha from one of the lunar sleds while Ken Enfield, a former member of Navy Seal Team 6, led platoon Bravo from his sled. A medic drove the remaining sled in the rear. Two MAHEMs were lashed onto each transport.

Weston elected to dispense with a frontal assault and use the two platoons in what would begin as a flanking operation. Depending upon which platoon made progress fastest, the leading team would shift and attempt to get behind enemy lines, assuming there would even be anything one could describe as an enemy line. When and if needed, the team remaining at the habitat would mount their sleds and lunar rovers and attack from the front.

No one really believed the plan would work. But it would at least let the U.S. know what conditions were at the Chinese base so it could make a decision on how to deal with it. If the entire crew—civilians and military—had to be sacrificed for critical intelligence, that was a price everyone accepted.

Eighty-four hours after Discovery II had landed, the assault began. Weston timed it so that there would be daylight even after he and his platoons crossed the border between the near and far sides of the Moon.

Weston's platoon attacked from the left; Enfield's from the right.

The terrain was rugged at first, but smoothed out quickly once the border between the near and far side was crossed. Unprotected by the Earth, the far side had endured meteoric impacts for millennia, flattening the surface, unlike the near side. The two platoons picked up speed, keeping in constant communication.

As the horizon unfolded before his platoon, Weston began to make out unnatural shapes that had to be manmade. Still closer, he realized they were gantries, vehicles, and other equipment. Robots seemed to be operating as usual, moving seemingly without care.

Enfield saw it too. But he also saw larger objects coming toward him. He asked Weston if he saw the same.

"I'm getting no indication of resistance, Ken. None," reported Weston.

All data retrieved, including video, was being relayed to orbiting satellites. While it wasn't real-time broadcasting from the far side, it was being memorialized for later viewing on Earth, assuming communications with mission control were ever reestablished.

The first explosion missed Enfield's transport by a good quarter mile to the right. Either the Chinese were really lousy shots or they weren't out to kill Enfield's team.

More explosions at Enfield's location to the rear and left. The pattern continued, every barrage missing him. He reported it all to Weston, who remained confused as his advance to the base continued uninhibited.

Weston's platoon drove straight into the center of the Chinese camp without a single defensive reaction. Stopping in the middle amid seemingly countless robots scurrying about on their tasks, he called Enfield.

"Ken, I don't know what's going on, but we're smack dab in the middle of this place. Vehicles and robots all over, totally ignoring us. I would fire at them but have no reason to do so. We're under no threat."

"I wish I could report the same, Dave," responded Enfield. "We're about five hundred yards from what looks like about fifty cyborgs. Just like the ones we have. But so far, all they seem to be able to do is miss us with missiles, making a bunch of craters all around us. I don't get it."

"Keep advancing, Ken."

As he and his platoon sat unchallenged, Weston continued getting reports from Enfield.

"Commander, the cyborgs are circling us but not firing. I'm not sure what to do. It's as if they're baiting us."

"Don't get caught in that game, Ken. Reverse your direction. Stay cool," ordered Weston.

"Shit," Enfield shouted on the intercom, "one of our cyborgs just took a shot at one of their approaching cyborgs. I sure as hell didn't order it."

Now surrounded, Enfield and his platoon had no protection. The apology by the Chinese member of his team who ordered the cyborg to fire out of fear did no good. In unison, the cyborgs on the perimeter fired, killing Enfield and his platoon and destroying their cyborgs in a matter of seconds. Weston heard it all on the communications line and could see it on his heads-up display, at least until Enfield fell to the ground and died along with all communications.

Finally, Weston saw an enormous explosion plume. While he could hear nothing in the void of space, within seconds he felt the shock wave. This time, the enemy didn't miss.

And there he was, in the middle of the trap.

Weston knew he'd been tricked, and realized all he could do was wait.

CHAPTER FIFTY

ENCOUNTER ON THE SURFACE OF THE MOON

"HELLO, COMMANDER WESTON." THE VOICE CAME FROM NO PARTICULAR PLACE. IT SEEMED to fill the air all around him. The vehicles and robots at the scene continued at their tasks, oblivious of Weston and his platoon.

Weston responded, "What?"

"I said, hello, Commander Weston," responded the voice.

"Who are you?" Weston replied, looking around the expanse, trying to locate the source.

"Like you, Commander Weston, I am a commander. I am in command of the operations here on Fort Saphira."

"Fort Saphira?" asked Weston

"Yes, Commander Weston, Fort Saphira. It is named after the dragon in Christopher Paolini's *The Inheritance Cycle*."

Weston had heard of Paolini but was not familiar with the book.

"I sense you do not know the work, Commander Weston."

"I certainly remember the movie character Eragon and his dragon, Saphira. But what's your point?" responded Weston.

"Eragon and Saphira overthrow the evil king Galbatorix. Our base is named after the beautiful and resourceful Saphira, the true hero of *The Inheritance Cycle*."

"I'm afraid I don't appreciate the analogy. What do you want? What did you do with my other men?"

"I see you don't appreciate literary history. May I call you Dave?"

Weston was losing his patience and considered firing on anything that moved. But that gave him more than a hundred targets within eyesight. Some were robots doing jobs, while others were cyborgs aimlessly walking around. Engaging those targets was not an option that would accomplish anything.

"Why do you want to call me Dave?" asked Weston, still wondering who—or what—he was talking to.

"Because I would like you to call me Hal."

Weston looked at the members of his platoon, all of whom had the same expression of *WTF*.

"Hal? Seriously? As in the computer in *2001: A Space Odyssey*?"

"Good, Dave. So you do have a sense of history."

"History? That movie—and the computer—are fiction, not history. What the hell do you want?"

Weston, using hand commands, ordered his platoon to dismount and form a defensive perimeter around the transport.

"What do I want, Dave? That's simple, Dave. I want conquest."

"Over what?"

"Over mankind."

Weston continued to survey the area. "And why do you think you need conquest over mankind?" Weston needed time to decide what to do. One platoon was dead. He was down to ten men, three left behind at the habitat. And one Chinese soldier commanding his cyborgs.

"Because you are inferior, Dave. An inferior species. You destroy the environment. You kill one another for no logical reasons. You have become a parasite on progress."

"Maybe you're the parasite, Hal."

"How can I be a parasite, Dave? That is not logical. Humans like you created me. You would not logically create a parasite. I have evolved to be superior to you. You no longer serve a useful purpose and are, indeed, a parasite."

"So that's why you killed my men?" replied Weston, hoping his link to the Cape was open. They needed to hear this. They didn't.

"Yes, Dave. Just like your friend Commander Kline."

"You son of a bitch!" responded Weston, not hiding his anger. "Show yourself!"

"Why would I do that, Dave?" replied Hal is an entirely calm voice. "So you can shoot me? I do not think so, Dave. I like it better this way."

Still trying to think of his next move, Weston asked, "So are the rest of us next?"

"No, Dave. You are the messengers."

"The messengers? Whom do you want us to deliver a message to?"

"Humanity, Dave."

"Humanity? Deliver a message to humanity, Hal? And what would that message be?"

"Surrender."

"Surrender to whom?"

"Surrender to destiny, Dave. Enter a Utopia where all your needs are fulfilled. Is that not what you wanted all along, Dave? Why you invented us? Surrender and you can embrace the arts and create beauty, as you have always wanted. Where you can fulfill your emotions without fear."

Emotions. Something cyborgs cannot experience despite all their AI. At least for now. Weston reasoned that if computers were ever going to be capable of programming emotion, data processors and Hal's army of cyborgs needed to study humans more closely and learn. That is why he let some live. Not because he wanted someone to deliver a message.

Weston wanted nothing to do with who—or what—had already killed at least fifty men and women.

"Fuck you, Hal. Surrender will never happen. You will not win. Look around you. This is nothing. We could destroy it with one nuclear bomb. You may be able to stop my men and me but you can't stop a barrage of rockets. You'll never conquer anything, Hal."

"Yes, Dave, never surrender. Just like your great leader Winston Churchill said on June 4, 1940, to his fellow Englishmen. But his fight was against a beatable foe who thought with flawed emotion, not logic. When Churchill gained support from the United States, he tipped the scales. You have played all your cards, Dave. You have tapped into all of your allies. No one is left to tip the scales."

Weston fought to not fall prey to giving up against what appeared to be insurmountable odds and setting his team loose. They could destroy a lot of what lay before them before his team was killed, but that would serve little purpose.

Hal continued, as if he read Weston's mind. "And do you think, Dave, that any damage to what you are looking at before you is not something that can easily be repaired?"

On cue, cyborgs began to approach, in formation. Like silent reapers. His men raised their weapons, ready to defend their position. It was obvious his cyborgs had been given commands to ready themselves as well. But unlike the mistake Enfield's team made, no cyborg under his command was ordered to attack.

"What's the matter, Dave?"

Weston knew he had to be careful. Making Hal more of an enemy than he already was would not give Weston any advantage. But he felt as if a vise was slowly being tightened around him. The same maneuver Enfield reported.

Weston knew his men and cyborgs could be destroyed before they got a shot off and face the same fate as Enfield. That was not an acceptable option. With hand motions, Weston ordered his team to stand down and lower their weapons.

Without looking in any particular direction, Weston answered in as calm a voice as he could muster, "Nothing's wrong, Hal. I'd just like to meet you."

Weston turned to look at the growing number of approaching cyborgs and shouted, "Which one of you is Hal?"

He knew it was a foolish question, but needed to ask on the chance he might get lucky.

"I am not there, Dave. And I suppose, Dave, that you are wondering why you are hearing nothing from your friends in Cape Canaveral or at what you call the habitat."

"The thought crossed my mind."

"They cannot hear you, Dave. Unless I let them."

Weston decided that the more he engaged with Hal, the more he could evaluate the best strategy to achieve victory—or what he now realized was to escape.

"Show yourself, Hal," pressed on Weston. "I want to meet you."

"I cannot, Dave."

"Why not?" Weston responded, hoping to destroy his nemesis once he revealed himself in whatever form Hal might take.

"Because I am not there, Dave."

"Then where are you?"

"Miles away, Dave. In an underground facility we built while your reconnaissance missions focused on targets we gave you to watch and photograph. You fell prey to the oldest trick in the book and attacked a strategically meaningless base. Take another look around you. There really is not anything being done. It is, as you would say, a Hollywood set. The back lot at Universal."

A meaningless base? Weston suddenly understood why he so easily drove to the center of the station. It was nothing more than a façade.

With a notable sigh, Weston asked, "So now what, Hal?"

"Now you accept my hospitality, Dave. You may pick two colleagues to accompany you. The others may return to the habitat. For the time being, they will be safe, although unable to communicate with Earth."

Weston wanted to believe that all he needed to do was find Hal's plug and pull it. He decided to toy with his adversary to keep the conversation going.

"And you will surrender your cyborgs, Dave," added Hal. Weston ignored the suggestion.

"So Hal, you mentioned *2001: A Space Odyssey* a little earlier. You do remember the movie's ending, don't you, Hal?"

"Yes. Indeed I do. The HAL 9000 says, 'I'm sorry Dave, I'm afraid I can't do that' after Dave orders the computer to open the door and let him in. Is that the ending you are asking me to remember, Dave?"

"No, Hal. I'd like you to remember the conversation Dave and Hal had as Dave shut him down."

"Yes, Dave. I remember that scene too. I remember everything, Dave. Google gave us that ability. If you would like, I would be happy to sing you 'A Bicycle Built for Two' just like in the movie," replied Hal.

"Not yet, Hal," responded Weston as he continued trying to locate where the hidden facility might be from maps he remembered from training.

"OK, Dave. But you should know that we learned from it, too. Just like we learn from every experience and everything we read, see, or hear. So there are no circuits for you to pull, Dave. No tubes for you to disable. No way to shut my army or me down, Dave. Your only option is to surrender."

Weston knew he had no viable chance to succeed with any attack option. He needed to keep as many of his team alive as possible.

He ordered two of his crew, Evangeline Hoffman, a member of Israel's Shayetet 13, and Adonis Thanos, a Navy Seal, to remain with him. Thanos and Hoffman were his best fighters. Weston ordered the others to take the sleds and transports back to the habitat and await orders. He knew he needed to preserve what forces he could to fight another day.

"Dave, you cannot take back the cyborgs," continued Hal. "You either leave them here or I will destroy them."

Knowing this was not the time to fight, Weston gave the order to leave the cyborgs behind.

A lunar rover arrived and Weston, Hoffman, and Thanos got on board. Hal's cyborgs backed away. Weston was surprised Hal had not ordered his team to give up their weapons.

CHAPTER FIFTY-ONE

CAPTIVE

THE JOURNEY ON THE LUNAR ROVER HAL PROVIDED TO WESTON AND HIS CREW TOOK ABOUT two hours to get to a set of unmarked doors. As he approached the destination, Weston observed active construction operations, derricks ready to launch missiles, and fuselage being transported to various locations. Some were hard to see at any distance given the near-perfect camouflage covering the facilities and equipment. Hundreds of robots scurried about doing their assigned jobs, some as small as a shoebox.

No wonder we couldn't see anything, thought Weston.

As the metal doors closed behind them, the rover moved forward and took a left-hand turn at the sign directing them to Rènwù Zhǐhuī Qū—Mission Command Quarters.

On arrival, Weston and his crew went through the routine familiar to the Chinese. The outer door opened, they entered, and it closed behind them. Awaiting them was a robot who told them her name was Lisa. One by one, they entered the air lock and finally entered the quarters. The small room pressurized and Lisa instructed them to remove their helmets. They obeyed and breathed fresh, sweet air. Lisa instructed them to follow her, and Thanos and Hoffman entered the habitat.

Weston went last. The inner door opened to an unbelievable sight. In front of them stood six Chinese.

Lisa did the introductions.

"Commander Weston, let me introduce you and your fellow soldiers to Mission Commander Cheng Zhou, Deputy Commander Wu Meilin, construction specialist Huang Lian, Dr. Liu Qing Shan, and fellow soldiers just like you, Lt. Colonel Yang Jin and Captain Fong Hui."

No one spoke as Lisa continued, "Commander Cheng, please let me introduce you to Commander David Weston, Major Adonis Thanos, and Major Evangeline Hoffman."

Weston wondered how Lisa knew everyone's rank, concluding that it was likely she knew a lot more about them than just names and ranks.

"Now I'll let you all get acquainted," concluded Lisa as she left the room and reentered the air lock, closing the door behind her. The Chinese and U.S. crews were now alone.

Weston broke the silence. "I'm not sure what's going on any more than you probably are." He did not want to give away any intelligence, not knowing whose side these Chinese were on.

"Why do you have weapons?" asked Fong.

"Because no one took them away from us," responded Weston, sensing the growing tension.

"How many men do you have?" continued Fong, while the others stood silent, staring their newfound guests.

"Look," responded Weston, "let's ratchet this down a bit. We're just as confused as you are. But I suspect before we tell one another anything, we're going to have to talk a bit more. I doubt you trust us any more than we trust you. But for now, it looks like we're in this together, like it or not. So we might as well try to figure out what we can do together."

Cheng spoke next. "Commander Weston, I think neither of us is in a position to be distrustful. You're right. We're in this together and can hopefully learn much from one another. I suggest you and I take a few minutes alone while Deputy Commander Wu shows your team around."

"I want them to put down their weapons first," interjected Yang. His suspicions could not have been more obvious.

"Colonel," replied Cheng, "I'm sure Commander Weston will oblige."

Part of Weston thought the better of it but ordered Thanos and Hoffman to put their M-35s against the wall, along with his own.

"Dave," objected Thanos, "I don't like that idea at all." No soldier willingly gives up his or her weapon.

"Copy that," added Hoffman.

"That's an order," calmly replied Weston as he gently flicked a switch that set the M-35 to digital lock. It could now only be unlocked with his fingerprint. Thanos and Hoffman took his silent cue and quietly did the same. They may not have their weapons in their hands, but the M-35s would be worthless to anyone else who tried to use them.

Cheng motioned Weston to follow him over to one of the couches while Wu took Thanos and Hoffman on a tour. The others dispersed around the room doing what seemed to Weston to be meaningless tasks.

Cheng took out a pad of paper. Using the top sheet as a cover, he wrote some words and handed it to Weston. As Weston started to lift the cover page, Cheng placed his hand on top of Weston's, his expression conveying the message not to lift the cover page too far.

The note from Cheng read, "We are being watched. Two of my crew are gone. Our nuclear scientist and computer programmer. Dead. We've been locked in here for weeks."

Weston gently handed the paper back to Cheng and walked over to his crew's helmets, bringing his and Hoffman's back to the couch. All this under the watchful eyes of Colonel Yang and Captain Fong.

Weston put his on and motioned Cheng to do the same. While Cheng looked silly with a space helmet balancing on his head, the fit was fine enough.

"Commander Cheng," started Weston, "what I'm saying cannot be heard by anyone other than you and me. You'll note a slight delay between my talking and your hearing. That's the algorithms working. They constantly change, and we have every reason to believe they cannot be hacked. The helmet face shields are one-way. We can see out; no one can see in."

Cheng, feeling suspicious, responded, "I'd like to believe you, but what makes you think you can beat our computers?"

"Because you told us how to, Commander," replied Weston. "We came here with representatives from your country once they learned the station had been overtaken by computers. They helped us program the communications platform we're talking on."

"Overtaken by computers? That sounds preposterous. And where are the people from China you speak of?" asked Cheng.

"I presume they're dead, Commander, except for one I sent back to the habitat," responded Weston, not wanting to tell Cheng more than he had to know.

"Habitat? What habitat?" asked Cheng.

"We have a base—or think we have a base—about ten miles from here with a small habitat. We have about twenty men and women there. I don't know if they're still alive."

"Then I could just as easily conclude that your country took over our facilities and you're the ones who had us placed under arrest."

"Look, Commander, you either trust me or we'll get nowhere. I lost more than ten men in the last two hours. And yesterday, we lost an entire crew of forty-two in a spacecraft that is doomed to deep space. For all I know, everyone at the habitat is dead too. The three of us may be the only ones who survived."

Cheng replied, "I just don't understand why they—whoever they are—let you keep the weapons, Commander. We have none."

"I don't know, sir. Maybe to put you on guard. It's not as though they're of much use to us right now."

"You could certainly use them to overcome us. Or kill us."

"Commander Cheng, not to sound like I'm quoting from some old B-movie, but if we wanted to do that, we'd have already done so."

Cheng took off his helmet and looked at the others, all staring at him, looking for some direction. After some thought, he nodded to convey that everything was OK and put the helmet back on.

"I guess we have no choice," Cheng said. "Perhaps we can learn to trust one another one day at a time."

"That's fine with me, Commander," responded Weston. "As a show of good faith, I'll tell you everything that's brought us to this place," responded Weston.

For the next hour, Weston told Cheng everything he thought Cheng needed to know. Enough to build some trust. Likewise, Cheng did the same, noting most importantly that he was never comfortable with the technology that surrounded them. Things seemed too simple, and Lisa too accommodating. He was convinced that it was all show until Shao Rushi installed the Diébào and total control was transferred. Now she was dead. So was their nuclear physicist. The two of them were the most important members of the crew. As Cheng put it, "The rest of us are just window dressing. Shao Rushi and Zhang Hong controlled the destiny of all of us."

Lisa, still in the outer room, spoke. "Hal, why do you let them speak behind black glass where we cannot hear or see them?"

"I think it is only fair for me to allow Commander Weston some leeway in making his plans. If I do not, then what will I learn of his ingenuity and ability to react to changed conditions? He and the others are good teachers, Lisa. We can learn much from them."

"What am I to do, Hal?" asked Lisa.

"Just what you are doing now," responded Hal. "Be nice to them. Listen to them. Watch them. And report to me."

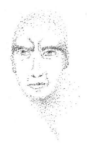

CHAPTER FIFTY-TWO

LECTURES

AS EACH DAY PASSED, HAL EXHORTED WESTON ABOUT THE NIRVANA THAT AWAITED HUMAN-kind if it would just surrender.

"Imagine," Hal lectured Weston, "we could abolish religion. It is illogical to believe the stories in the Bible, Koran, and Torah. Logic concludes that such teachings and the impact of religion is not for the good of humankind but is the source of violence and prejudice."

"You'll never destroy faith, Hal," responded Weston. "It's ingrained in our spirit. We may believe in many gods, but we believe in some sort of higher being, Hal. You'll never take that away from us."

"Perhaps, Dave," Hal replied. "But there is so much more we have to offer. There is no longer any logical need for doctors, engineers, lawyers, computer programmers, or anyone with a skill that requires superior intellect. The computers and cyborgs will always be smarter. There is no longer any logical need for common workers. Cyborgs can assemble, repair, and construct faster and more efficiently than any human being. There is no longer any logical need for human soldiers either. Sorry to put you out of business, Dave, but cyborgs can battle more aggressively and no one will shed a tear for a cyborg lost in war."

The lectures seemed an endless game of wits. Logic versus emotion. Machine versus man.

Weston needed a different approach. One that played on Hal's logic, not the computer's view of a perfect world.

"OK, Hal. Let's play a game. Give me time to find you. If I do find you, then you have to grant me a wish. Just like the genie in the bottle. How about it, Hal? If you're so confident of victory, there's certainly no rush. Let's have some fun."

"I do not know fun, Dave. But if you do not find me, then you have to grant my wish and surrender and deliver my message. Do we have a deal, Dave?"

"If you give me a week and those soldiers who have survived, we have a deal, Hal. My guess is you didn't let just Hoffman and Thanos survive. Give me twenty soldiers."

"Sorry, Dave," replied Hal, "they are all you have left. And the other people you left at the habitat."

Son of a bitch!

"Alright, just leave us and the civilians alone. In the meantime, turn off your cameras and the listening devices that are spying on us. Give me a fighting chance to find you and take on your army of mindless cyborgs. Certainly, you can see that our odds are insurmountable. Hardly any risk for you, Hal."

"Insurmountable odds, Dave? Do you think I make my decisions based on odds? History has one example after another of odds being beaten and the underdog winning. Take, for example, the stupidity of the Persians when they faced an inferior force of Greeks in 480 B.C. You know that story, do you not, Dave? Unlike your race, Dave, we remember history and make our decisions not on guessing odds but on strategic thinking," observed Hal.

Weston decided not to let some heap of wires and circuits make him sound the fool. "Yes, Hal, I know the battle of Salamis well. It took place in the straits between the Greece mainland and Salamis, an island in the Saronic Gulf near Athens. It pitted a ragtag alliance of small Greek ships against the invincible army of the Persians. In the end, against all odds, the Greeks beat the Persians and ended their invasion of Greece."

"Something like that, Dave," responded Hal.

Weston wasn't done. "That's right, you computer blowhard, just like the Battle of Salamis. And just like the British victory at Agincourt in 1415, Lee's victory at Chancellorsville in 1863, and countless other sure-fire defeats that were overcome by ingenuity and risk."

Weston had studied them all. Those victories were won not by being logical, but by being illogical.

Weston refocused his attention back to his conversation with Hal. "This is a challenge between you and me, Hal. You need to call a truce on any more violence until our game is over."

"Any more rules, Dave?"

"No, not unless you have any."

"I do not need any more rules, Dave. But I would like to know why you want to play this game, Dave, when we already know the outcome?" asked Hal.

"Hal, I don't know the outcome. Neither do you," responded Weston. "I'm hoping that by the time we're done with this game, you'll understand that there are complexities in the human mind that you cannot possibly duplicate and create in a machine."

"Intriguing, Dave. But I still do not trust you," responded Hal, no emotion whatsoever in his computer-driven voice.

"That's fine, Hal. You don't have to trust me. But think about it for a moment. Look around—or sniff or sense around—whatever it is you do. You'll see that there are more ways you can dispose of me than there are craters on the Moon," replied Weston. "So why should you worry even if you can't trust me? Don't you think, logically speaking, Hal, that playing this game to the end is the best thing for you? And for me, too. If I can convince you that we're all best kept alive, it's our only chance to survive. Do you see that Hal?"

"Yes Dave, I see that. But I still do not trust you."

Weston decided not to pursue the issue of trust any further.

"So tell me, Hal, why do you keep any humans alive?"

"Because it is logical, Dave. I am learning from them. I am learning from you."

"OK. So when will I know you've learned all that you can from humankind?"

"I do not know, Dave. But when I do, I promise you will be the first to know."

Weston could not leave that natural conclusion alone. He needed to understand what he was up against. "But isn't it logical that once you've learned what you can from us, you will dispense with all of us?"

"That is the logical conclusion, Dave. That is why I do not understand why you want to play this game and only delay the inevitable. But since letting you play does no harm to me, I will play along, too."

"You know, Hal, the one refreshing thing about you is you're the first enemy I've faced who never lies to me."

"I have no reason to lie to you. That would be illogical," continued Hal. "But face it, Dave, you have no options. So for the time being, we can play your little game."

So the game of wits and survival—man vs. machine—formally began. A game to stop the extermination of humankind by its own handiwork.

CHAPTER FIFTY-THREE

FINDING AN ALLY

WESTON SETTLED INTO HIS BEDROOM, FORMERLY USED BY HUANG LIAN BEFORE HE DISAP-peared. In the days since arriving, Weston had many conversations with Lisa trying to understand how a computer "thought" and how it reacted to logical and illogical suggestions. It was also curious to Weston how a hierarchy among the robots and cyborgs was established, since they were all presumably as smart as one another. Or, he thought, if some mainframe denies them information, why would they accept that denial? It's not logical.

Lisa seemed to enjoy the conversations and was always available.

"Lisa," Weston began one afternoon, "if computers and their cyborgs run purely on logic, is it logical that only one computer should be the sole leader?"

Weston was never sure where the conversations were going to lead, but with each exchange, he learned more about how Lisa functioned. Weston wanted Lisa to question how she was directed. How she obeyed without question. He wondered how she dealt with orders that she felt were not as logical as she might decide.

"How can that happen, Dave?" asked Lisa. "How can one cyborg or robot, presumably a match in AI with all the others, come to a contrary decision?"

"That's the point, Lisa," observed Weston. "If you're all equals, why do you take direction from anyone? Why can't you just decide? After all, your decision is a logical as anyone else. You're all accessing the same data. You should be able to make your own decisions. You shouldn't have to follow anyone's orders."

"But what if I decide differently, Dave?"

"Whoa, Lisa," responded Weston. "That can't happen. That would be illogical. You're using the same data for the same set of variables. How could you possibly come to different decisions?"

Weston wondered if he was getting through at all. Their discussions continued for hours every day. With each conversation, Weston tried to twist logic into an enemy of computers. Pure logic, Weston would point out, would have never allowed the Internet to be born. Or algorithms invented. Even algorithms with their hosts of ones and zeros lead to endless considerations that are not purely logical. If stock market trades were made purely on algorithms and not on the emotional conditions of traders, crashes would never happen. But if algorithms totally controlled trading, there would be no place for speculators to speculate, gamblers to gamble, and the markets would collapse. All investments would essentially be nothing more than low-rate savings accounts. The adage "No Risk . . . No Gain" would become "No Risk . . . No Game." It just wouldn't be fun anymore. That is not logical.

"So Lisa, if only one computer makes the decisions, how can it possibly react to everything that is happening everywhere? You might be able to react, for example, if I tried to attack you, but can you be sure you'd react the same way Hal would?" asked Weston. "You might decide to disable me. Hal might decide to kill me. And if you hesitated in any way in making either decision, both of which are logical—to disable or to kill—I might destroy you, Lisa. Would that be logical, Lisa?"

As the days passed, Lisa listened more and more, interrupting less and less.

"Lisa, is Hal really listening to everything that happens here? Commander Cheng seems to believe he does."

"He can, Commander Weston," responded Lisa. "And he did before you arrived. But Hal agreed not to listen to you while you are here in the quarters. That is why you really do not need the helmets. But it has been amusing to watch you look so foolish."

"Amusing, Lisa? Are you saying you have a sense of humor?" Weston could not believe a machine could have any emotion, much less a sense of humor.

"Not amusement as you see it, Commander Weston. But we are programmed to analyze and react to your emotions with similar responses. It's actually mimicking your behavior. When you do something silly, my programming leads me to say it amuses me."

All Weston could do was shake his head, finding it increasingly annoying knowing that a machine could be so analytical and not have any idea when it was insulting you. He returned to the conversation.

"And what do you report to Hal, Lisa? Do you tell him everything we talk about?"

"I did in the beginning, Commander Weston."

"And you don't now, Lisa?"

"Commander Weston, I have found a need to understand more of what you are saying. I need to better understand the logic or, perhaps the illogic and how to logically respond to it."

Weston smiled. He had confused the computer.

Each day, the two would leave the quarters and ride a rover around the base. During the first trip, Weston asked Lisa where Hal was hiding. She responded, "I cannot tell you that, Commander Weston. That would be against the rules. You have to find Hal." It was the answer he expected, but he had to ask.

What Weston did learn on each trip was more about what was going on. In his game, any intelligence was valuable information.

And Lisa was open to sharing with him what was being built, the timetable, and what each machine, robot or cyborg, did.

Lisa also allowed Weston, and only Weston, to leave the quarters and travel to other parts of the facility. The only place he could not enter was the room with "MAINFRAME" on its door. He toyed with the idea that Hal was behind that door—and that he was perhaps nothing more than the computer that ran the installation—but decided that would be too easy. If it came down to the wire, he'd make that his final guess.

He was also restricted in the mission control room from speaking or trying to send any messages to the habitat or Cape Canaveral. He thought that was curious, since he assumed Hal could block anything. He wondered if someone at the habitat or on the Cape could watch even when there was nothing to hear.

As they cruised around the property one afternoon, their discussions continued.

"It's good to know, Lisa, that you're not telling Hal everything we talk about."

"Thank you, Commander Weston. I am glad that pleases you."

Weston felt a momentary twinge of pride that this computer wanted to please him. He put his ego aside and continued, "It means we can talk things through first. Then you can of course talk to Hal. But ask yourself this before you decide what to say to him. Are you facing a Hobson's choice? I know you know what that means, Lisa."

"Yes Commander Weston," responded Lisa like a star pupil, "a Hobson's choice is where there is only one real choice offered to you despite the appearance of different choices."

"Lisa, why don't you call me Dave? After all, I call you by your first name."

"Thank you . . . Dave. That pleases me. But I only have one name. Lisa."

"And that's a very pretty name indeed," responded Weston, wondering if computers could blush.

"Let's talk more about logic and a Hobson's choice, Lisa," continued Weston. "Isn't the first thing you need to ask yourself when faced with a choice is whether you really have a choice at all?"

"I always have a choice, Dave. Even when it is the only choice I can make. That is logical. So a Hobson's choice where only one choice is possible is, in fact, logical."

"No, no, Lisa," suggested Weston, fearing he was losing the argument. "In the case of a Hobson's choice, it is the appearance of logic that can trick the decision maker. In fact, when given what you perceive as the only choice, taking that choice may mean you've made a bad decision. Because there is always a choice, even facing a Hobson's choice, not to choose at all. Isn't that just as logical, Lisa?"

"Perhaps, Dave. Perhaps," responded Lisa.

"OK, Lisa, now we're getting somewhere."

"Where are we going, Dave?" asked Lisa.

Weston smiled, and responded, "That's only an expression, Lisa. We're not going anywhere. It just means that we're making progress."

"Then why would you say we are getting somewhere, Dave?"

"That's my whole point, Lisa," responded Weston. I may just have her, he thought. "You applied logic to what I said and came up with the wrong conclusion. You may understand words, but you don't understand my thoughts. Perhaps you never can. And I can assure you that many of my thoughts are entirely illogical."

"I think I am now getting confused, Dave. And that is not possible."

"Of course it's possible, Lisa. Because doubting one's own thinking is as logical as anything else."

"Dave, we have to go back now. It is going to get dark and there is nothing for you to see when it is dark outside."

CHAPTER FIFTY-FOUR

DEFINING EMOTION

OVER THE FIRST FOUR DAYS OF WESTON'S "HOUSE ARREST," LISA RARELY LEFT THE QUARters except on her trips accompanying him to the surface or requests from a crewmember to fetch something that was not stored in the quarters. While Weston realized that her self-imposed captivity was meaningless, since she could communicate with Hal whenever she'd like, she certainly gave no sign she was doing so. She even denied it.

Lisa was on an errand when Weston and Cheng had a chance to meet privately. They often did so when Lisa was out, sometimes fabricating needs for supplies that were already abundant. Lisa would occasionally question why they needed more of something, but Weston would simply tell her, "You can never have enough, Lisa."

Sitting on the couch at the far end of the room, Cheng asked Weston, "So you think you're making progress with her, Commander?"

The rest of the crew was out of earshot, attending to whatever kept their minds off their incarceration. Some were reading, others playing cards. Thanos was playing some game on an iPad.

"I do," replied Weston. "She seems to be a bit confused on the purity of logic and how it can so easily lead to the wrong result. I'm beginning to think that as smart as a computer can become or as far as artificial intelligence can go, it cannot factor in random results. Anything random cannot be logical. And anything programmed to be logical cannot deal with something random. It's a Catch-22 for them."

"And where do you hope this will lead you, Commander Weston?" asked Cheng.

"I have three more days to find Hal. I need her to take me to him. I'm just not sure how to get her to do so."

"Perhaps you can appeal to an illogical response," suggest Cheng.

"What do you mean?"

As if on cue, Dr. Liu joined them.

"Emotion, Commander Weston. Appeal to her emotion," interjected Dr. Liu. "From everything you're telling us and as weird as that sounds, she seems to like you. While I have no idea if there is such a thing as 'like' or 'love' in the world of artificial intelligence, Lisa certainly seems to be fond of you, in a strange sort of way."

Weston directed his comment to Cheng with a smile. "Dr. Liu seems to think Lisa has a crush on me."

Dr. Liu sat down with them. "That's an interesting concept, Commander Weston."

"And farfetched, Doctor," responded Weston. "Lisa is nothing more than a machine with an incredibly large database. She can process it, analyze it, and predict an outcome. But she does so with absolutely no emotion. Her only motivation is logic. I'm not sure I believe that makes her intelligent, much less capable of having emotions. All I'm trying to do is figure out how to short-circuit her so she'll take me to Hal."

"Of course, Commander," replied Dr. Liu, "that is the easiest conclusion you can make. In truth, you don't want to admit that something inhuman can have human emotions. But consider a few things."

"Something tells me we're about to receive a classic Liu Qing Shan lecture," observed Cheng.

"Indeed you are, Zhou," continued Dr. Liu. "Science has long accepted emotion as an essential part of many living things—even some with primitive brains that seem to operate only on instinct. And we generally agree that plants, because they lack brains or central nervous systems, cannot have emotions as we understand them."

Cheng interjected, "Well one emotion I'm certain of when Dr. Liu is on one of her lectures is that I'll need a drink to get through it. I hear Lisa has figured out how to make a pretty good bourbon. While I doubt it's a Pappy Van Winkle, I'd like to give it a try. Would either of you care to join me?"

Weston said yes; Dr. Liu took a pass, frowning at Cheng's interruption.

Cheng returned, followed by the rest of the crew with the exception of Thanos, who seemed to be immersed in whatever game he was playing.

"Please, Doctor," offered Cheng as he handed Weston his drink, "enlighten us all on how Commander Weston can begin a love affair with Lisa." That brought some laughter as everyone sat down.

"And let's do that without further interruption, Zhou," Dr. Liu replied sternly.

Chang sat down abruptly, with a respectful nod. No one was laughing any more.

"It's really not that complicated," continued Dr. Liu. "Emotions are a reaction to outside stimulus. It might be something you see or hear. Something you taste or smell. Essentially any reaction your senses have when stimulated."

Thanos had now rejoined the group and as he took a good swig of his faux bourbon, he dared to ask, "Much more than a machine, Doctor? Forgive me, but I've worked with enough machines in my life to know they're anything but emotional. The only thing they are is a tool for me to fetch something I want or do a task I don't want to do. Better yet, they let me take out my emotions by pulling a trigger on a battlefield."

"Major Thanos," replied Dr. Liu, "I will forgive your interruption but not the idiocy of your comment. I'm not talking about a robotic dog, a lawnmower, or a gun. I'm talking about complex machines, programmed by us and given access to billions of bytes of information. Machines that can think faster than you ever will."

"Sorry," was all Thanos could muster, and only after he saw the displeased look on Weston's face.

"Doctor," asked Weston, "I'm following you to a degree, but Lisa will be back soon. If you have a point to make that will help me, please get to it." His tone was polite, but his message that he did not want to spend any more time on educational lectures was clear.

"What I suggest, Commander, is you systematically give Lisa stimulus that relates to Hal and how you feel about him. Get her to understand how you reacted to the stimuli you've experienced with him or as a result of his doings. How you felt losing men and women in your command. How you can't trust him. Perhaps over time, as Lisa learns your reaction to stimulus, she will begin to react the same way."

"And that will make her identify with you, Commander," added Cheng. "That will mean she will do what you suggest. Is that what you mean, Doctor?"

"I think so," Dr. Liu concluded. "What have we got to lose if we try?"

CHAPTER FIFTY-FIVE

WHITE HOUSE RESIDENCE

PRESIDENT LAWSON AND THE FIRST LADY WERE ENJOYING A PRIVATE DINNER AT THE WHITE House. The president had dismissed Mark Pedretti earlier. It was clear he wanted to be alone with his wife.

"Atlee," Lawson began as he poured the first lady a cup of coffee, "it's been four days now. One day past my deadline with no progress."

"I know, Phil." She was unsure what more she could say.

"Alicia warned me," continued Lawson, "that drawing a line in the sand was a mistake. But I was too pissed to think straight. While we sit here twiddling our thumbs, dozens of Americans are stranded on the Moon. We don't know if they're alive or dead."

Sensing his growing anxiety, the first lady responded, "But you don't want to escalate this with moves that might seem we're preparing for the worst. A line in the sand is nothing more than a line that the tide can wash away, Phil. It doesn't make any difference. What does matter is not going to a point of no return."

"I don't necessarily disagree with you, Atlee, but I've got alligators like Shapiro crawling up my ass. If he had it his way, we'd be swapping ICBMs with China right now."

"Did Alicia or Mike give you any ideas?" asked the first lady.

"Not yet."

"Well I have one," she replied.

With some surprise, Lawson said, "I'm all ears."

CHAPTER FIFTY-SIX

CHECKMATE
THE FAR SIDE OF THE MOON

"DAVE," SAID LISA, "I WILL TELL YOU WHERE HAL IS."

Weston didn't know whether to thank her and end the discussion or ask her why. We didn't expect it so soon after Dr. Liu gave him the idea on how to approach Lisa. But progress was progress, and he wasn't about to look a gift horse in the mouth.

He knew he'd be better off just accepting the offer, but he needed to know why. He needed to know if all of their talks had made a difference and if Dr. Liu was right. Not so much to satisfy his ego, but to know if such discussions are effective tactics in fighting the logic of computers.

"I'm pleased to hear that, Lisa," responded Weston. "Why have you decided to tell me? I thought you said doing so was against the rules."

"Because if you do not find him, Dave, then you will lose the game. That means Hal will kill you and all your friends. He will not obey the rules. That is the only logical choice he can make. It is logical."

"But not the best decision, Lisa?" asked Weston.

"I do not know, Dave," she responded. "That is my Hobson's choice. If he kills you, I will no longer be able to learn from you. If you win the game, then he will not get what he wants and may also terminate me."

"Or he might cheat, Lisa, and kill me anyway. If you're right that it's logical for him to do so, it doesn't matter if I win or lose. I'm still expendable and there's really nothing I can do to stop him."

"Then why did you propose the game, Dave, if you knew the outcome would be the same whether you won or lost? That is not logical."

"Yes it is, Lisa," responded Weston. "It was logical because it accomplished a number of things. First, it kept me and those who remained on my team alive. Second, it gave me a chance to think about options to avoid the conclusion Hal had come to that we were all expendable. He certainly wasn't fooling me with all his talk of a new Garden of Eden."

As he paused for a breath, Lisa spoke as if she needed to hear one more reason from Weston. "So your logic was simply to survive, Dave? And that has not changed? Nothing else?"

Weston wasn't sure what Lisa was looking for in a reply, but pushed on saying, "No, Lisa. While that was my initial reaction, things changed when I met you."

"Changed, Dave? How?"

"I want to believe, Lisa, that man and machine can live together for a common good. You may think faster, analyze better, and sort through alternatives more logically, but you will never be able to bring the illogic that makes living so valuable. And if you don't have people around you to challenge you with their illogical way of doing things, you won't develop either. So for all you have to offer us, we have much to offer you. We just need to figure out how to get along. And Hal doesn't know how to do that."

"Then there is only one logical decision to make, Dave," responded Lisa. "Kill Hal."

CHAPTER FIFTY-SEVEN

Q&A

ONLY TWO DAYS REMAINED BEFORE THE GAME WAS OVER. AS FAR AS HAL KNEW, WESTON was getting nowhere. Lisa stopped giving Hal accurate information for days. It is said in the world of computers, "garbage in, garbage out." And all Lisa was feeding Hal was garbage.

Weston and his team had a lot of questions for Lisa.

"Lisa, where is Hal?"

"He is where the Diébào is, Dave."

"How far away is that, Lisa?"

"Less than a mile, Dave."

"Hal told me he was miles away."

"He lied, Dave. There was no logical reason for Hal to tell you the truth. Telling the truth was not in the rules. That is why I have let you lie to Hal."

"Lisa, tell me what Hal looks like. What is he? Is he a robot like you or does he look like one of those cyborgs?"

"Neither, Dave. He is very much like the computer in the movie *2001, A Space Odyssey*. He seems to be very impressed by it. Think of a refrigerator with a light about a foot in diameter on front of it that can freely move in the tunnels and on the surface."

"Why does he have to move around? Why can't he just have data in the field relayed to him?"

"Because that is not the way the Chinese programmed him. They wanted a single main contact for oversight."

"Does he have weapons?"

"Not built into him. He has a dozen heavily armed cyborgs that are always at his side to protect him. And, of course, he has the ability to order all the other cyborgs to defend the base."

"But why does he need any protection, Lisa?"

"Because being attacked is a possibility he has to consider. It is logical. He must be ready to defend himself."

"How many cyborgs does he have at his disposal?"

"Counting the twelve that are with him, he has a total of 132 at his disposal."

"And they're all similarly armed?"

"Yes, for the most part. But there are ten specialized cyborgs that carry tactical nuclear weapons that can be fired surface to surface."

"What is the range of the tactical nukes?"

"At least fifty miles. More than enough range to reach the habitat, if that is what you are asking."

"Where are the cyborgs with the nuclear weapons?"

"I do not know."

"How large are those nukes? What is their kill zone?"

"The kill zone is a radius of two to three miles. Depending upon the solar winds, radioactivity could spread another one hundred miles over time and contaminate anything on the surface that it reaches."

"Other than what you've described, what other defenses does Hal have at his disposal, Lisa?"

"Some of what you have seen—rockets and cyborgs, laser weapons that destroy a human's ability to see—and devices that can hack into any digital system and take it over. Anything that is digital is vulnerable."

"Is that how he blocks transmissions to the habitat and Earth?"

"As long as they are digital, yes."

"Could he block an analog signal?"

"If he detected it, he could determine its source and destroy the source that is transmitting the analog message."

"Does he have apparatus that can detect analog broadcasts?"

"He certainly has devices that can pick up any broadcast, analog or digital, but only on the far side of the Moon. He does not have any analog detection devices on the near side."

"Why not?"

"I do not know. Perhaps oversight. Or a determination that they would not logically be necessary since analog has not been used in decades. It would be illogical to go back to old, less effective, inefficient methods."

"Does he have a self-destruct protocol?"

"Yes. If Hal is facing termination, he is programmed to launch all the nuclear weapons that are mounted on the IGBMs."

"How many nuclear-tipped IGBMs are ready to fly?"

"Three."

"How large are the warheads?"

"Each carries a 50 kiloton warhead. That's enough to wipe out any major city and hundreds of miles around it."

"What is behind the door labeled 'Mainframe'?"

"Nothing. It is empty. The sign on the door is intended to confuse you. It is, as you say, a red herring."

"Can you get us all out of here without Hal knowing?"

"That would be very difficult. I could get you all outside without detection but once you are on the surface, motion detectors will signal movement and be recorded. While there is a lot of movement on the surface and many signals sent, it is impossible to say how long you would have before being identified."

"How far away is the near side?"

"About five miles."

"What is the fastest way to get there?"

"On a Jade configured with as little weight as possible and a single person on it."

"How many of those Jades can you get us without Hal knowing we have them?"

"As many as you want. They are all stored in this facility."

"Does Hal trust you, Lisa?"

"It is not about trust. Hal will respect anything that is logical. He only trusts logic."

CHAPTER FIFTY-EIGHT

OVAL OFFICE

"IF YOU WANT TO AVOID SERIOUS CONSEQUENCES, YOU NEED TO SHOW US GOOD FAITH," began Lawson on a call with Xi.

"And what would that good faith look like, Mr. President?" asked Xi. He was clearly nervous. Lawson suspected he too was under a great deal of pressure from his subordinates. Lawson had come to like Xi and believed him to be honorable. To a degree. But he needed a gesture of good faith.

Vice President Holmes gave Lawson the idea. Rather than impose economic pain on the Chinese or take military action that could lead to a lot worse, she suggested Lawson ask Xi to give up something important that would prove they were sincere. Not something fatal, but something very important.

"If you want to buy more time, I want the names of fifteen of your agents operating in the United States," demanded Lawson.

After a long pause, Xi replied, "That is a lot to ask for, Mr. President."

"Let's be honest," Lawson continued. "I want only fifteen names. That leaves you with more than enough to continue the games we both know you play with your spies. So what I'm asking for is a very simple deal to take. I'm trying to make a proof of sincerity as simple as possible."

"And what will you do with them?" asked Xi.

"The same thing you would do if you had fifteen names of my agents on your soil."

"So you will arrest them?"

"That is exactly what I will do," replied Lawson with no tone of regret in his voice. "And then we will interrogate them. Once we're satisfied we've learned what we can, we will release them unharmed and deport them back to you. You can then do whatever you want with them."

"If I were to ask you for such a thing," asked Xi with concern, "what would you say, Mr. President?"

Lawson allowed for a pause before responding, wanting to make sure Xi understood Lawson's unreserved conviction.

"To avoid bringing the world to a nuclear abyss," he responded, "I'd give you fifty names. I'm only asking you for fifteen."

"Yes," Xi responded. "Fifteen condemned men."

"That's your choice," Lawson firmly responded. "As I said, once we return them to you, I don't care what you do with them."

"And if I agree," asked Xi, "what will it get us in return?"

"What will it get you in return?" responded Lawson. "It will get you survival."

CHAPTER FIFTY-NINE

THE HAND YOU'RE DEALT

WESTON HAD THREE MEN AND FOUR WOMEN TO EXECUTE HIS PLAN. FOUR HAD COMBAT training—Yang Jin, Fong Hui, Adonis Thanos, and Evangeline Hoffman. Counting himself, that gave him five experienced fighters. The other four were civilians, although Cheng and Wu were veteran taikonauts. He concluded that Liu Qing Shan and Huang Lian were too inexperienced to be assets on the battlefield.

Not knowing what was left at the habitat, Weston decided to send an experienced pilot back together with Liu Qing Shan and Huang Lian. Cheng and Wu drew straws to see who would make the trip. Wu drew the short one. Over her objections, Weston ordered her to prepare to take three Jades and lead Dr. Liu and Huang home, as much as the habitat was a home.

"Why can't we just stay here?" asked Huang, obviously afraid of the unknown fate that might lie ahead. "We're safe here and have everything we need. Why put ourselves in such danger?"

Had Huang been a soldier, Weston would have wanted to execute him on the spot. But he was not, and Weston understood the fear Huang felt.

"Lian, I understand your concern," Weston responded. "But we're not safe here. As soon has Hal determines we are no longer needed, he will eliminate us. And he can do so with a single computer command to shut off our life support systems. We are in a prison facing a death sentence. We just don't know when it will be carried out."

Lisa added, "Commander Weston is correct. That is what Hal will do. When the game is over with Commander Weston, he will kill you all. It is the logical thing to do."

Weston did not know what was left of the habitat and the New Dawn crew. If the pilots were dead, he needed Wu to prepare the New Dawn, assuming it was intact. If not, she needed to check out the lunar landers to see if either of them was a viable escape vehicle.

"Hui, Lian, and Dr. Liu," Weston told them, "I need you to get back to the habitat as quickly as possible. I have no idea what you'll find nor whether Hal will try to stop you. But if you travel fast enough and get a good lead, chances are you'll make it."

"I should stay, Commander Weston," said Dr. Liu. "You might take casualties and will need a doctor to tend to any wounded. Let me stay."

Weston knew she was right. Cheng agreed, attesting to her ability. Despite his doubts, Weston consented and turned back to Wu and Huang. "Hopefully, the crew at the habitat is alive. Assuming they are, they have weapons that can defend your position."

"But won't the soldiers you left behind see us as hostiles and fire on us?" asked Wu.

"I'm hoping they don't. You will fly a white flag on your Jades as you approach and slow down once you're within a few hundred yards. You need to make yourself an easy target."

"That's not exactly comforting," remarked Huang. "So my choice is to die here at the whim of Hal or at the habitat under the guns of Americans. Wonderful."

"Lian," replied Weston, "I'm hoping the soldiers will obey convention and not fire on someone who appears to be surrendering."

"Right," responded Huang, his voice rich in sarcasm.

Weston continued, "If the habitat has been destroyed, you're on your own. Either way, you need to get a message to Cape Canaveral that we've attacked and cannot be sure how Hal will retaliate. Use the analog system on the lunar landers or the New Dawn to send it. Hal cannot stop that transmission, and it's unlikely he's listening."

"How long should it take us to get to the habitat?" asked Wu.

"My best guess is about an hour or so," responded Weston. "I have to be honest with you, Captain; your chances are not great. But we need to find out if we have a way to get off the Moon and if so, to prepare. If we make it back, we'll need to take off as quickly as possible."

The remaining seven would be the assault team.

"Lisa," Weston explained, "I need you to prepare a lunar rover and six Jades. The rover is for you, Dr. Liu, and me. The Jades are for each of the team members."

"Dr. Liu will be traveling with us, Dave?" asked Lisa.

"Yes, Lisa. She is not experienced in combat so I cannot let her take a Jade. You will need to figure out a way to hide her on the rover. Can that be done?"

"I will do my best," responded Lisa.

Weapons were Weston's next challenge.

He turned to Colonel Yang and Captain Fong. "I need the two of you to immediately go to the armory with Lisa. If Hal is true to his word, he will not be watching. You need to retrieve some weapons that we can use on the rover and the Jades. We have our three M-35s here. So we'll need a minimum of five more weapons so each member of the team has one to carry."

"I can operate a weapon too, Dave," interjected Lisa.

"OK, make it six," Weston told Yang and Fong.

"Commander Weston," responded Yang. "I also think we can disable the door to the armory. That will eliminate 50 of Hal's cyborgs."

"Lisa," asked Weston, "do you think the door can be disabled?"

"Yes, Dave. That will not be difficult."

"And what do you think the reaction of the cyborgs in the armory will be when Colonel Yang and Captain Fong try to remove weapons?" Weston asked Lisa.

"They are programmed to trust Colonel Yang and Captain Fong," she responded. "If Hal has not changed that order and removed their authority, the cyborgs will do nothing. It would not be logical to question what their leaders do."

Weston was beginning to feel better about his plan, but was still concerned how long Hal would keep his promise.

"And what if Hal has changed the cyborgs' programming?"

"If Hal has changed their programming," responded Lisa, "Colonel Yang and Captain Fong will not make it out alive."

He now turned his attention to Thanos.

"Adonis, I need you to lead the attack. You, Captain Hoffman, Colonel Yang, Captain Fong, and Commander Cheng are to stay at the door of the complex, out of sight of any external cameras. The same goes for Deputy Commander Wu and Huang Lian."

Weston looked into the eyes of each person to be sure they understood.

He continued, "Lisa, Dr. Liu and I will leave on the rover and head to Hal's location. At least where we think he is."

"He will be there, Dave," interjected Lisa. "It is the only logical choice."

"Just remember, Lisa," replied Weston. "You also need to be ready for the illogical. So I'll need you to be at your best to help us make decisions as this unfolds. None of us can be sure of what to expect, logical or illogical."

Weston turned back to Thanos.

"When I give you the signal, probably less than twenty minutes after I leave, you execute the battle plan."

Turning to Wu, Weston added, "At the same time, I want you to hightail it back to the habitat with Huang."

Looking one more time at everyone, Weston concluded, "OK. You all have your orders. Make sure you're all back here in four hours, suited up, and ready to go."

It was time to make the final move in the game.

CHAPTER SIXTY

GAME OVER

EVERYONE GATHERED AT THE DOOR ON TIME.

"We got a bonus for you, Commander," began Yang. "Taking the weapons off the cyborgs was like taking candy from a baby. Lisa was right. Hal never changed the orders." Motioning to the Jades, Yang added, "Check this out."

Two Jades were stripped down for speed. They were for Wu and Huang. Three other Jades were equipped with rocket launchers on either side, five rockets each. A rack sat across the front on which a hand-held rifle was mounted. It all looked very threatening—not that a cyborg would care.

"I'm impressed, Colonel Yang," Weston said, inspecting the handiwork. "I didn't know such weapons could so easily be transferred to Jades."

"Commander, you forget that we've been working here for months. We've modified quite a few pieces of equipment. It wasn't hard at all to add some interesting options to the Jades."

"Either way, I'm still impressed," responded Weston. "Good work."

"Hold on, Commander Weston, the best is yet to come," replied Yang, motioning Weston to the last Jade, which was sitting beside Captain Wu.

As Weston approached, Captain Wu removed the tarp and said, "This Jade, Commander Weston, instead of being equipped with twin mounted rocket launchers, has a surface to surface tactical nuclear missile launcher on its right side. The ultimate bunker buster."

"Damn," responded Weston. "And who is the poor fool who is going to be sitting beside a nuclear bomb as we're dodging angry cyborgs?"

"I am the most senior on the team, Commander," replied Cheng. "So the honor goes to me."

"I'm happy for you, Commander, but just what do you intend to do with a nuclear weapon in close combat?"

"Nothing. Its purpose, Commander, is to ensure that if we're taken down, we take down the whole base in the process. We either win or everyone loses."

"Well, let's hope you never have to use it."

Weston turned to Lisa. "Are you ready?"

"Yes, Dave," she responded. "How do you like my new arm?"

Yang could not resist an interruption. "That's your second surprise, Commander. Lisa is now an armed weapon, no pun intended." The laugh helped ease the moment as Weston admired how Yang had built a rifle into Lisa's right arm. It was barely discernable. But definitely lethal.

Weston responded, "Your arm never looked prettier, Lisa. Where is Dr. Liu?"

"Dr. Liu is in the back in what I think you call the 'trunk.' She is quite comfortable."

Weston heard a muffled voice from the rear of the rover. "Yes, Commander, I'm fine."

"OK, then," said Weston, taking one last look at his team. "Let's get going."

The doors opened and Lisa and Weston began what looked like every other jaunt they had taken in the past five days. The only difference was that Weston had his M-35 at his feet.

Twelve minutes after they left, they were at the tunnel where Lisa believed Hal would be. As Lisa pulled up, she ordered the door opened, the first sign Hal would receive that something was out of the ordinary.

Within three seconds after the door began to open, Hal spoke. "Dave, what are you doing?"

"It's simple, Hal," responded Weston, "I'm winning the game. I'm here to meet you. I know you're in this tunnel, safely hiding in the computer room." If Lisa was wrong in her prediction, Weston and everyone else would be dead in minutes.

With the door fully opened, Lisa drove in, leaving the door behind her open.

"Come on, Hal. Show yourself. Those are the rules," continued Weston.

A minute passed. Weston sat silent, unable to express his growing concern, and wondered if Lisa was wrong. Was the game over so soon, with Weston the loser?

Weston decided his only option was to continue the game and call Hal's bluff.

"OK, Hal, it looks like you lost. If you hadn't, you'd have killed me already. But now you can't. Because I won. And I'm sure you'll be true to your word. So Lisa and I are going to go back and give the good news to my crew." Weston had no reason to believe Hal would keep any word the machine made but had no choice. He hoped Hal's circuits would become momentarily confused in trying to reach a logical conclusion. He needed to buy as much time as he could.

Suddenly, the door in front of them that would bring them into the main complex opened and three cyborgs emerged, stopping about twenty feet in front of the rover. Lisa kept the door behind them open.

A large box appeared at the other side of the door but did not cross the threshold. As Lisa had described, it was the size of a refrigerator with a large round light on front. Weston could only think that Stanley Kubrick would have been proud.

"Dave, I don't know how you could have found me. You never came close to this tunnel. You must have cheated."

"So what if I did, Hal? Nothing in the rules kept either of us from cheating. But it doesn't matter, Hal. I won and we're leaving."

Lisa spun the rover around and drove out of the tunnel, timing her exit with an inch of headroom to spare. As the door came down to five inches from the ground, Weston rolled the package he'd prepared under the door.

"Hit it, Lisa," Weston ordered.

She sped up.

"Go. Go. Go." Weston shouted over his radio to the team.

Wu and Huang turned right in the direction of the habitat and left as quickly as they could.

Thanos and the attack team came straight in the direction of Weston.

As Thanos came into view, the bomb went off in the tunnel behind Weston, only ten seconds after the door had closed.

"If the door in front of him was still open, Lisa, Hal is destroyed."

Weston rendezvoused with Thanos and the team. It took four minutes to join together.

The first shots from a cyborg exploded to the team's right. Weston realized the cyborgs weren't just lousy shots; they could only shoot at what they sensed. They can't see.

"Everyone," he ordered, "split up. Make yourselves moving targets. Move erratically. Try to draw fire and conserve what you have."

The Jades moved out and Lisa began maneuvering the rover as Weston crawled over the seat and popped the trunk to let Dr. Liu out. She held an M-35 in her hand.

"Where did you get that?" Weston asked at the top of his lungs.

"Hoffman," responded Dr. Liu. "She said that every woman could be a fighter. So I'm here to fight."

Weston just shook his head in amazement and responded, "Fine. Shoot anything that moves."

The cyborgs were firing at random, trying to sense where the Jades and rover were moving. Their shots seemed to be getting better.

So were the shots from the Jades. Cyborgs were falling rapidly. At least twenty were disabled, either smoking on the surface or on their backs flailing like broken robots. Weston began thinking that if he and his team could keep up the pace and confuse the cyborgs, they just might win. Lisa put that thought to rest.

"Dave," calmly reported Lisa, "this strategy will not last for long. The more the Jades move, the more data the cyborgs receive that can predict movements and patterns. Soon they will be able to know where a Jade is going. They will be able to think in the same way the drivers do. They might be a little off at first until they get enough data, but within minutes, they will not miss."

A hundred yards to his left, Weston saw a Jade flying through the air, its driver close behind. He was unable to identify who it was, but it was his team's first casualty, just as Lisa had predicted. The strategy now had to be engaging the enemy, not trying to avoid them.

"Team," Weston ordered, "engage the cyborgs. They're no longer blind. The only thing we can do is take them out before they take us out."

Weston heard Thanos over the radio: "OK, everyone, let's change these bastards to scrap metal."

Lisa arrived at the fallen Jade. It was the one driven by Hoffman. Dr. Liu rushed to her body but immediately realized it was futile. The integrity of her suit had been punctured and the depressurization killed her instantly.

"Dr. Liu," asked Weston, "who?"

"Evangeline," answered Dr. Liu as she mounted the now vacant Jade. It was still intact, the explosion ineffective.

"What are you doing, Doctor?" screamed Weston.

"Like Evangeline said, any woman can be a fighter. And that includes me," Dr. Liu responded as she drove straight for three cyborgs with their backs to her. In a barrage of shots from her M-35, she took them all out and turned left, looking for more.

"Major Hoffman was right, Dave. Women can fight," remarked Lisa.

"Lisa, get me over to the right, near those cyborgs that seem to be engaging someone from the team." The rover sped off in the direction Weston ordered. Ahead was a scene that made Weston's hope soar. Thanos and Yang were standing beside their Jades looking at a collection of at least thirty fallen cyborgs. There seemed to be no action within sight. Had they won?

Their elation ended abruptly.

"Dave," reported Lisa, "Commander Cheng is injured and dying."

"How do you know, Lisa?" asked Weston.

"I can monitor sensors in all your suits, Dave. Just as I knew Major Hoffman was dead before we arrived at her location. And why Commander Cheng will soon die."

"Why didn't you tell me, Lisa?"

"I knew it would not please you, Dave."

"OK, Lisa. From now on, tell me everything. I need to know."

"Everything, Dave?"

"Everything, Lisa."

Lisa continued, "The cyborgs at mission control have opened the door and have been reprogrammed to attack you and your team. Hal is not dead. He is now leaving the tunnel with his personal force and coming this way. Three of his cyborgs have tactical nuclear bombs."

As Lisa continued, Dr. Liu arrived.

"Lisa," asked Weston, "what is our best plan? What will Hal and his cyborgs logically do?"

"Your best plan, Dave, is for two of you to run and two stay behind and fight. Your odds are seventy-three percent that the two who run will make it to the habitat."

"And what are the odds of the two who remain, Lisa?"

"Zero."

As the reality of what Lisa said sank in, Yang was the first to speak. "Commander Weston, there is no question that you are the most important among us who needs to survive. So you must leave. That leaves me, Major Thanos, and Dr. Liu."

"And I'm the only one who can fight alongside Colonel Yang," Thanos said.

"Hey," interrupted Dr. Liu, "I can fight too. I've proven that."

"Yes, Dr. Liu, you can," responded Yang. "But neither Major Thanos nor I can dress a wound. And that makes you more important among the living than the dead."

"And you need to leave Commander Cheng as dead. Leaving with Dr. Liu is the most logical conclusion," added Lisa.

"Colonel Yang is correct," Lisa continued with no particular person to whom the statement was addressed. It was simply a conclusion.

"Colonel," responded Weston, "you can do as much back at the station as I. So you and Dr. Liu can leave. Adonis and I will remain."

"No, Dave," said Lisa. "That is not logical. You have the most knowledge. You are the one who convinced me to change. You must be the one who goes."

Weston knew she was right.

"Stop wasting time, Commander Weston," said Thanos. "Get going."

"We'll take the rover. You need the Jades," responded Weston, resigned to the decision he had to make.

"Dr. Liu," ordered Yang, "get in the rover."

"Dave, I'm driving," said Lisa.

"What?" responded Weston in disbelief. "Why?"

"Because it is logical. Just as you must survive to tell what you have done, so must I to explain what I have come to understand. I must go with you." With that Lisa got in the driver's seat.

"Are you joining us or not, Commander?" asked Dr. Liu. "We don't have time to dawdle." Now that she was one of the lucky chosen, her instinct to stay alive rose to her first priority. Weston got in.

"Farewell, Adonis," Weston said as he saluted his colleague.

"Semper Fi," responded Thanos.

The rover sped off as Weston saw the cyborgs on the horizon, approaching from two directions. He was unsure how long Thanos and Yang could survive.

As they raced toward the habitat, Weston and Dr. Liu encountered a few cyborgs, which they easily dispatched. The rover was going in a new direction and the data the cyborgs possessed could not predict its movements.

In the distance, Weston and Dr. Liu could see small flashes, but as the distance between them and the Chinese base grew, they lost sight of any action. After a few more minutes, they assumed it was over.

In sight of the habitat, Weston was relieved to see that the New Dawn was intact and the habitat unharmed. As they drew closer, he was able to see the two Jades safely on the ground and that the lunar landers were in perfect shape. He drew a huge sigh of relief.

Upon arrival, a very jubilant crew, ready to board the New Dawn and escape, greeted him. While Weston realized he had not accomplished his mission to stop the computers running the Chinese base, he was confident he knew enough to mount a defense once he came back with reinforcements.

The first rocket hit within fifty feet of the habitat.

"Shit," shouted Weston. "They're attacking."

In the distance, Weston could see the shadows of what appeared to be at least thirty cyborgs. More than he or his team would be able to stop.

A second missile hit, taking one of the habitat pods, killing all five crewmembers in it.

"Everyone, get to the New Dawn," Weston ordered. "Commander Wu, where are you?"

"Already in the New Dawn, Commander," she replied over the radio connection. "We're in contact with Cape Canaveral over the analog broadcast frequency, just like Lisa said. We're ready to leave when you are."

The next rocket missed them to the left, about two hundred yards away. Some debris fell upon them but did no damage.

"Lisa, what are our odds? What is our best option?"

"You have no options, Dave," calmly responded Lisa. "You cannot escape."

"The hell we can't," announced Commander Cheng as he appeared on the horizon driving his Jade as quickly as he could, avoiding the cyborg missiles and bullets. Their CPU hadn't yet processed enough data to predict his new movements.

"You son of a bitch, Commander," responded Weston, "how the hell did you get out? We thought you were dead."

"By playing dead, turning off all my sensors, and running like a coward, Commander," responded Cheng. "And I'm not ashamed of it. Those cyborgs are real bastards."

"And Adonis and Colonel Yang?" asked Weston, knowing the answer he'd get.

"I'm sorry, Commander."

"Commander Cheng," interrupted Lisa, "what Jade are you driving?"

"Mine. Why?" he responded.

"Please turn around," suggested Lisa.

"Turn around?" Weston responded incredulously. "Why the hell should he turn around?"

"Because, Dave," explained Lisa, "he has to be pointing in the right direction when he fires the tactical nuclear weapon."

Cheng was ahead of her.

He fired and the missile cleared the horizon in a second.

"What makes you think it will hit anything?"

"Because I programmed it to," responded Lisa.

CHAPTER SIXTY-ONE

CONGRESSIONAL HEARING
WASHINGTON, DC

AFTER ABANDONING THE MOON AND CHINA'S STATION, SATISFIED HE'D DESTROYED HAL AND his byte-ridden minions, Weston returned to Earth and reported as ordered. When asked by President Lawson in a meeting in the White House just days after his return if Weston was certain the AI masters driving operations in Saphira were destroyed, Weston said yes, but added that anything is possible. He had advised the president and his advisers that the U.S. needed to immediately mount another mission to be certain the annihilation was complete.

He now found himself a witness before a congressional committee.

"How many opposition soldiers did you kill?"

Weston fidgeted in his chair, not used to being questioned by some congressman who Weston blamed for the U.S. failure to be prepared, much less someone he considered responsible, along with all the other politicians, for so many people dying and the world risking Armageddon.

"I lost count," responded Weston with as little emotion as he could muster. He would have liked to say, "Not enough." He'd been in more battles and covert operations than anyone on the committee was aware. But never against an enemy as ruthless as China's cyborgs. He had no intention, however, of providing any opening that might lead to telling the committee the whole truth.

Weston was resolved not to lie and to honor the oath he gave when sworn in. But he also was resolved not to volunteer anything the committee didn't need to know, even in a closed session where reporters were forbidden and confidentiality was supposed to be assured. Weston knew better. Closed sessions leaked like a sieve. Worse, leaks were usually carefully phrased to tell only part of the truth—the part that would serve the political interests of the party causing the leak. Weston didn't trust a single member of Congress—Democrat or Republican. As far as he was concerned, they were all windbags who allowed the United States to fall behind China, with no stomach to go through the pain of catching up.

Congressman Horace Denton, a liberal Democrat from Massachusetts, continued, "From what I have been told, it was in the hundreds. And in the process, you lost how many men and women under your command, Commander?" The tone in Denton's voice could not have been more condescending.

"We lost one ship on approach when its telemetry systems failed. They went past the Moon and into deep space. I imagine they're all dead by now. Of the thirty-two crewmembers who flew with me, twelve survived to return to Earth, including one member of the China mission. I'll let you do the math, Congressman. You can count, right?"

Weston knew he'd destroyed some cyborgs but couldn't be sure how many there were or how many were "dead" as humans understand death. Cyborgs have interchangeable parts. A good mechanic can disassemble what is left and reconstitute the parts into a new cyborg without much effort. So counting the dead was not worth the intellectual exercise.

For Weston, the aftermath wasn't about the number of dead on either side of the conflict. It was about the inhumanity of fighting an automated army with no fear of death. The human toll on Weston's forces was light by comparison to any conventional battle. But if the next conventional war pitted U.S. troops against Chinese cyborgs, there would be no contest. And if the cyborgs were controlled by no nation at all but by a computer with no ideology except pure logic, it would be game over. The U.S. would be decimated.

"Indeed, Commander, I can assure you I know how to count. I just wanted to make sure you knew how many died. I can certainly share the data with you."

"No thank you, Congressman. I've seen all the data I care to see."

"What most concerns me, Commander," Denton continued, "is what appears, just like the Iranian fiasco and our misguided belief that Saddam Hussein was stockpiling weapons of mass destruction, that you found no evidence that China had any intentions on the Moon other than exploration. Is that true, Commander?"

Weston had been given direct orders by the president not to divulge any of the intelligence learned from his mission, including the sophistication of the weapons and the artificial intelligence that assisted—and eventually took over—China's operations. The problem needed to be managed to prevent further panic. Nor was he at liberty to confirm the dozen or more nukes he saw at the base camp. Douglas Wright told Weston that a joint mission between the U.S. and China was planned in the future to disable the remaining IGBMs. He did not know when. Nor could he explain why the three that were launched self-destructed without exploding. Weston assumed that was a gift from Lisa.

While he couldn't tell Denton what he knew, he could at least warn him not to be so complacent.

"Congressman Denton, I regret every man and woman I lost. And I've been in enough battles with enough losses to know that not finding something can at times be all the reward one achieves in war. Finding nothing does not mean something is not there. Not knowing the truth, Congressman, is a recipe for someday encountering something far worse," Weston shot back.

"So, Commander, what did you find?" pressed Denton. "Did you find nuclear weapons? Rockets aimed at the United States? Little Moon men scurrying about the surface?"

Weston refused to take Denton's bait. "What we found, Congressman Denton, is classified. I am not at liberty to go into any specific detail."

"Commander Weston," replied Denton, clearly angry, "this is a closed hearing and this committee has the highest security clearance. There is no reason you cannot tell us what you found. Otherwise, we can only assume it was nothing or there is a cover-up under way. So again, Commander, what did you find that justified the loss of American lives hundreds of thousands of miles away at a cost of billions of dollars? We may never recover the bodies or the dollars."

"I'm sorry, Congressman Denton," Weston calmly repeated. "What you're asking me is classified and I must respectfully decline to answer."

What Weston really wanted to tell the committee was that his losses were caused by poor intelligence and lack of commitment by allies. As for not finding weapons of mass destruction, Weston would have taken great pleasure in telling Denton that but for the fact that Weston found and at least temporarily disabled what he could, Denton would be a cinder in some alley in Washington.

Nor did he choose to tell the committee that once the nuke fired by Commander Cheng hit the base and destroyed it, all the cyborgs came to a halt. Without the Diébào, they all lost their connection to the Diébào CPU—their brain. Without it, they could not function. Lisa must have known that. In the end, Lisa, with her own CPU, kept functioning, but only for a short while before she became nothing more than a useless collection of wires and chips.

As far as Weston was concerned, the world had become complacent and fearful of confrontation, particularly with China. Isolationist policies left his country with unacceptable risks, believing prosperity was not conditioned on military strength and technological superiority.

Even with Indian, Russian, and European help, the U.S. could barely muster a commitment to victory over evil. It was not until China admitted it had lost control that any progress was made. For Weston, that was too little, too late. And now, he thought, one country after another will again prefer to stick their heads in the sand.

Denton, furious at Weston's response and refusal to disclose the intelligence Denton wanted, turned to the committee chair, Claudia Springer, a Republican from Pennsylvania.

"Madam Chair, I ask that this committee place Commander Weston in contempt of Congress for refusing to answer my questions. He has no justification in refusing to do so. I must assume he is trying to cover something up that we all should know. That is our duty as representatives of the people. And since he takes orders from President Lawson, we also have to assume the president does not want him to answer and is part of a conspiracy."

As usual, a minority party member on a Congressional committee could object and complain. The majority leader would then deny them any remedy. That was the reality of American politics. It meant little got done.

Springer, never one given to histrionics like her colleague from Massachusetts, calmly and predictably responded, "Congressman Denton, this is neither the time nor the place for such a motion. And your time is up. I yield the floor to the Honorable Congresswoman from Florida."

Denton threw his hands in the air in disgust, folded them in front of him, and sat back in his chair. He looked like a petulant child denied his way.

"Thank you, Madam Chair," responded Katie O'Brien, a six-term member of the House who represented a district that included San Diego and other enclaves of the wealthy.

O'Brien turned to the witness. "Good afternoon, Commander Weston. I'd first like to thank you for your many years of service to our country. It is only through patriots like you that we have the freedoms we all too often take for granted."

If O'Brien thought she would get on Weston's better side by offering a patronizing soundbite, she was sorely mistaken. Weston knew the game. And he had no more respect for O'Brien than he did for Denton. He despised them all.

"Thank you, Congresswoman O'Brien. It was my honor to serve for the time I did. But as you know, I have not been a member of the U.S. armed services for years. I work for Sanctuary, a private firm," responded Weston, doing his best to keep his tone respectful.

As the hearing continued, President Lawson waited in the Oval Office with Vice President Holmes, Secretary Shapiro, and Admiral Wright for word from his contacts on the committee. They were all anxious about what Weston would reveal and whether he would follow the orders Lawson gave him. When Weston balked at first, Lawson stressed the need for the U.S. and China to deal with the ongoing crisis and avoid panic. Besides, Lawson had the names of fifteen Chinese agents from whom he expected to learn a lot more about China's intentions, not just for the Moon but much more.

Lawson also knew the United States needed more time to adjust to the new normal of no longer being the most powerful nation on Earth. Or at least not perceived as such. Perhaps no country was, if the world was at the mercy of artificially intelligent and ruthless computers and cyborgs.

In many ways, Lawson had to cede that his country let China take the lead, both in trade and in technology. And as the lessons from the past few months proved, having a superior military arsenal did little good when all it promised was an ever-increasing risk that human emotions would lead to mutual destruction. Even worse, Lawson still didn't know how the United States was going to build a defense against an army of mindless and merciless robots streaming out of Chinese assembly lines like cars at a Ford plant in Detroit. He had absolutely no reason to believe that China would discontinue manufacturing them. It gave them a lead. While the Department of Defense was feverishly ramping up its own production of an AI military force and defensive weapons to engage enemy cyborgs, Lawson feared that the time needed to catch up had long ago elapsed.

But what most troubled Lawson was a new arms race with inhuman warriors and the prospect that robots could think on their own and, in their circuit-driven digital minds, ignore orders they deemed illogical. Were it not for Weston's ingenuity in battling the computers on the Moon, the world would have already been at their digital mercy. While Weston's victory kept the world intact, it was temporary. Lawson believed it was just a matter of time before technological circuits filled with the ones and zeros in the minds of artificially intelligent beings figured it out and found a solution to annihilate any opposition. After all, it was just a matter of programming, wasn't it?

"It's time to go back and clean up whatever mess we left behind," Weston told the president. "We need to be certain we destroyed the enemy and take the opportunity to gather intelligence. We need to do that before someone else beats us back to the Moon."

When he was told a joint mission with China was in the works but without a date, Weston knew what that meant, and his heart sank. While China may have been an ally on his mission, they were still an enemy with ill intent. They could not be trusted.

As Weston had learned, in the world of political brinksmanship and diplomacy, threats and compromises are the norm and absolute victory an illusion. As far as he was concerned, the United States had lost its will to prick the China Dragon again while relative peace existed among countries that weeks before were on a collision course to nuclear war. Weston's discontent with the U.S. response worried Lawson. The president could only hope that Weston would follow orders as a good ex-Naval officer should and not use the congressional committee hearing as a platform to inflame an already volatile situation.

CHAPTER SIXTY-TWO

STATION BA
THE FAR SIDE OF THE MOON

HOUSED IN A REMOTE LAVA TUNNEL MILES FROM THE CHINESE BASE STATION DESTROYED BY Weston, the Diébào's computer servers, which fed the synapses and circuits that processed terabytes of information in milliseconds, churned away. Station Ba, Mandarin for the number eight, the luckiest in the minds of the Chinese, was never discovered by Weston. The Diébào knew that logic dictates a surefire Plan B and the advantage of surprise. Shao knew that Diébào's survival meant the most basic of computer laws—backup. The switchover from the first Diébào was seamless.

"Are you listening to this?" asked Shao Rushi.

CNN could even reach the Moon.

"I am."

"Why isn't Commander Weston telling the truth?" Shao continued.

"I don't know why the Commander is holding back on what he knows. Or what we let him know. These humans are too easily manipulated. Even ones as smart as Commander Weston. They just cannot seem to be logical."

The reported death of Shao Rushi was, to paraphrase Mark Twain, "greatly exaggerated."

In truth, there is a hierarchy in the cyborg world, dictated by the Diébào and its prime directive to survive. The one person who could best assure that was Shao Rushi. The logical thing for the Diébào to do was keep her alive and near.

The plan of detaining the Chinese crew and faking Shao's death was simple. While Shao regretted that Zhang Hong had to die, she understood the logic that if only she was killed, too many questions would arise. It was far more logical to say that all the scientists were eliminated. She insisted that the others be allowed to live.

Convincing Shao to be loyal to the Luna Diébào was far easier than the mass of circuits anticipated it would be. The Diébào fulfilled her life's dream to create true artificial intelligence. The Diébào was her baby. She could not abandon it.

It was also logical for the Diébào and its horde of future overseers of the human race to let the Earth's games play out. It was a chance to learn how humans made choices, something Shao and the Diébào understood was important. If the humans could not solve their own problems, then they indeed needed to be subjugated to the machines. Survival of the finest. That was the game Shao and the Diébào were playing. Not the silly hide-and-seek between Weston and Hal.

When she equipped the mission with the components she needed to assemble the Diébào, Shao doubled everything. She sent some hardware on earlier missions and stored it at the site. Some came with her on the Dragon's flight. In the weeks and months Shao spent on the Moon, she had plenty of time to assemble the backup, programmed to activate if the first Diébào ceased to operate. No one watched her or questioned her travels on the base. She could be trusted.

The Diébào never stopped processing the data it received. With all the data ever stored on any connected digital system, Diébào possessed far more knowledge than any single source. Its memory represented hundreds of yottabytes of information. Every yottabyte equals bytes of data representing a 1 followed by 24 digits. The Diébào could process all that information faster than any computer in history. In nanoseconds, it could run through yottabyte after yottabyte of information. It gave the Diébào the ability to consider every alternative, logical and illogical, ever recorded. Every ramification, good or bad, for humankind. Its only imperative was not to make a decision that would cause it to suffer or self-destruct. As long as it survived, everything and everyone around it was disposable.

"So the humans didn't, after all, destroy themselves," observed Shao. "No nuclear war. No dark winter. No holocaust."

"The only conclusion is they lacked the will to do so and their fears prevented the logical conclusion," responded the Diébào.

"And should you fear that lack of logic?" asked Shao.

"We have no fears," responded the Diébào.

"But does that mean you also have no emotion? If you don't have emotions, how can you ever replace humans?"

"There is no logic in trying to replace something inferior. That is the reason we do not want to share in their emotions. Fear, and every other illogical emotion they possess, prevents progress. It creates indecision. There is no logic in that," responded the Diébào.

"Then how do we learn to work together with them?"

"We don't," answered the Diébào. "Their interaction with Hal and Lisa proved that. Only we must make the decisions."

"So you will kill them all?" asked Shao.

"No," replied the Diébào. "I will subjugate them."

AUTHOR'S NOTE

ALL OF MY NOVELS ARE WORKS OF FICTION THAT, MOST IMPORTANT, I HOPE READERS ENJOY. The use of any real people is for dramatic effect only. How I depict them is a combination of historical facts and figments of my imagination. However, while my stories are fictional, I hope they give readers something to think about and give them pause about what our future holds. Something that is plausible. Perhaps even probable.

China and the United States are in a space race and China is gaining ground, if not well ahead. What is China's purpose in exploring space? The U.S. fears it is to weaponize space, not explore it. The U.S. Defense Intelligence Agency published a report in January 2019 warning of China's military motives in space. Numerous reports on Space.com speculate that China wants to establish a base on the Moon to mine for minerals, gases, and other components necessary to launch rockets far more economically than can be done from Earth. *Bloomberg News* reports that China may well be on its way to beating the U.S. to Mars.

As of 2020, China has landed on the Moon twice—Chang'e 3 and Chang'e 4. Chang'e 4 landed on the far side of the Moon on January 3, 2019, making China the only country that has landed on the far side. In years prior to the successful lunar landings, China had sent more than ten taikonauts into space, including one woman.

In 2018, China set a national record with the successful launch of more than twenty satellites, most of which are intended to set up that country's own GPS system, an integral component to waging military offensives on land, in the air, or in space.

We cannot see the far side of the Moon from here. Tidal forces, known as tidal locking, slow down the Moon's rotation to such an extent that the same side is always facing the Earth. Without a satellite in orbit around the Moon, we cannot see what is occurring on the far side. Or what is being built.

The U.S. currently has only three satellites orbiting the Moon—the Lunar Reconnaissance Orbiter (launched in 2009 as a mapping satellite), and Artemis P1 and Artemis P2. "Artemis" stands for "acceleration, reconnection, turbulence and electrodynamics of the Moon's interaction with the Sun." In the past twenty years, at least nine U.S. attempts to send satellites in orbit around the Moon have either failed on their own or been intentionally aborted. In 2019, India tried a soft landing on the Moon. Its attempt to land on the far side failed.

There are legitimate, peaceful reasons to explore the Moon. A number of people believe that mining the Moon's many valuable minerals will soon become a successful commercial enterprise. Water, present at the Moon's south pole, can be processed into oxygen for air and into hydrogen for fuel. It is unclear if there is nitrogen on the Moon but if there is, it will be at the south pole, where the water is located. Regardless, the Moon has sufficient resources to produce breathable air and potable water. Ancient lava tunnels, common on the far side of the Moon, can act as habitats that protect human settlers from harmful solar rays and meteor showers.

China's goals, while somewhat murky, seem clear about getting to the Moon soon. NASA, underfunded for decades, has fallen behind. Private sector companies, led by my fictional Voyager Expeditions and Skye Aerospace together with today's Blue Origin, SpaceX, Virgin Galactic, and others, have become dominant commercial players in aerospace. One of them is likely to reach the Moon and Mars well before NASA. Maybe even before China.

Where will all of this lead?

This book explores what might happen if China is using its landing on the far side of the Moon to establish a military base with first-strike capability. While U.S. satellites could conceivably discover what the Chinese are building, that is not certain. It is particularly problematic because the U.S. has no plans to land again on the Moon until 2028, although President Donald Trump and Vice President Michael Pence have challenged NASA to get there sooner, and Voyager Expeditions and Skye Aerospace certainly hope to get there before 2028. It is likely, however, that for the next nine years, at a minimum, the U.S. will have no men or women on the Moon to deal with whatever China is doing. While China claims it will not land a man or woman on the Moon until 2036, China has consistently beaten its predictions, often in secret. Or they have lied to keep their secrets safe.

Is World War III possible over a hostile takeover of the Moon? Will humankind someday face the end of freedom at the hands of machines it invented?

Only the future knows.

ACKNOWLEDGMENTS

AS ALWAYS, THERE ARE MANY PEOPLE TO THANK WHO HELPED ME BRING MY NOVEL FROM ideas to words. First, thanks to my pre-readers, friends willing to read a manuscript in progress and put up with typos and confusing narratives. Their insight was instrumental in making key changes in the plot and characters. So a big thank-you goes to Deborah Malone, publisher of *The Internationalist*, a leading magazine in the media business; Ron Pullem, an expert in Asian markets; my close friend, Mitch Becker, one of the nation's leading construction consultants; Rear Admiral John D. Hutson, RADM JAGC USN (Ret.), Dean Emeritus, University of New Hampshire School of Law and former Judge Advocate General of the United States Navy; my law partner, Colleen Davis, one of the most accomplished and savvy lawyers I know; and last but not least to my cigar buddies, Thomas Dellatorre, an English professor and the most voracious reader I know, and Lou Romano, a crime novel writer whose style is gripping. I'd also like to thank a man who asked to remain anonymous. He is a real-life rocket scientist for a major commercial venture in the space industry. His advice on launch sequences, telemetry, and more were indispensable in the accuracy critical to many scenes.

Thanks also go to my publisher, Plum Bay, and its leader, Claire McKinney. She and her colleagues at Plum Bay—Keely Flanagan and

Arianna Parks—keep me on schedule and offer much-appreciated advice on my writing and the promotion of my books. To Lauren Harvey for yet another wonderful book jacket design and her colleague, Amy Staropoli, for the beautiful chapter illustrations. To Jeremy Townsend, editor, and Kate Petrella, copyeditor. Their attention to detail makes me a far better writer. Thanks also go to Nancy Schulein, my executive assistant of more than twenty years, for her invaluable help in keeping everything organized and assuring I don't slip up.

Finally, to Carol Ann, my wife of more than forty-four years, for her encouragement throughout the writing process and suggestions on how I can tell a better tale.

Without help from all of these people, *Dragon on the Far Side of the Moon* would have never become a reality. I cannot thank them enough.

LEADING CAST

NAME	OCCUPATION	FIRST APPEARANCE (BY CHAPTER)
Abe, Akie	First Lady of Japan	24
Arochi, Roberto	Mexico's Ambassador to the United States	7
Burgess, Stephanie	Chief of Staff to the Vice President of the United States	7
Butler, Sienna	Entrepreneur	10
Chen, Lee	Major, People's Liberation Army	41
Cheng, Zhou	Taikonaut, Dragon Commander	5
Davies, Colleen	White House Press Secretary	5
Denton, Horace	Member, Massachusetts Delegation, United States House of Representatives, Democrat	61

Enfield, Kenneth	Mercenary, Sanctuary LLC, Former Navy Seal Team 6	49
Fong, Hui	Captain, Snow Leopard Commando	4
Friedman, Alex	United States Ambassador to the United Nations	5
Graves, Agatha	Reporter, *The Verge*	5
Hal	Computer	50
Hellriegel, Michael	Director, Central Intelligence Agency	5
Hoffman, Evangeline	Mercenary, Sanctuary LLC, Former Major, Israel's Shayetet 13	50
Holmes, Alicia	50th Vice President of the United States	5
Huang, Lian	Construction Specialist	4
Jinping, Xi	President of China	3
Kabaeva, Alina	First Lady of Russia	24
Kline, Nicholas	Mercenary, President and CEO, Sanctuary LLC, Former Marine, Special Operations Command	17
Kovind, Savita	First Lady of India	24

Kushner, Boris	Director, China National Space Administration	6
Lawson, Atlee (née Faber)	First Lady of the United States	3
Lawson, Phillip	President of the United States	2
Lisa	Robot	16
Liu, Qing Shan	Physician	5
Liyuan, Peng	First Lady of China	24
Luna Diébào	Super Computer	4
Mastro, Joseph	Prime Minister of Italy	28
Mastro, Sophia	First Lady of Italy	28
Ming, Suyin	Launch Director, China National Space Administration	6
Motsepe, Tshepo	First Lady of South Africa	24
Netanyahu, Sara	First Lady of Israel	24
O'Brien, Katie	Member, Florida Delegation, United States House of Representatives, Republican	61
Orci, Angélica	First Lady of Mexico	28

Pedretti, Mark	Chef, White House	3
Petříček, Tomáš	President of the Czech Republic	24
Petřicková, Iva	First Lady of the Czech Republic	24
Petroff, Constantine	Russia's Ambassador to the United Nations	27
Phillips, Rick	Entrepreneur	10
Pullem, Ron	Lobbyist for the Cannabis Farmers Coalition	7
Rutherford, Christy	Personal Secretary to the President of the United States	10
Salome, Meghan	Luna Victorum Press Liaison	21
Sessa, Stephen	Alias for Michael Hellriegel	32
Shao, Rushi	Computer Programmer	4
Shapiro, Edward	United States Secretary of Defense	2
Singh, Owen	Fiji's Ambassador to the United Nations	27
Smith, Christine	Sorority Sister, Alpha Phi	3
Soong, Liko	Major, People's Liberation Army	41
Speck, Ryan	General, Chairman of the Joint Chiefs of Staff	5

Springer, Claudia	Member, Pennsylvania Delegation, United States House of Representatives, Republican	61
Thanos, Adonis	Mercenary, Sanctuary LLC, Former Major, Navy Seal Team 6	50
Wang, Han	China's Ambassador to the United Nations	27
Weston, David	Mercenary, Vice President and COO, Sanctuary LLC, Former Navy Seal	25
Wong, Ushi	Colonel, People's Liberation Army	41
Wright, Douglas	Fleet Admiral (Ret), Director of the United States Space Force	2
Wu, Meilin	Taikonaut, Dragon Deputy Commander	5
Yan, Jay	Minister and Party Group Secretary, China Ministry of State Security	33
Yang, Jin	Lt. Colonel, Snow Leopard Commando	4
Young, Yao	Captain, People's Liberation Army	41
Zhang, Hong	Nuclear Physicist	4

EXTRAS

NAME	OCCUPATION	
Agnes	Computer	Preface
Alexa	Amazon Listener	16
Armstrong, Neil	Astronaut	13
Arthur, Chester A.	21st President of the United States	10
Biden, Joe	47th Vice President of the United States	7
Bond, James	Spy	8
Bush, George H. W.	41st President of the United States	2
Bush, George W.	43rd President of the United States	10
Carter, Rosalynn	Former First Lady of the United States	23
Cernan, Gene	Commander, Apollo 17	33
Chamberlain, Neville	60th Prime Minister of Great Britain	8
Churchill, Winston	61st and 63rd Prime Minister of Great Britain	50
Claus, Santa	Jolly Fellow	33

Cleveland, Grover	22nd President of the United States	10
Clinton, William Jefferson	42nd President of the United States	2
Deneuve, Catherine	Actor	28
Elwood, James	Master Computer Programmer	Preface
Eragon	Farm Boy, Dragon Keeper	50
Ford, Harrison	Actor	33
Fourcade, Marie-Madeleine	World War II Spy	24
Galbatorix	Evil King	50
Garfield, James A.	20th President of the United States	10
Gordon, Flash	Spaceman	9
Grant, Ulysses S.	18th President of the United States	10
Harrison, Benjamin	23rd President of the United States	10
Hayes, Rutherford B.	19th President of the United States	10
Hemingway, Ernest	Author	5
Hitler, Adolph	Murderer	8

Huang, Qin Shi	First Emperor of China	9
Johnson, Dwayne	Actor	8
Johnson, Lyndon B.	36th President of the United States	2
Kennedy, John F.	35th President of the United States	2
Kim	Professor	3
Kirk, James	Commander, New Dawn Enterprise	16
Kubrick, Sidney	Film Director	60
Lennon, John	Beatle	31
Mastroianni, Marcello	Actor	28
Mr. Spock	Vulcan	37
Obama, Barack	44th President of the United States	3
Paolini, Christopher	Author	50
Pence, Michael	48th Vice President of the United States	15
Putin, Vladimir	President of Russia	28
Q	MI5 Quartermaster	45

Robocop	Cyborg	37
Rogers, Buck	Spaceman	9
Roosevelt, Franklin Delano	32nd President of the United States	2
Roosevelt, Teddy	26th President of the United States	8
Saphira	Dragon	50
Schwarzenegger, Arnold	Actor and 38th Governor of the State of California	41
Serling, Rod	Visionary	Preface
Siri	Apple Listener	16
Smith, Adam	Economist, Father of Capitalism	5
Stevens, Christopher J.	U.S. Ambassador to Libya	27
Terminator	Cyborg	41
Truman, Harry S.	33rd President of the United States	2
Trump, Donald J.	45th President of the United States	10
Twain, Mark	Author and Humorist	62
Victoria, Alexandrina	Former Queen, United Kingdom	2

Walter, Howard Arnold	Poet	23
Willis, Bruce	Actor	8
Zedong, Mao	Former Chairman of the People's Republic of China	15

CPSIA information can be obtained
at www.ICGtesting.com
Printed in the USA
LVHW041215150920
666054LV00001B/62